"The real problem is that I find you very attractive,"

Max said huskily, "but I don't want to take advantage of you."

The heat in his eyes sent a surge of excitement through her. "You wouldn't be taking advantage of me. You would be participating in my adventure."

"I wish I could see it that way," he replied.

Bernadette stood looking at him. The moment of real decision had come. If she was truly serious about having an intimate relationship, this was her opportunity. All she had to do was convince him. The excitement grew more intense. She took a step toward him. Reaching up, she began to remove his tie.

"I really don't think you've given this enough thought," he warned, catching her by the wrists and holding her hands away from him.

"I have given it all the thought I'm going to give it," she assured him. "My mind is made up."

Max was sure he'd never heard a woman sound more determined. "I'll be part of your adventure," he said gruffly.

Dear Reader,

This March brings you a very special event—the publication of *Convincing Alex*, by Nora Roberts. This extraspecial SILHOUETTE SPECIAL EDITION title is the fourth tale in Nora's bestselling THOSE WILD UKRAINIANS series, and features Alex Stanislaski—definitely the sexiest detective in New York! Don't miss this wonderful story—it's destined to become a classic!

The March selection of our THAT SPECIAL WOMAN! promotion is *One Last Fling!* by Elizabeth August. This warm, wonderful tale is sure to win hearts! Our THAT SPECIAL WOMAN! series is a celebration of our heroines—and the wonderful men that they fall in love with.

This month also brings you stories from more of your favorite authors—Emilie Richards, Diana Whitney and Trisha Alexander—as well as a super debut book in the Special Edition lineup by Kate Freiman. A wonderful March will be had by all!

I hope that you enjoy this book and all of the stories to come.

Sincerely,

Tara Gavin
Senior Editor

Please address questions and book requests to:
Reader Service
U.S.: P.O. Box 1325, Buffalo, NY 14269
Canadian: P.O. Box 1050, Niagara Falls, Ont. L2E 7G7

ELIZABETH AUGUST

ONE LAST FLING!

Silhouette®

SPECIAL EDITION®

Published by Silhouette Books

America's Publisher of Contemporary Romance

To unexpected turns of fate: may even the most
unsettling, in the end, prove to be to your advantage

 SILHOUETTE BOOKS

ISBN 0-373-09871-5

ONE LAST FLING!

Copyright © 1994 by Elizabeth August

ELIZABETH AUGUST

lives in western North Carolina with her husband, Doug, and her three boys, Douglas, Benjamin and Matthew. She began writing romances soon after Matthew was born. She's always wanted to write.

Elizabeth does counted cross-stitching to keep from eating at night. It doesn't always work. "I love to bowl, but I'm not very good. I keep my team's handicap high. I like hiking in the Shenandoahs, as long as we start up the mountain so the return trip is down rather than vice versa." She loves to go to Cape Hatteras to watch the sun rise over the ocean.

Elizabeth August has also published books under the pseudonym Betsy Page.

Chapter One

"I wish I could be more specific," Dr. Harold Riley said. "But the truth is, there's no telling when it will burst. I'm sorry."

Bernadette Dowd stared at him trying to concentrate on what he was saying. But the words "inoperable aneurysm" were echoing so loudly in her head she was only catching bits and snatches.

Her attention focused on the gray at his temples. When she'd first seen him she'd thought that touch of age made him look distinguished. Now it simply made him look old...something she would never be.

The doctor extended a small white business card toward her. "Here's the name of an excellent psychologist. She's been able to help several of my patients under similar circumstances."

As her gaze shifted to his hand, Bernadette wanted to scream out of sheer fear. Instead, with the calm self-control she always maintained over herself, she accepted the card, thanked him politely, then left.

Still in shock, she was only vaguely aware of her movement out of his office and through the building. But as she stepped out into the late afternoon sunshine, the lingering brightness of this June day made her blink. That tiny reaction brought her mind back into focus. She glanced down at her watch. The hands indicated it was nearly five-thirty.

When Dr. Riley's secretary had called and asked her to stop by to see the doctor, Bernadette had assumed he had some last minute information he wanted to give her for her article concerning the medical research he and his group were conducting. While writing the story, in order to fully understand the tests the doctor and his group were using, she'd even volunteered to be a control subject and gone through the program herself. "But I never expected him to discover anything wrong," she murmured, still finding what he'd told her difficult to believe.

Continuing toward her car she tried to come up with a plan of action. Nothing definite took form. Again fear shook her. She nearly always had a running mental schedule of what she was going to do and when she was going to do it. When anything new cropped up, she'd immediately insert it and continue along in a steady flow. Before coming here, she'd finished her assignment for the day and handed the copy in. Her scheduled intention had been to take the doctor's information home, read through it and incorporate it into the medical research article when she went in to work the next morning.

Now, for the first time in years, she felt lost, without direction. The only thing she was certain of was that the thought of going back to her empty house left her cold. Her gaze flicked to the business card she was still holding. A frown creased her brow. She wasn't interested in contacting a psychologist either. Stuffing the card in her pocket, she continued to her car.

Sliding in behind the wheel, she inserted her key in the ignition. But as she started to turn it, she suddenly froze then she began to shiver. The truth which she'd been attempting to face slowly hit her full force. She was going to die! And, it was most likely going to be some day real soon!

Her hands gripped the wheel. "It isn't fair!" she gasped, fighting back the hot tears burning at the back of her eyes. "I've always played by the rules. Why me!" The tears began to roll down her cheeks.

She saw a passing nurse look in at her worriedly. From force of habit, she quickly brushed the tears away and a stoic mask descended over her features. She'd never liked her inner emotions put on display.

She drew a steadying breath. This time of year, the days were continuing to lengthen as the calendar approached the date of the summer solstice. She guessed there would still be light until nearly nine.

"I could go for a walk in the park. Take time to smell the roses," she murmured aloud, seeking courage in the sound of her own voice.

But solitude didn't appeal to her. On the other hand, she didn't want company or to be in a crowd either. The newsroom suddenly flashed into her mind. She could go back to work. There would only be a few people around at this time of day and they'd only be there because they had work to do. If she sat at her desk and pretended to be working on an article, no one would bother her and yet she wouldn't be totally alone. "Terrific solution," she stated, relieved to have a plan, at least for the moment.

A few minutes later she was parking in the garage in the basement of the multistoried building, which housed the *St. Louis Daily Tribune*. As she climbed out of her car, and dropped her keys into her purse, she remembered the business card Dr. Riley had given her. Taking it out of her pocket, it occurred to her that waiting until the next day to talk to the psychologist might be too late. What would she care, she'd be dead, came the retort and the urge to giggle became acute. Realizing this was more panic than humor, she stifled the impulse and shoved the card into her purse.

"Anyone know where Ben or Max is?" Grace Glee was yelling as Bernadette stepped off the elevator. Grace was in her mid-fifties and had worked at the newspaper for better than twenty-five years. She wasn't a reporter. She had more clout. She was Ben Kealy's secretary. Ben was the editor of the news department. Grace was his sentry and all-round girl Friday.

The news department occupied about half the space on this floor of the building. Ben had a private office and there were a couple of rooms along the west wall that were used for editorial meetings and confidential interviews. But the reporters all worked in one huge open area crammed with desks. This was the "newsroom" and earlier in the day it had been bustling with people. But right now, as Bernadette had surmised, nearly everyone was gone, either finished for the day or out catching a quick bite to see them through the night.

"I think they're at The Late Edition getting some dinner," Gordon Hedley called back as he started to step onto the elevator. "I'm on my way there to get a hamburger. You want me to give either of them a message?"

"No," Grace yelled back. "I was on my way home anyway. I'll stop by and give them the message."

"Right," Gordon called back as the elevator door closed.

Bernadette frowned thoughtfully. The Late Edition was a small bar-restaurant across the street from the newspaper offices. In spite of its close proximity, she knew it was unusual for Grace to make a special trip there just to give Ben a message. Normally the secretary would simply have left a note on his desk.

"Something wrong?" she asked approaching Grace's desk as the woman covered her computer console and reached for her purse.

"A call just came in on the News Tip line," Grace replied in hushed tones. "Some woman said that if we were interested in uncovering a dangerous consumer rip-off we should keep an eye on a man by the name of Chuck Lang. He'll be at the All Night Saloon, west of town, tonight." She grimaced disapprovingly. "If I remember correctly that place shows up on the police reports at least three times a month."

Shrugging off this thought, Grace finished conspiratorially, "I didn't want to mention it to Gordon. You know how gung ho he can be. He'd take the story and run. I figure Ben will want Max to handle this."

Of course Ben would want Max to handle this, Bernadette mused dryly as Grace cast her a motherly smile and started toward the elevators. Ben always assigned Max Laird, Ace Investigative Reporter, to every important story.

Bernadette also knew Grace felt safe telling her about the tip because the secretary was sure Bernadette wouldn't try to grab it. "Because I'm never pushy and always polite," Bernadette muttered under her breath as she forced a smile and waved as Grace stepped into the elevator. "That's why I always get to interview the centenarians and the mother of the firstborn child on New Year's Eve." A sour taste began to form in her mouth.

She frowned as she moved toward her desk. During the four years she'd worked here, she'd never before minded the assignments she'd been given. Now she found herself thinking that they'd been somewhat dull, certainly unexciting. Although there had been that fistfight at the school board meeting a couple of months ago, she reminded herself. A tiny smile tilted one corner of her mouth. Now that had been invigorating, especially when Mrs. Charles had punched out Alderman Nesbit.

The smile returned to being a frown. But normally the stories she handled were less dramatic. And she'd never balked at being given them because she honestly preferred a peaceful life.

Had preferred a peaceful life! she corrected as rebellion surged through her. If she was going to die anyway, she should have a little excitement before the end. Even more, exposing a scheme to defraud consumers and possibly even put them in danger would make her life seem as if it had served some real purpose. Changing direction, she headed back to her car.

Max Laird sat on a stool at the bar of the All Night Saloon watching the woman at the pinball machine. When he'd first noticed her, he'd thought she looked familiar. It had taken him a minute or two before he realized she was Bernadette Dowd. That had been a shock. He'd always thought of Ms. Dowd as the office wallflower. Admittedly she had a pleasant-featured face. He'd even classify it as cute. But there was a dullness about her that caused her to seem to blend in with the desks and other furnishings. Tonight, however, she was standing out like a neon light. Sipping a beer, he began a thorough inspection. Her long, thick hickory hair, which she normally wore pulled back and twisted into a bun at her nape or piled up on her head in a nondescript fashion, was hanging freely, swinging seductively with each movement of her body. He'd never think of those locks as being mousy again.

His frown deepened as his gaze traveled downward along her five-foot-seven-inch form. The Bernadette Dowd he'd seen around the newsroom was ultraconservative in her choice of clothing. But the woman standing at the machine was wearing a pair of jeans that looked as if she'd been poured into them and a tank top that fitted like a glove. Nice curves, he admitted, very nice. Unexpectedly he found himself wondering how those curves would feel to his touch. Then he scowled at himself. Rule two, stay away from females who work in the same office or even in the same building, he recited from his list of do's and don't's concerning his private life. He shifted his attention upward.

At the moment he couldn't see her face, just the back of her head. But when he'd first entered the bar, he'd wandered unobtrusively around the perimeter. That's when he'd gotten a good look at her and recognized her. Again he recalled his stunned disbelief. Normally she wore only a moderate amount of makeup. Tonight she looked painted for war. The possibility that the woman might lead a double life occurred to him. But the jeans and boots were obviously new. And he found it hard to believe that her being in this particular bar was merely a coincidence.

"A woman playing a pinball machine can sure hold a man's attention," the man sitting next to Max said with a knowing grin. "And that one has one hell of a cute wiggle when she's flipping those paddles."

Cute but dangerous, Max thought, observing the glances a few of the other patrons were casting Bernadette's way.

"Been watching her for a while," the man continued. "Looks to me like she's angling for a particular fish . . . one of those four in that booth."

Following the direction of the man's gaze, Max studied the four men huddled in private conversation. "Lucky them," he said, hoping to keep his bar mate talking. The man was clearly observant and there was always the chance he might know Chuck Lang.

"Not for her," the man replied. "Two of them are married. The third's got a steady live-in. That don't mean they won't play around a bit. And she'd be better off with one of them. The fourth guy, the wiry dark-haired one, Lang, he likes to treat his women rough."

He'd definitely found the right man to talk to, Max thought, congratulating himself on his good fortune. He owed Bernadette Dowd a favor for this. And watching her, he was pretty sure she'd need that favor tonight.

Releasing the spring lever that shot another silver orb into the pinball machine, Bernadette hoped she could keep this ball alive longer than half a minute. At this rate, I'm going to be broke in less than an hour and this place doesn't look like it takes credit cards, she moaned silently as the ball disappeared. Surreptitiously she glanced out of the corner of her eye at the four men in the booth a little to her right.

Before leaving the newspaper offices, she'd called the All Night Saloon. Pretending to be a reporter doing a story on night spots, she'd learned that the place had a Western motif and its customers were generally blue-collar workers. She'd also scanned the police reports. Grace had been right. They'd been called to break up fights on a regular basis. For one brief moment her resolve had faltered. In the next instant, she'd tossed caution to the wind. She'd made a quick stop at one of the larger malls to acquire the proper clothing and some extra makeup. She'd changed at the store, applied the extra makeup in her car, then come directly to the bar.

When she first arrived, she'd sat in the darkest corner of one of the booths watching customers entering and leaving, listening for Chuck Lang's name to be mentioned. She'd wanted her meeting with him to look accidental. But after about half an hour, she'd been ready to ask the waitress if she knew him and would point him out. Then a short, slender dark-haired man entered.

"Lang! Over here," a heavyset man sitting with two others had yelled out to him.

Once she knew her quarry, Bernadette had left her corner, gone over to the pinball machine and tried to coquettishly catch Lang's eye. That had been nearly an hour ago. As she lost another silver ball, she grudgingly admitted she hadn't had enough practice attracting men. "I'm clearly amateur night stuff," she muttered under her breath.

Well maybe not entirely amateur night, she conceded. A couple of the patrons had made passes. She just hadn't sparked Chuck Lang's interest. He was too involved in the conversation he was having with his companions.

Trying to keep the last ball in the machine alive, she wished she could be a fly on the wall and hear what they were saying. It had to be important and private because she'd noticed that when anyone approached, they quickly became silent.

Suddenly an arm was wrapped around the back of her waist, the large hairy hand attached to it coming to rest on her hip. "You about ready to give that machine a rest?" a husky male voice questioned, then added in a seductive leer, "Whatever you're selling, lady, I'm ready to buy."

The strong stench of alcohol-laced breath wafted around her. Turning her head, she found herself looking up into a heavily bearded face with mildly glazed eyes. It was one of the men who had made a previous pass back for another try. Typical of the others in this place, he wore cowboy boots along with a Stetson, jeans and a Western-cut shirt. The shirt, embroidered on the yoke, strained at the lower buttons keeping it fastened over a large potbelly.

A momentary rush of fear that questioned her sanity in coming alone to this place brought a knot to her stomach. Curtly she reminded herself she had very little to lose. Tossing the man a "get lost" glare, she returned her attention to the machine only to discover she'd lost the last ball. The interruption was going to cost her another quarter and, to make matters worse, the "get lost" glance hadn't worked. The chunky, unwelcome arm remained around her like a persistent leech.

"I ain't opposed to a little conversation first," the man was saying, obviously attempting to make amends for his less than subtle approach. "How about if I buy you another beer. You've been nursing that one," he nodded at the half-empty glass sitting near the machine, "for over an hour. It's bound to be flat."

Lifting his hand from her hip as if it was a distasteful insect, she regarded him coldly. "I like flat beer."

Anger etched itself into the man's features. "Lady, you've been standing at this machine for nearly an hour, wiggling around like bait on a hook," he growled, replacing his hand on her hip.

Bernadette didn't want to cause a scene and she didn't want to do anything that would keep Chuck Lang from approaching her. Fighting back a second rush of fear that again questioned the rationale of her behavior, she wished she had more experience in dealing with this segment of the male population.

"You about ready to leave, Lou Ellen?" a male voice drawled in a heavy Texas accent from close behind her.

There was something familiar about that voice, she thought. Glancing over her shoulder, she was startled to see Max Laird. Like her, he was dressed to blend in with the crowd. And, she had to admit, he fit in well. Unlike her, his jeans weren't new but showed signs of having been worn and his boots were scuffed. Even his fake drawl didn't sound artificial. And the easy way he carried his six-foot-two-inch athletic frame made him look like he could have just climbed off a horse instead of out from behind a desk.

"If you've run out of quarters," he continued, those cold blue eyes of his holding a threat as they traveled over the man with his hand on her hip, "I'd like to go home."

Bernadette saw the momentary fear in the bearded man's eyes, then came defiance. "Where'd you come from?" he challenged, his hold on her hip tightening.

"From over there." Max nodded toward a darkened corner of the bar. "And if you don't take your hand off my wife, I'm going to have to put a fist down your throat."

"Hey! No fighting in here," the bartender yelled. "Take it outside."

Bernadette had wanted a little excitement during her last days, but that hadn't included being the cause of a bar-room brawl. "I'm really not worth fighting over," she assured the bearded man.

Momentarily he hesitated, clearly struggling with his pride. Then as if a solution had presented itself, his expression became self-righteous. "I don't fool around with married women." Releasing her as if letting go of a hot potato, he added with curt disapproval, "And, if she was my wife, I wouldn't let her play one of those machines in public."

"She says it turns her on." Max shrugged with a "what's a man supposed to do" expression.

Shaking his head, a leering smile played across the bearded man's face. "In that case, I suppose a fight once in a while might be worth it." Then returning to the bar, he said something to his fellow drinkers that sent them into spasms of laughter.

Flushing with embarrassment, Bernadette said nothing as Max slipped his arm around her waist and guided her out the door. But once they were in the parking lot, she jerked loose from the contact and glared up at him. "You had no right to interfere. If I want to do some investigative reporting, that's my business."

"What kind of story were you planning to write?" he growled, keeping his voice low. "An up close and personal article on the life of a prostitute?"

"I know about the consumer rip-off scam," she snapped back, following his lead and keeping her voice low so anyone passing couldn't hear.

So he'd guessed right, Max congratulated himself for a second time this evening. Her being there hadn't been a mere coincidence. But didn't this idiot woman know what kind of danger she'd placed herself in? he fumed. He continued to regard her darkly. "Dressed like that, you look like a ten-cent trick and those men in there play rough. You could have gotten yourself in a lot of trouble."

In her present state of mind, the fact that he was right only irked Bernadette more. "Ten-cent trick!" she seethed.

"Well, maybe a quarter," he amended dryly, admitting even he'd experienced an unexpected attraction.

His pompous, self-righteous attitude fed her fury. Unable to think of anything to say, she glared at him in mute rage.

A hint of a smile played at the corners of his mouth. He'd never thought Ms. Dowd possessed such a fiery temper. "Okay, a fifty-dollar trick."

The hairs on the back of her neck bristled. He was laughing at her. He'd ruined her chances of making contact with Chuck Lang, embarrassed her in front of all of the patrons and now he had the nerve to laugh at her! Too furious to remain in his presence a moment longer, she turned and stalked toward her car.

Max was tempted to let her go. The last thing he wanted was Bernadette Dowd cluttering his landscape. But he was smart enough to know that letting her walk away now didn't mean he was getting rid of her. Catching up with her, he captured her by the wrist, forcing her to a halt. "We have to talk," he said. "In private . . . my car." As he spoke, he began walking toward the other side of the parking lot, pulling her along.

"There's nothing to talk about!" she replied, trying to jerk free.

"We can't be stumbling over each other. That will blow the investigation. We're going to have to work out some arrangement," he growled back, continuing to hold on to her while at the same time picking up his pace.

Forced to nearly jog to keep up with him, Bernadette glowered at him. She was in no mood to work out an arrangement with anyone, especially Max Laird, who until tonight hadn't even given her the time of day.

Out of the corner of his eye, Max saw the resolute set of her jaw. She was going to be difficult, he knew. But then weren't most women, he added. He led her to a far corner of the parking lot. There, he unlocked the passenger side of his blue Mustang and motioned for her to get inside.

For a moment when he released her, she considered walking away. But before she could act on this impulse, her common sense intervened. She might be dying but that was no reason to behave totally stupidly, she admonished herself. Stoically she obeyed.

Seated inside the car, she watched him as he rounded the front and climbed in behind the wheel. He didn't look any happier to have her there than she was to be there, she noted. Taking a couple of deep breaths, she ordered herself to behave rationally and coherently. "You were right about my maybe getting into trouble in there," she said stiffly. When he greeted this admission with an of-course-I-was look, her jaw hardened with determination. "And you're right about us interfering with each other. So I'd suggest you let me handle this story and you go find something else to work on."

The frown on his face darkened. She wasn't being difficult, she was being impossible. "You're great at the stories you do. Stick to them."

His patronizing manner threatened her control. "If you're inferring that all I'm good for reporting is local bazaars, charity drives and all those other assignments you think are beneath you, then you're going to discover you're wrong." The concern that she might be biting off more than she could chew flashed through her mind but she refused to acknowledge it. She was not going out with a whimper.

For a long moment, Max regarded her in silence. He'd never thought of Bernadette Dowd as being the belligerent type. She'd always been more like a Milquetoast. But the woman seated beside him looked more determined than any female he'd ever seen ... than any person, male or female, he'd ever seen, he corrected. But she lacked experience. That was obvious. If he let her continue on her own she could get hurt.

Her life isn't my problem, he snarled silently. However, he still didn't know what Lang was up to. It could be something minor or it could be something that threatened lives. If it was the latter, Lang had to be exposed. He couldn't, in good conscience, simply turn this investigation over to a rank amateur. "How about if we pool our information and work together?" he suggested.

Bernadette was forced to admit she was fumbling around in the dark. Besides, catching Lane at whatever he was doing was the important issue. "Sure," she replied. "You first."

Max started to balk. Rule four on his list was never to go first when divulging information. He liked to keep an ace in the hole. But, he reasoned, he didn't know all that much. He might as well humor her for the moment. "I was here on a tip about Chuck Lang. The barfly seated next to me told me Lang's the owner of a company called Pure Liquid Refreshment. It's a bottled water distributor. That's all I've learned so far. Now it's your turn."

"That's about all I know, too," she replied, feeling triumphant she'd made him go first. He'd found out a lot more than she had. But if he hadn't interfered she would have uncovered some information on her own, she assured herself. She cast him a disgruntled look. "I was trying to meet Lang in hopes of learning more."

"My guess is you'd have gotten a very unpleasant lesson and not learned anything about whatever Lang is up to. My new drinking buddy told me the guy likes to knock his women around."

Inwardly Bernadette shivered. Just how much trouble she could have gotten into hadn't occurred to her. She'd just wanted to do something important before the end.

Max studied her narrowly. She'd known about this place and she'd known about Lang. She had to have an informant. That meant she had to know more than she was admitting. "How'd you find out about Chuck Lang?" he asked, breaking the silence that had fallen between them.

Bernadette considered fabricating an informer but decided against it. He was bound to find out the truth from Grace. "I was at the office right after the call came in," she replied. Not wanting to get the secretary in trouble, she added, "Grace mentioned it to me because she was sure I wouldn't do anything about it."

Max cursed under his breath. Bernadette Dowd was beginning to feel like an albatross around his neck. "First time I've ever known Grace to be wrong."

Bernadette shifted her gaze back to the bar. "Life takes some unexpected paths."

"So it would seem." Max's gaze narrowed on the woman beside him. At the moment, her expression was again stoic and cool. But he'd seen the momentary flash of anxiety mingled with fear that had crossed her features when she spoke. His gut instinct told him something that had nothing to do with Chuck Lang or this investigation was bothering Ms. Dowd. *She's not my problem,* he grumbled at himself again. The story was all that was important.

Bernadette jerked her mind away from the morbid path it had begun to travel. "What do we do now?" she asked.

I get rid of Ms. Dowd, Max answered silently. Aloud he said, "You go home and get out of that outfit before it cuts off your circulation and take off that makeup before it hardens and you have to use a paint scraper to get rid of it. Then, get some rest. I'll stay here and watch for Lang to leave and follow him."

Bernadette scowled at him. Granted, her current appearance wasn't the real her, but she'd thought she'd looked at least somewhat sexy in this outfit. Max Laird made her feel like a kid at Halloween who'd chosen an inappropriate costume. And, she seethed, did he think she was stupid?! His ploy to get rid of her was as transparent as glass. "In the first place, you're not my father. In the second, I will not just walk away from this story and leave it to you."

Max groaned inwardly. He should never have made those comments about her clothes and makeup. But she made him uneasy. She had some dangerously enticing curves and they were tempting him a lot more than he wanted to be tempted. "Look, there's no sense in both of us staying up all night. One of us should be fresh in the morning."

"Then you go get some rest and I'll follow Lang," she returned, reaching for the handle of her door.

Max knew when he was fighting a losing battle. Capturing her by the wrist, he stopped her. "We'll both follow Lang."

Chapter Two

Bernadette glanced out of the corner of her eye at Max Laird. An hour ago, he'd told her to wake him in a couple of hours. Then he'd lowered the driver's seat into as much of a reclining position as it would go, and gone to sleep.

She knew from all the ribbing he'd taken on his birthday last year that he was only thirty-one. That made him a mere four years older than her but his demeanor suggested he considered himself much more mature than her and considerably wiser. Well, he had lived a fuller life than she had, she admitted, but that didn't make him smarter or more clever than her. That merely gave him more experience to draw from.

Assured that he was truly asleep, she allowed herself a more thorough inspection. During the past three years, she'd seen him at work on nearly a daily basis. In fact his desk was just across the aisle from hers. But he'd always behaved coolly toward her and she'd never been one to force her company on anyone who didn't want it. As a result, she'd probably spoken less than ten words to him before tonight and never taken a really close look at him.

His jaw, she decided was a little too square. An outward sign of his stubborn, authoritarian nature, she mused. Her attention shifted to his nose. It was medium in size and fitted his face well. But there was a slight crook in it that ruined the symmetry. Considering the way he'd managed to irritate her so quickly this evening, she decided he'd probably said the wrong thing to the wrong person and gotten punched.

Her gaze traveled to his mouth. It was average looking in shape and size. The lips were medium in fullness. Continuing to his chin, she decided it fitted the rest of his features well. It was strong but didn't jut out. All in all he wasn't bad-looking. He wasn't handsome but he was passable.

Bernadette's mouth pursed into a thoughtful pout. Of course, there were women who thought he was a great deal more than passable. She recalled a scene she'd witnessed in the office last Wednesday.

It had begun with the sound of spiked heels accompanied by the scent of expensive perfume announcing the arrival of Sabrina Baron, the newspaper's gossip columnist. Passing Bernadette without a pause, the strikingly lovely, natural blonde had shifted the clutter on a corner of Max's desk with a carefully manicured finger, then perched herself on the cleared space.

Bernadette had learned long ago that those delicate boned features masked a competitive drive equal to none. It was rumored that Sabrina was willing to go to any lengths to get a story and could, herself, fill several years worth of columns if her antics were ever put into print. That day her hair had been gathered in an upward sweep then artistically arranged into a soft cascade of curls and she was clothed in a daringly low-cut cocktail dress. "I'm on my way to Merriweather Neily's garden party this afternoon," she purred, leaning forward to provide Max with the full effect her dress was designed to create. "How do I look?"

"Like a very tasty morsel," he replied with a suggestive smile that caused an extra sparkle in the woman's eyes.

Laughing, she leaned closer. "Do you think I'll be able to get any of the guests to reveal some deep dark secret that's definitely not fit to print but will make great copy?"

"I'm sure you will," he replied, raising and lowering his eyebrows in Groucho Marx fashion. Then abruptly, his expression became serious and a cautionary note entered his voice. "But if I were you, I'd stay away from Neily. He's a very powerful man and only likes the nicest things written about him."

Sabrina gave him an impatient look. "From what I know, there are only nice things to write about him. He doesn't even cheat on his wife. And he's one of the most charming men I've ever met." Her gaze narrowed on Max. "But you do seem to always be warning me about him. Do you know something I should know?"

"I don't know anything about him that would interest you," Max assured her. "However, I'm sure Neily isn't perfect. I just wouldn't go searching for the imperfections if I were you."

Sabrina's expression relaxed into a confident smile. "I know my business. Merriweather could see that I'm cut from every important guest list in this town." Her eyes glistened with purpose. "And I do love parties."

Max's expression relaxed and he grinned. "I'm sure you'll have a great time this afternoon."

Sabrina leaned even more closely to him. "If I don't, will you be available to see that I enjoy my evening?"

"I'm sure a classy lady like yourself can find a better companion than me," came his friendly but firm refusal. "Besides, I have to catch up on my work tonight."

"That's right. Tomorrow night is the weekly male poker game." Sabrina's mouth formed a petulant pout as she lifted her hand to examine her blood-red fingernails. "That final bastion of male sovereignty. I'll bet I could pick up enough gossip for a week's worth of columns." Her gaze leveled on Max. "How about sneaking me in?"

Mock horror descended over his features. "And lose my position as top male chauvinist?"

"You could take me as your servant," the blonde coaxed. "You know...the browbeaten subservient female who waits on you hand and foot, massaging your shoulders and pouring your drinks."

"Sorry, but no nonplayers allowed."

"I've never been accused of being a nonplayer," the woman purred. Then glancing at her watch, she slipped off the desk and, with a final regretful smile, waved goodbye.

Bernadette was not normally an eavesdropper, but she'd found herself following the exchange. It wasn't new. Sabrina had been making a play for Max for as long as Bernadette had been with the newspaper and, according to office gossip, even before that. However, in spite of Sabrina's striking good looks and no-strings-attached attitude, he refused to succumb to her charms.

Bernadette knew about Max's rule never to date anyone he worked with. She'd heard Sabrina chiding him about it once. But she was surprised he hadn't made an exception in the blonde's case. Not very many men, she guessed, would have refused such an open invitation from such a beautiful female.

"Is there something on your mind, you want to say to me?"

Bernadette blinked as the sound of Max's voice caused her mind to snap back to the present. Realizing she'd been staring at him, she frowned to cover her embarrassment. "I was just wondering if you were still asleep."

"Not anymore," he growled, shifting his seat into an upright position. As he turned his attention to the door of the bar, he admitted he was more angry with himself than with her. He'd trained himself to sleep anywhere and at anytime. He'd especially trained himself to ignore anyone he chose. When he'd closed his eyes an hour ago, he'd told himself to forget about Ms. Dowd, relax and get some rest. Instead, she'd lingered on the fringes of his consciousness. And he'd been as aware of her studying him as if she'd actually reached over and touched him. "You sleep. I'll watch for a while."

His obvious irritation with her presence grated on Bernadette's nerves. "I think I'll watch from my car," she said and in the next instant she was out of his and moving across the parking lot.

For a moment Max considered stopping her, then dismissed the notion. "With any luck, she'll get tired, fall asleep and I'll lose her," he muttered to himself. "She's one nuisance I don't need." He watched her until she was safely in her car, then turned his full attention to the door of the bar.

Max glanced at his watch. It was a few minutes past midnight. He hoped Chuck Lang wasn't going to close the bar down. As if in answer to this wish, the man in question came out, waved goodbye to his buddies and walked toward a late model Porsche.

"Nice car," Max observed. "His business must be doing real well." As he started his engine, he glanced toward Bernadette's car. She'd flicked her lights on. "Damn," he groaned. They were going to look like a circus parade.

Hanging back, he let her leave behind Lang. "Okay, Ms. Dowd, just don't hang too close and let him spot you," he cautioned under his breath as he pulled out behind her. He didn't relish the idea of her getting spotted and him having to come to her rescue. That would blow both of their covers.

"She did all right," he conceded a few minutes later as he guided his car into a parking spot several cars away from where she'd just parked. They were at an apartment complex. Lang had parked in front of the building on the other side of the lot and was now making his way to the entrance of that building.

Bernadette turned off her car and sat watching the building Lang had entered. Had he come to see someone or did he live there? she wondered. She recalled that in the movies the detective usually got that answer by checking the names on the mailboxes. She glanced at her watch. She'd give him ten minutes then take a quick look.

A knock on her window startled her. Glancing to her side, she saw Max.

"Looks like he's home," he said when she rolled down her window.

Bernadette frowned up at him. "How do you know this is 'home'?"

"I keep a phone book in my car. There's a Charles Lang listed as living here."

Bernadette mentally kicked herself. Why hadn't she thought of that? Max was a step ahead of her again.

"It's my guess he's in for the night," Max continued. Giving in to the inevitable, he added, "And since we don't want to look like a parade tomorrow, I'd suggest you go home and fix some sandwiches and a thermos of coffee. I'll wait here for an hour or so. If he hasn't moved by then, I'll know he's gone to bed and I'll swing by and pick you up."

Challenge flickered in her eyes. "Why don't you go fix the sandwiches and coffee and I'll swing by and pick you up in an hour."

"Because I'm not the one who needs to wash my face and change clothes," he replied impatiently, then silently berated himself when he saw the anger flair in her eyes. If they weren't going to blow this story, they needed to cooperate and that meant not making her angry with him. But that outfit was a strain on his control.

Bernadette silently admitted the thought of changing out of the tight jeans and taking the makeup off her face was appealing, but she was in no mood to be ordered around. "I'm quite comfortable, thank you."

Well, he wasn't, Max returned mentally. The urge to break rule number two was growing stronger by the moment. But Bernadette Dowd was not a woman he wanted to mingle with. The first time he'd seen her, he'd labeled her as a female who'd want a commitment and rule number one was that he stayed away from women like that. He intended to remain totally unencumbered. "The one thing a person doing surveillance doesn't want to be is conspicuous," he explained, trying to keep the annoyance out of his voice. "Not only are those clothes bound to catch people's eyes, but your makeup is already smearing. By morning you're going to look like you were in a cat fight."

Bernadette glanced at herself in the rearview mirror. He was right about the makeup. Not used to wearing so much, she'd forgotten about it a couple of times and rubbed her eyes. Now the mascara and eyeliner had formed a wide circle of black. But she wasn't ready to give in just yet. "What if you're wrong and he leaves?"

"Then I'll call you as soon as I can get to a phone. What's your number?"

She wasn't so sure he would call but she did agree that he was probably right about Lang being in for the night. The man's driving had been erratic enough for her to guess he was fairly drunk. By now, he's probably already passed out on his bed, she guessed. She scribbled her number and her address on a sheet of paper and handed it to Max.

Bernadette paced around her living room. She'd changed into a pair of slacks, a loose fitting pullover top and sneakers. The heavy makeup was gone. She should have felt more comfortable but she didn't.

What she felt was tense. In the kitchen was a grocery bag filled with sandwiches, water and snack food. Beside it was a thermos of coffee. "I packed enough food to feed an army," she muttered, thinking she should go unpack some of it. Instead she came to an abrupt halt and let her gaze travel around the room.

The single story, three-bedroom house located in a quiet suburb in northern St. Louis county had belonged to her maternal grandmother, Claire Birkely. Bernadette's parents had died when she was a child. Claire, widowed and with her only child now gone, had taken her granddaughter in and raised her. When Grandma Birkely had died, she'd left all she had to Bernadette. The major part of the inheritance had been this house and its contents. Here, among the handmade afghans, pillows and doilies her grandmother had knitted and crocheted, surrounded by photos of her grandparents, her parents and herself, Bernadette had always felt safe and comfortable. This was her sanctuary. But tonight it seemed barren and cold and very lonely.

She glanced at her watch. She'd give Max five more minutes to show up, then she was going back to Lang's place. As if in response to this silent promise, two blurred orbs of light showed on the curtain drawn across her living-room window. They were accompanied by the sound of a car pulling into her driveway.

"You got a couch I can sleep on?" Max asked as he entered. "I was going to go back to my place, but I figured if I called and told you that, you wouldn't believe me."

Silently Bernadette admitted he was right. Aloud, she said, "I thought we were going to keep an eye on Lang."

He shrugged as he passed her and seated himself on her sofa. "He's in for the night. I figure our best bet is to get some rest and follow him on his rounds tomorrow. That way we'll get a list of some of his customers in case we need to talk to them. And, with any luck, we'll be able to spot what he's up to that has our anonymous tipper so upset."

Taking off his shoes as he spoke, he added, "I've got a friend at the Better Business Bureau. I'll give him a call tomorrow morning and see if anyone's filed a complaint against the Pure Liquid Refreshment Company and what that complaint is." Pausing, he glanced at his watch. "Set your alarm for five. That'll give us a couple of hours to sleep."

The way he was mapping out their strategy without even asking her opinion, grated on Bernadette's nerves. Even more, remembering how tense she'd been before he'd arrived, she was worried about being able to keep her calm mask in place if she was forced to sit idly around. However, his plan was sensible. For her to insist on going back to Lang's place would only make her appear totally amateurish. "You might as well stretch out on the bed in my guest room. You'll be more comfortable," she heard herself saying.

Rising, Max nodded. "Which way?"

"The door to the right at the end of the hall," she replied.

Watching him walk away, she wondered if her sanity would last as long as her life. With him there the walls suddenly didn't feel so confining. In fact, the house actually felt almost comfortable. That she found solace in Max Laird's company was not rational. The man considered her a nuisance. "Well, as they say in the navy, any port will do in a storm. Or, in this case, any living presence just so I'm not totally alone seems to be a help," she murmured under her breath.

Following his lead, she went into her own bedroom. After setting the alarm, she kicked off her shoes and laid down on top of the covers. She was sure she wouldn't sleep. The prayer her grandmother had taught her as a child began to play through her mind.... "Now I lay me down to sleep. I pray the Lord my soul to keep. If I should die before I wake..." Her jaw tensed and she pushed the rest of the words from her mind. Think of something else . . . anything else, she ordered herself. The sound of the bed in the guest room creaking caused Max's image to fill her mind.

"I'd hoped I'd come up with something a little more enjoyable," she grumbled dryly. Then exhaustion suddenly overwhelmed her and she drifted into a restless sleep.

Chapter Three

Bernadette awoke with a groan of disgust as her alarm rang. Groggily she hit the Snooze button to give herself ten more minutes before facing the day.

"If you're coming with me, you'd better get up now."

Bernadette's eyes popped open at the sound of the male voice. She looked in the direction from which it had come to see Max Laird standing in the doorway of her bedroom. For a moment confusion prevailed, then suddenly the events of the day before all came back to her. "I'm up," she said, shifting into a sitting position on the side of the bed.

Max drew a disgusted breath. He'd been standing in the doorway watching her for several minutes before he'd said anything. She'd looked cute curled up with her hair in disarray over her pillow. Too cute and much too appealing. For a while he'd considered sneaking out without her. But he was sure she'd simply follow him and they'd be a parade behind Lang. Angry to find himself caught in this dilemma, he headed for the kitchen.

Bernadette had looked up in time to see the expression of disgust on Max's face. She'd never liked confrontations. For a second, she considered letting him pursue this story on his own. But that would mean going into the office and getting stuck with the Board of Adjustment meeting. "I just can't sit through one of those sessions today," she growled under her breath. Besides, hadn't she promised herself she would do something worthwhile with the time she had left?

Her jaw firmed as she reached for the phone and punched in the private line to Ben Kealy's phone. Grace's voice sounded on the answering machine and Bernadette left a message saying she was feeling ill and wouldn't be in to work for a couple of days.

"You coming or not?" Max yelled impatiently from the living room.

"Be with you in a minute," she called back heading for the bathroom.

He'd hoped she'd changed her mind. "Don't you have a zoning hearing you're supposed to be covering today?" he asked as she came down the hall still brushing her hair.

"I called in sick. Maybe Ben will send Sabrina. That should stir the meeting up some."

Max grinned at the image of Sabrina striding into that conference room. He'd never thought of Ms. Dowd as having such a dry sense of humor. In fact, he'd never thought of her as having much of a sense of humor at all. "Considering the dirt she probably has tucked away in that gossip-collecting mind of hers, it's my bet a few of those board members would probably start squirming."

The mischief she saw in his eyes surprised her and, in spite of her tenseness, she grinned back. In the next moment, she found herself wondering just what Sabrina knew about Max Laird. The thought of asking the woman even occurred to her. *He's not the kind of man you've been looking for,* she berated herself, stunned by the path her thoughts were taking. Everyone knew about his vow to remain uncommitted.

Of course, any relationship she might form wouldn't last long enough to be considered a commitment, she reminded herself.

Max saw the haunted look that suddenly shadowed Bernadette's features. Again, he felt sure that something other than his unwanted presence was bothering this woman. But he refused to get involved in her private life. She'll work whatever it is out on her own, he assured himself. His grin disappeared and his manner became businesslike. "Come on, we have to get going if we're going to find a good spot to observe our quarry."

As she'd watched the cool, distant expression return to Max's face, Bernadette had the sensation of a door being closed between them. Mentally she mocked herself for having even momentarily experienced an interest in him. Clearly he would never consider pursuing any relationship with her. And, I'd be a fool to consider one with him, she told herself. If she did decide to have a final romantic fling, it was going to be with a man who was kind and gentle and cared about pleasing the woman he was with. And, she doubted Max Laird possessed any of these characteristics in any great quantity. "I've got food packed in the kitchen," she said over her shoulder hurrying to retrieve the sandwiches and coffee she'd made the night before.

Max dubiously eyed the large bag of food she set on the back seat before sliding into the passenger side of his car. "Looks like you prepared for a week's siege."

"I don't like to get caught unprepared," she returned flippantly while mentally kicking herself for not leaving some behind.

"Then where's your video camera?" he tossed back.

Bernadette stared at him. "I'm a newspaper reporter, not a television personality."

Max regarded her patronizingly. "If we're going to accuse this guy of something, we need proof. In the past, pictures used to be enough. But today the public wants to see the culprit in live action. So we get the tape, we print the story, then we distribute the proof to the television stations.''

She hated looking like an amateur but, she admitted, she was when it came to investigative reporting. ''All right so I'm new at this.'' Suddenly tired of being on the defensive, she regarded him wryly. ''However, I'm sure you, O'Honorable Ace Investigative Reporter, have one we can share.''

Max couldn't stop himself from grinning. She had spunk. ''As long as we both agree that O'Ace here is in charge and can make the rules, I'll let you play with my toys,'' he returned.

Bernadette was startled by how handsome he looked when he smiled. ''As long as you keep the rules within the limits of fair play,'' she specified.

''Agreed.'' Max offered her his hand. But the moment she slipped her hand into his, he wished he'd skipped the handshake. He found himself very aware of the softness of her skin and he couldn't believe how much he wanted to continue to prolong the contact. Obviously I've been neglecting my social life much too long, he told himself, releasing her quickly and starting the car.

Bernadette had shaken many hands but she'd never experienced the rush of heat that traveled up her arm when Max's hand closed around hers. His abrupt release startled her. Clearly, although he'd agreed to her presence, he wasn't pleased with it, she noted. Well, she didn't care. This could be her last chance to do something important.

''Our Mr. Lang obviously doesn't believe in getting an early start,'' Bernadette commented dryly. It was nearly eight o'clock and, for the past two hours, she and Max had been sitting in Max's car in the parking lot of Lang's apartment building waiting for the man to come out.

They'd barely spoken. Max had slept. He'd offered to keep watch while she napped but she'd been too tense to sleep. She'd also been too tense to just sit and watch the door of the apartment. To pass the time, she'd gotten out Max's video camera and read through the instruction manual five times. She was pretty sure she could disassemble the thing and put it back together without any great difficulty.

Breathing a bored sigh, she again glanced at the apartment building door. Suddenly her body tensed and her boredom vanished. Lang was coming out. "He's on the move," she said, nudging Max sharply with her elbow.

"Ouch!" came an irritated growl, followed by an impatient, "I see him."

Glancing to her left, she saw Max alert behind the wheel. She'd been sure he'd been sound asleep just a moment earlier.

Max tried to concentrate on Lang and forget about the woman beside him. But even as he watched his quarry crossing the parking lot, his mind was on Bernadette Dowd. For the past hour he'd been covertly studying her. When she'd started reading the instruction manual for his camera, he'd thought that was in character. She'd always struck him as the efficient, professional type. But when she'd begun reading it a second time he'd begun to study her more closely.

Again he was sure he saw a hint of panic on her face. He tried telling himself she was probably just one of those people who was intimidated by new technology. But almost immediately, he'd had to discard that notion. She was always one of the first people in the newsroom to master any new software for the computers.

Then she'd shifted her attention to Lang's apartment building. What he'd thought would be a glance had turned into a stare. Then he'd seen unabashed fear etching itself into her features. As if forcing her mind away from a path she didn't want it to take, she'd jerked her attention back to the manual.

Continuing to covertly observe her, he'd noted the increasing lines of strain around her mouth. Again, his gut instinct insisted something totally unconnected to the Lang investigation was bothering Ms. Dowd. However, whatever problem she's working through, it's her problem not mine, he told himself as he followed Lang out of the parking lot. And she clearly wanted it that way, too, he added, noting she'd made no attempt to talk to him about anything other than their investigation.

Bernadette jotted down the address of the house to which Lang had just delivered two large bottles of water and retrieved two empty bottles from. They'd been following the man all morning. He'd gone first to the warehouse in which his small, one man operation was located, gotten into his truck and begun his route. At each stop he delivered filled bottles of purified spring water and picked up the empties.

"That truck of his can't hold too many more bottles," Max said as Lang drove away and they followed. "He must be full of empties by now."

Bernadette nodded. "It's coffee break time. He'll probably be heading back to his warehouse."

"Looks like he's going to stop for gas first," Max noted, passing the gas station Lang had pulled into and parking a little farther down the street.

Bernadette watched in the side mirror as the man filled up his gas tank. An attendant came out of the repair bay to collect his money. She squinted for a better look at the new arrival. "That man he just paid looks a lot like one of the men he was with at the bar last night," she said, turning around in her seat for a better look.

"Sure does," Max agreed.

"I don't believe this," Bernadette groaned in frustration as she saw Lang climb into his truck, pull it over to one of the bay doors and then back it in. "We start following him around on a day when he's bringing his truck in for maintenance.''

Max breathed a disgusted sigh as the garage bay door closed. "Looks like our dogging is done for today."

"Maybe he'll borrow a truck from his buddy," Bernadette said, impatience strong in her voice.

Max hoped she was right. He usually didn't mind getting stuck sitting for long periods waiting and watching. He kept a portable computer in the back seat and he'd use the time to work. But the information he kept stored in that little machine was not something he wanted anyone else to see just yet. And he wasn't willing to take a chance on Ms. Dowd reading over his shoulder.

On the other hand, he hated wasting time. Glancing to the back, he noticed the bag of food. His stomach growled reminding him he hadn't eaten anything other than the doughnut and coffee they'd picked up on their way to Lang's warehouse. "Now's as good a time as any for a snack," he said, reaching behind him and lifting the bag into the front seat.

As he began to eat, he noticed that although he'd handed Bernadette a sandwich and she'd unwrapped it, she was barely nibbling at it. He recalled she hadn't eaten more than a bite of her doughnut, either. "If you're on a diet, forget it," he ordered. "When you're doing a stakeout, you have to eat when you can because you never know for sure when you'll be able to eat again. And I don't want you fainting from hunger at a crucial moment."

Bernadette wondered how he'd react if she died at a crucial moment. Then shoving that thought out of her mind, she forced herself to follow his instructions and eat.

Max had finished a second sandwich and was considering ways of working on his computer without letting Ms. Dowd get a glimpse of the screen when the door of the garage bay opened.

"That was a fast tune-up," Bernadette said with a breath of relief. "I guess it pays to know the mechanic."

"Guess so," Max replied as Lang passed them and he pulled out behind the delivery truck once again.

To Bernadette's surprise, instead of heading back to his warehouse, Lang turned west. His next stop was a nursing home where he delivered several bottles of water and picked up more empties. Next he stopped at a bakery where he dropped off five more bottles.

As he carried the empties back to his truck, Bernadette turned to Max. "I feel like I'm watching one of those clown acts at the circus, the one where a zillion clowns come out of a little car."

Max nodded. "That truck does seem to have an inordinate amount of storage room."

"I suppose he could have a stash of bottles stored at the gas station so he wouldn't have to go all the way back to his warehouse," she suggested dubiously.

"But wouldn't that be a little crowded if they were stored in one of the work bays?" Max asked. He frowned thoughtfully. "Of course there could have been a door we couldn't see leading to a storage shed in the back."

Another incongruity suddenly occurred to Bernadette. "While Lang was backing his truck into the repair area, the mechanic closed the other two bay doors then they closed the door of the one Lang had backed into. Why would they shut themselves in on such a beautiful spring day?"

"I doubt it was because they like the smell of gas and oil," Max replied.

Bernadette nodded in agreement. She was beginning to form a theory but she didn't like what she was thinking and she wasn't ready to share it just yet. Besides, she was pretty sure Max was also forming the same theory and he wasn't talking about it, either.

As they followed Lang through a few more deliveries, she began keeping a running total of how many bottles of water he was delivering. The number was mounting fast when he turned into one of the older residential areas. The homes here were small two-story brick affairs. Some had bars on the lower windows, an outward sign the people inside didn't feel their neighborhood was as safe as they would like. But the majority of the yards were well kept, the exterior of the homes looked cared for and the sidewalks and gutters along the street were clear of trash. Blue-collar, hardworking, law-abiding people lived here, Bernadette thought, mentally picturing the residents.

Well maybe not all of them were law-abiding, she amended as Lang backed into one of the driveways while another of the men she'd seen him with at the bar came out the front door and watched. The driveway ended in a carport and Lang continued backing until the roof of his truck nearly hit the overhang. The other man joined him as he climbed out of the vehicle and both headed for the back of the house. Bernadette reached for the video camera.

"You stay here and out of sight," Max ordered, grabbing the camera ahead of her.

"I will not," she returned, her hand already on her door handle.

Max caught her by the wrist. "Those two look like the type to play rough. Besides, I'm probably going to have to climb a couple of fences to sneak up on them and get close enough to film what they're doing."

"I can climb fences as good as you," she announced, jerking free from his grasp and continuing out of the car.

Max breathed a disgusted sigh. "I'd argue with you but it's my guess we don't have time. Just stay close and be quiet."

"Yes, master," she tossed back dryly.

Max had been scanning the neighborhood. Because Lang or his cohort could come around to the front at any moment, he decided he should start his approach from at least two houses away. Both of the ones to his right looked at if their occupants were gone, at least for the moment. There were no cars in the carports and the doors were shut. Quickly he made his way to the backyard of the farthest house. A glance at the windows revealed no one watching.

Breathing a sigh of relief he sprinted across the yard, then cursed under his breath at the chain-link fence bordering the next. Well, Ms. Dowd would just have to take care of herself, he told himself as he slung the camera strap around his neck, then climbed over the fence.

"Try to use just one foothold on your way over," he instructed her when he had landed on the other side. "That will make as little noise as possible. Between Lang and his pal talking and the sound of the water running, hopefully they won't notice us."

Bernadette frowned at the fence. She refused to tell Max she'd never climbed one before. For a brief moment, she considered letting him handle this part of the story himself. But this thought brought a rush of rebellion. The fence was less than five feet high, she pointed out to herself. She could get over it. Imitating Max's motions, she did.

Max had seen her hesitation. Immediately he'd guessed she probably hadn't climbed very many fences in her day. The fear that she would make a racket loud enough to raise the dead made him start to urge her to wait for him where she was. But before he could speak, she joined him and, to his relief, with only a modicum of noise.

He glanced at the windows of the house whose yard they'd just entered and saw no one peeking out. So far, so good, he thought as they made their way across the yard to the fence line separating this property from the property belonging to Lang's friend. Beyond the fence, a thick line of evergreens formed a foliage wall encasing the yard in which Lang and his friend were working. Good coverage, Max thought as he climbed this side of the chain-link fence and came down in the midst of the sticky branches.

"You sure know how to show a girl a good time," Bernadette muttered in a whisper as she joined him and one of the branches left a bloodied scratch along her cheek.

"You could have waited in the car," he returned, irritated because he felt bad she was hurt. He didn't like having someone around he had to worry about.

Bernadette wished she hadn't complained. This was what investigative reporting was all about and coming along had been her choice. It wasn't Max's fault she was standing in the midst of these pricking needles with sticky sap smeared on her arm.

Abruptly a snarl caused her to forget her discomfort. Looking to her right, she saw a pit bull about five feet away, his teeth bared.

"Damn!" Max cursed in a harsh whisper. "Get back over the fence," he ordered in the next breath, keeping his voice low. "I'll watch your tail."

Bernadette looked at the dog with its ears laid back. She'd been given a death sentence and that mean little beast was standing between her and a final goal she'd set for her life. A rage at the unfairness in the world filled her. It showed on her face and an ice came into her eyes as she met the dog's gaze. "Go away!" she growled in a voice low enough not to carry to the two men by the house but loud enough for the dog to hear. For a moment longer, the compact little beast stood looking at her, then slowly he took a couple of steps back. In the next instant, he was running yapping in the direction of Lang and the other man.

Reaching them he came to a halt and growled at Lang threateningly.

"You know I don't like that dog of yours," Lang complained to his companion. "I don't trust any dog that's been trained to attack."

"He won't bother you as long as I tell him to leave you alone," the heavier man said patronizingly.

"I'm not in the mood to argue with you about your dog. Put him inside," Lang ordered. "I want to get done so's I can have time to eat some lunch."

The heavier man gave Lang an impatient glance, then waved to the dog. "Come on, Buddy."

The small beast glanced once more in Bernadette's and Max's direction, then followed his master into the house.

"That's quite a way you have with animals," Max remarked in Bernadette's ear. "Next time I hear of any openings as a lion tamer in a circus, I'll be sure to keep you in mind."

Bernadette's heart was pounding double time. She couldn't believe she'd faced that pit bull down. She'd never faced any animal down before. Even her grandmother's poodle had never obeyed her. "Let's get those pictures," she said to Max, wanting only to get finished and get out of there.

Max glanced at the woman beside him. A minute ago she'd looked as if she could have taken on an army single-handed. Now she looked shaken. He was used to women being unpredictable, but he'd never meet anyone quite so unpredictable as Ms. Dowd. Better get this job done and get out of here before she displays any more surprises, he told himself.

He nodded for her to move farther down the fence line away from the house.

Realizing he was trying to get a clear view of the back of the carport, she worked her way along as quickly as possible. To her relief, the line of shrubs continued around the entire perimeter of the yard thus providing them with coverage. It didn't take long to reach a position where they could see past the small storage shed at the rear of the carport and into the back of the truck.

Lang and his friend had lifted a medium-size box from the truck and hooked a hose to whatever was inside. A second hose ran from the box into the truck where Lang's bar buddy was using the water running from it to refill the bottles while Lang sealed the newly filled bottles to make them look as if they'd just come from the real spring water distributor.

"It's my guess that what they have housed in that box is a filter to get rid of any residue in the water," Max said as he adjusted the zoom lens on his camera for a close-up shot.

"I suppose even if his customers did notice residue, he could claim they were simply getting an added bonus of a few healthy minerals from a real spring," Bernadette replied. "And they'd probably believe him."

"Most likely," Max agreed. "Last night, before I came by your place, I was able to get in touch with a friend of mine on the police force. Seems this Lang's a real con-artist. He's been accused several times of fraud in various business dealings but he's never been convicted, never even been brought to trial. In some cases it was bad for business for whoever he conned to prosecute rather than settle out of court. In others, the people he fleeced were too embarrassed to go to court."

Max frowned at himself. He'd never before shared information until it was absolutely necessary. Ms. Dowd was having as unsettling an effect on him as she'd had on Buddy. "Let's get out of here," he whispered, then began making his way along the fence line once again. The sooner this story was in print and their alliance severed the better.

When they reached the side of the yard where they'd crossed the fence before, Max waited until both men were in the back of the truck moving bottles, then waved Bernadette over. He followed as soon as her feet hit the ground.

"Do you think we could use the gate this time?" Bernadette asked as they started across the yard and she spotted this more conventional exit on the other side of the house they were passing. "We can still slip into the adjacent backyard without being seen."

Mentally Max kicked himself for not noticing the gate earlier. "I suppose if you want to do this the easy way," he replied, feigning a regret that he wasn't going to get to go over the fence yet again.

Bernadette gave him an impatient glance. "My grandmother used to say the simplest way was generally the best." A sudden gleam of amusement showed in her eyes as they left through the gate and made their way across the next yard. "Of course she did also like to point out that it was one of those 'men things' to do whatever had to be done in the most complicated or difficult manner possible."

Max glanced at her. "Men things?"

"Things men do differently than women," Bernadette elaborated as they casually strolled to his car, pretending to be a perfectly normal couple on their way out for the afternoon.

Max raised an eyebrow. "Why do I get the feeling we aren't talking about flattering comparisons?"

"They aren't necessarily unflattering," she replied. "They're simply demonstrations of how men and women view things differently."

"Such as?" Max asked as they reached his car and he opened the passenger door for her.

Bernadette thought for a moment, then said, "Such as leaving the tops off tubes of toothpaste and screwing lids on bottles so tightly you need a pair of pliers to get them off."

Max frowned down at her. "I'm beginning to get the impression you think men are a nuisance." As he closed the door and walked around the car to the driver's side, he told himself he should feel relieved. Obviously she was a feminist of the highest order and he'd never mixed well with radical females. No need to worry any longer about the unwanted feelings of attraction to her he'd been experiencing, he assured himself.

Watching him rounding the car, Bernadette considered letting his assessment stand. She couldn't believe she'd been so open with him. But she didn't want him believing she was unreasonably judgmental. "On the whole, I don't consider men nuisances," she said as he slid in behind the wheel. Then without thinking, she heard herself adding, "They have their uses." A flush reddened her cheeks. That was her grandmother's usual finish but Bernadette couldn't believe she said it to Max.

"How very chauvinistic of you," he remarked wryly. Still, he found himself wondering just what being of use to Ms. Dowd would be like. Put thoughts like that out of your mind, he ordered himself curtly and turned his full attention to Lang who was pulling out of the driveway and heading down the street.

Bernadette started to say she'd only been repeating a joke of her grandmother's, then stopped herself. She seemed to be putting her foot into her mouth every time she opened it. Maybe it would be prudent to shut up, she reasoned.

"Now that we know the game," Max said as he again began to follow their quarry, "I'd suggest I continue to tail Lang while you go back and interview a few of his customers. Find out how long they've been doing business with him and why they chose his company, that sort of thing. Then we can meet at the office and put the story together for tomorrow morning's edition."

Bernadette nodded in agreement. She'd actually enjoyed jumping the fences but riding around following the delivery truck had begun to wear on her nerves. There was too much time to think. "I'll get out at the next corner," she agreed readily. "And call a cab."

"Looks like we were both wearing on each other's nerves," Max muttered a couple of minutes later as he pulled away from the stoplight alone. Glancing in the rearview mirror, he saw Ms. Dowd heading for a pay phone. His back muscles relaxed and he breathed a relieved sigh. He preferred working alone.

At the next light he glanced at the computer on his back seat. When he got the chance, he'd check it to see if Lang's name showed up on any of his files. Experience had taught him it was always smart to know who all the players in any game were. "I don't want any surprises," he growled.

Chapter Four

Pretending to be doing a story on why people used bottled water in place of the regular tap supply, Bernadette had interviewed several of Lang's customers. And, although she didn't want Lang tipped off that he was being investigated, she'd managed to plant a few seeds of doubt about his product. Now she was sitting in front of her word processor typing out a rough draft of the story while she waited for Max to arrive.

Hearing the elevator doors open, she looked up to see him coming her way. During the years she'd worked here, she'd concluded that the women who thought he was handsome were simply those who liked a challenge. Now, as her gaze traveled over him, she admitted she'd been wrong.

Max nearly always wore a suit. Last night and today were the first times she could recall seeing him in jeans and a shirt. Without his suit coat, she had a clear view of his broad shoulders and flat abdomen. She also noticed the way his jeans stretched across sturdy-looking thighs. And, recalling how easily he'd gone over those fences, she knew he was as strong as he looked. The entire package taken into account, he was attractive in a very masculine way. She suddenly found herself wondering exactly what he looked like under those clothes.

She jerked her gaze back to the screen in front of her. Her mind had started down a path she usually didn't follow and a flush was creeping up her neck.

"What's Ben think of our story?" Max asked, coming to a halt in front of her desk. He'd seen her watching him and he'd seen her turn away quickly. He'd also been sure he'd caught a look of feminine interest in her eyes. That had surprised him. But he chose to ignore it. Business was all that was ever going to transpire between him and Ms. Dowd, he vowed. Still, he couldn't help noticing the way her pullover clung to the soft, generous curves of her breasts and there was that cute little way she pursed her lips when she was concentrating.

"I haven't told him yet," she replied. "I thought we should tell him together after we had consolidated our facts."

The way she'd grabbed onto this story and insisted on staying with it, Max had been sure she'd go directly to Ben and attempt to take ninety-five percent of the credit. Ms. Dowd was turning out to be a constant surprise, he mused as he rounded her desk so that he could read her screen over her shoulder. "Let's see what you have."

Bernadette sat in her chair and stared at the blank screen in front of her. The past hour had been hectic. She and Max had gone over her draft of the story. He'd suggested a few changes, then they had taken the story and their videotape into Ben's office. The editor had been pleased.

Now the story was on its way to the front page. The video tape was being used to extract a photo to accompany the story. Then the tape would be copied and the copies would be delivered to the proper authorities. Arrangements would also be made for other copies to arrive at the local television stations in time for the noonday news. But the newspaper would have the pleasure of breaking the story to their readers over that first cup of coffee of the day.

Bernadette had been excited, even elated when she'd left Ben's office, his words of "good job" ringing in her ears. But when she'd reached her desk, reality had brought her down fast. There was a message taped to her word processor saying she had a call from Dr. Harold Riley's secretary. When she'd returned the call, the woman had reminded her of the scan she was scheduled for midafternoon of the next day.

"The doctor is concerned and wants to keep track of your progress," the woman had said.

Bernadette had been tempted to say she didn't feel like being a human guinea pig. But she'd heard the uneasiness in the secretary's voice and knew the woman was uncomfortable enough already. "Yes, sure. I'll be there," she'd said instead.

Now she sat staring at her word processor and wondering how she was going to make it through the night. With nothing to do to keep her mind occupied, fear was closing in on her. *I should do something I've always wanted to do but never gotten around to,* she told herself. Her grandmother's income had been limited and her parents hadn't left much insurance. All her life, she'd worked and saved. During high school, she earned all her own spending money and she'd put herself through college. She'd never treated herself to anything extravagant. Maybe now was the time.

"I could go to dinner at one of the more expensive restaurants in town," she murmured under her breath. And she knew just the one, she added feeling better already. She'd heard a lot of people talk about Joe's Place. It was supposed to have some of the best Italian food in the state, maybe even in the country.

Pulling out the phone book, she looked up the number and dialed. A couple of minutes later she was hanging up and her black mood was returning. They'd been fully booked for the night. She tried telling herself she should be grateful to have saved herself a bundle of money. Instead, she wanted to scream in frustration.

Max had found himself watching Bernadette Dowd from the door of Ben's office. Again he'd seen the anger, then the fear on her face. She's not my problem, he'd repeated to himself as he'd forced his attention away from her and strode to the elevators. He'd put in a good day and night's work. Gordon was on duty for tonight, he could cover Lang's arrest. It was time for a beer, a burger and some work on his private files. But as he pushed the button, he glanced back.

He'd noticed her getting out her phone book when he'd passed her desk. Seeing her frown as she hung up, he concluded her call hadn't gone well. The elevator came and he ordered himself to get in. Instead he approached her desk. "Got a problem?" he asked coming to a halt in front of her.

Just a death warrant hanging over my head, Bernadette returned mentally wondering how he'd react if she actually said that aloud. But she didn't. This was her own private hell and she'd handle it herself. She gave a shrug as if to say what was bothering her was inconsequential. "I wanted to go out to eat at a very exclusive restaurant to celebrate my first investigative story. But they're booked solid."

This was not a serious problem, Max told himself and ordered himself to go home. Instead he asked, "What restaurant?"

Bernadette shrugged out the name, feeling foolish for even considering such an extravagance.

Immediately Max picked up the phone and hit the redial. Within a couple of minutes, he was speaking with the owner and making reservations for two.

"One. Reservations for one," Bernadette whispered to him, amazed he knew the proprietor and was held in such high regard the man was not only willing to set up a special table for him but even eager.

"Reservation for one," he corrected.

"You seem to have a lot of friends in this town," she remarked as he hung up.

"I get around," he replied. Again heading to the elevators, he added over his shoulder. "I know you'll have a great meal."

But as he started to press the button, he couldn't stop himself from glancing back at her. Sometime during the early morning ride to Lang's place, she'd pulled her hair back into the tight little chignon that was her usual style. Unexpectedly he found himself recalling how she'd looked that morning when he'd gone in to wake her. Relaxed in sleep and with those chestnut tresses in wild disarray, there had been an appealing gentleness about her. But there was nothing gentle about her now. The line of her jaw was set in a hard line and her entire body seemed stiff when she moved.

Bernadette felt a prickling on the side of her neck. Glancing toward the elevators, she saw Max watching her out of the corner of his eye. She guessed he was thinking she couldn't get a date and that was why she was dining alone. The thought that maybe she should call someone and ask them to join her played through her mind. But there wasn't anyone she felt comfortable calling. She didn't want sympathy or advice and friends always felt they had to offer both at times like this. "I need to go home and change," she ordered herself, hoping action would ease the growing strain she was feeling. But as she reached for her purse, she accidentally knocked it off the side of her desk. The contents spilled. She couldn't hold back a small shriek of disgust. It seemed as if nothing was going right for her.

Max frowned as he watched her stoop to gather the contents of her purse. She'd been much more angered by that little accident than was normal. Something really has that lady rattled, he grumbled to himself, wanting to walk away and knowing he wasn't going to. You'll regret this, he warned himself as he strode back to her desk.

Bernadette's gaze traveled from the spilt contents of her purse up the pair of sturdy male legs to Max's face.

"I was wondering if you'd mind if I join your little celebration? I haven't had a really good Italian meal in a long time," he said. Employing the same technique he used when he was bullheadedly working on a story, he added, "I'll pick you up at your place in an hour and a half," then walked away before she could refuse. He even took the stairs down to the garage so she couldn't catch up with him at the elevator. "I know I'm going to regret this," he muttered to himself as he climbed into his car.

Bernadette had absently shoved the remaining articles back into her purse as she'd watched Max's retreating back. Under normal circumstances she would have steered clear of any socializing with him. She was sure they had nothing in common except their work. But, she admitted, she hadn't been looking forward to spending the evening alone. That had been another reason for going out to dinner in a crowded restaurant. And Max's company would do as well as anyone else's. Besides, she was a little curious as to why he'd invited himself along. She'd been certain he would be relieved to be free of her.

Feeling less frantic about the hours stretching before her, she headed for the elevator.

Bernadette glanced surreptitiously at Max's clean-shaven jaw as he drove to the restaurant. He'd showered, shaved and changed into a suit before coming to pick her up. To her surprise, she found herself missing the stubble that had grown during the hours they spent pursuing Lang. She wondered what the rough growth would have felt like if she'd run her hand over it. Again startled by the paths her mind was taking, she scowled at herself. This aneurysm was definitely affecting her sanity, she decided.

Max sensed her watching him even before he glanced at her to confirm this suspicion. He seemed to be unusually aware of her, he admitted. But only because my reporter's instinct is curious about why she's suddenly acting so differently, he assured himself.

Noticing the flicker of a scowl cross over her features, he again chided himself for acting on the impulse to invite himself along. On his way home, it had dawned on him that she might be acting so peculiar because she'd just broken up with a boyfriend. Rule number three on his list was never get involved in other peoples' love lives. And considering the depth of anger he'd seen on her face a couple of times during the past day, he had to consider the possibility she might be feeling hostile toward all men at the moment. That would definitely lead to a tense evening. "Look, there's one thing I want to get out in the open," he said, deciding to take the bull by the horns. "You seem to be angry at someone or something. If you've just broken up with your boyfriend, keep in mind I'm not him and I don't have any romantic designs on you. All I'm here for is the food."

"I didn't just break up with a boyfriend and I'm not harboring any grudges," Bernadette replied, mildly shaken by the fact that he'd seen the anger she was trying so hard to hide. Her body stiffened in her effort not to allow any further emotion to show.

Max mentally kicked himself as the temperature in the car chilled. "The only reason I asked about a fight with a boyfriend is because that usually precipitates one of those 'women things,'" he said, attempting to return the atmosphere in the car to a more comfortable level.

Bernadette cocked an eyebrow. "Women things?" she asked, knowing she'd set herself up for this one.

Max grinned dryly. "You know, one of those ways of behaving that make women different from men. It's been my observation that when a woman breaks up with a long-standing boyfriend or when her marriage goes sour, she suddenly decides to completely alter her life-style. With women a little change is never enough. You seem to have to go whole hog."

Payback time, Bernadette told herself, recalling her remarks about "men things." And she couldn't fault him for applying this particular description to her. "Touché," she replied with a matching grin.

She looked kind of cute when she smiled like that, Max thought, then jerked his attention back to the street. He was here to do some detecting, not to think about her as if she was a date. Mentally he frowned. He'd hoped his crack about women changing their life-style might trigger conversation about her recent behavior. But instead, she'd fallen silent again.

Staring out the window, Bernadette wondered if maybe she would have been better off refusing Max's company for the evening. The urge to talk about what was happening to her was suddenly strong but he was the last person she wanted to confide in. "Do you have much family here in Missouri?" she heard herself asking. Feeling the need to make some sort of conversation, she'd been trying to think of something to say regarding their work but thoughts about family were weighing heavily on her mind.

"My mom and dad live here in St. Louis and my younger brother and his family reside in Jefferson City. My sister and her family live in Delaware. What about you?"

Bernadette stared out the front window at the traffic in front of them. "No one in Missouri," she replied. "My mother was from here and after my parents died I came here to live with her mother. My mother was an only child and Grandma Birkely was widowed. Now she's gone, too. My father's family was from Montana. His parents are gone now, too, but I have an aunt and uncle who still live there. My father's other brother is in the Navy and stationed in California.''

Max glanced at her out of the corner of his eye. He'd thought he'd detected an underlying sadness when she'd asked him about his family. That had caused him to believe that whatever was bothering her might involve hers. But that didn't seem to be the case. She rattled off the information about both the living and dead almost absently.

They were nearing the restaurant now and he was again having second thoughts about butting into Ms. Dowd's private life. I might be smarter not to find out what's bothering her, he cautioned himself as he parked. Keeping that thought in mind, he decided to let her guide the conversation.

Feeling uneasy discussing any topic even remotely personal for fear it might lead her to reveal her current situation, Bernadette decided to turn to comfortably impersonal subjects. As she climbed out of his car, she made a comment about how pleasant the weather was. And when they entered the restaurant, she immediately began, with a reporter's eye, analyzing the warm yet subtly expensive decor. To her relief, Max seemed willing to follow her lead.

It took only moments for them to be seated, but already Bernadette was being lulled into a sense of well-being by the atmosphere of the place. Then she opened the menu. She'd thought she was prepared for the shock the cost of this meal might be, but when she saw the prices on the menu, her eyes rounded.

Watching her, Max felt a surge of unexpected protectiveness. ''Would you like to just have a drink and go somewhere else for dinner,'' he asked.

For a brief moment, her conservative nature made her consider taking him up on this offer. Then she dismissed that notion. The money she'd saved wasn't going to do her any good in the grave. ''The prices were just a momentary surprise,'' she replied, her facial muscles relaxing into a self-mocking smile. ''But now that it's over, I can hardly wait to taste the food and see if this place deserves its reputation.''

''You won't be disappointed,'' Max assured her, still uncertain if he should say something more to let her know that it would be perfectly all right if they left. But before he could say anything, the waiter appeared and Bernadette ordered the most expensive appetizer on the menu.

''It's nice to see you here again, Max.'' A heavyset man dressed in a finely tailored blue pin-striped suit approached their table as the waiter left. ''It's been a long time.''

''I've been busy,'' Max replied. He'd thought coming here wouldn't bother him after all this time, but it did. He forced a smile. ''The years have been good to you.'' He turned to Bernadette. ''I'd like you to meet Joe Colomaro, the owner of this place. Joe, meet Bernadette Dowd, she works with me at the newspaper.''

''It's a pleasure,'' Joe said, lifting Bernadette's hand in a cavalier fashion and kissing the back lightly. ''You brighten my place with your beauty.''

He spoke with such genuine feeling, Bernadette flushed with pleasure.

Watching her, Max was surprised by her very feminine reaction to Joe's flattery. He also found himself being irritated by Joe's kiss on her hand. I just think he's overdoing his ''charming the ladies'' routine a little, he told himself. Aloud, he said dryly, ''Apparently that old-world charm works every time. You even have Ms. Dowd blushing like a teenager.''

Embarrassment swept through Bernadette. It was not normal for her to let flattery go to her head. However, what harm can it do in this case, she reasoned unexpectedly. Wasn't it time she started enjoying a few things in life instead of always being so skeptical? Forgetting her embarrassment, she tossed Max a haughty glance. ''A woman always appreciates being made to feel as if she's special.''

Joe turned to Max and frowned. "You've grown cynical. I was hoping time would have mellowed you."

"A good reporter always looks at the world through skeptical eyes," Max returned.

A fatherly expression spread over the other man's face as he studied Max closely. "You can't fool me. You haven't put the past behind you, have you?"

Bernadette had noticed an uneasiness in Max when they'd entered the restaurant. She'd thought that maybe he was having second thoughts about being seen with her in public, that he was worried people might think they were a couple. Now it occurred to her that his uneasiness might not have anything to do with her.

The proprietor placed a large hand on Max's shoulder and gave the shoulder a squeeze. "We must learn to bury our dead." Then turning to her, he smiled warmly. "I'm sure a lovely lady like you can convince Max to look to the future." His smile warmed even more. "Enjoy your meal." Then with a final squeeze on Max's shoulder, he left to greet a couple who had just entered.

Bernadette's curiosity was peaked. She told herself Max's personal life was none of her business. But then, she hadn't been listening to her rational mind for two days. Why start now? "It would seem that you and Mr. Colomaro go back a long way," she said, easing into her probing gently.

"His family and my mother's family lived next door on the Hill," Max replied with practiced indifference.

The Hill, Bernadette knew, was the Italian section of town. "Someone once told me there was a place there with the best fresh baked bread in St. Louis. I can't remember the name but they said all I had to do was follow my nose early in the morning."

"Yeah, I suppose," Max replied, returning his attention to his menu.

That he didn't want to talk about the Hill or his connection with Joe Colomaro was pointedly clear. But Joe's remark about burying the dead was ringing in her ears. A good reporter doesn't back down easily, she told herself. Besides having someone other than herself to concentrate on was a relief. "I guess, with your grandparents living next door to Mr. Colomaro, you've been friends all your life."

Max shifted his gaze from the menu to her. He couldn't fault her for being inquisitive. That was part of a reporter's makeup. But he had no intention of talking about his past. "Our families were close. They still are. I like Joe but he can be overly dramatic. Now, have you decided what you want for dinner?"

Bernadette knew she was being told very firmly she was trotting where she wasn't welcome. For a moment, she considered attempting to probe further anyway. But the set of Max's jaw let her know that would only put an added strain on the evening and get her nowhere. Besides fair was fair. She had no intention of telling him her troubles so she shouldn't expect him to tell her his. Just enjoy the dinner, she ordered herself. Turning to her own menu, she began to ask his opinion about various items listed.

For the next couple of hours, they discussed the food, the weather and what kind of legal recourse might be taken against Lang.

Max noticed that although there were moments when she seemed to actually relax, the tension would abruptly return. After he'd so firmly refused to talk about himself, he doubted she would openly talk about herself. Still, as they finished their desserts, he knew he had to try. She'd become a puzzle he was determined to solve. "Until yesterday, I had you pictured as the quiet, conservative type," he said. "The type who likes a safe, comfortable life."

"I thought I did," she replied honestly. A wistfulness suddenly seemed to overwhelm her. "I even planned on having a family one day and only working part-time so I could devote more time to my children." Realizing the wine had lowered her guard, she clamped her mouth shut.

"Why this sudden change of plans?" he prodded when she remained silent.

Bernadette gave what she hoped was a nonchalant shrug. "I got bored."

Max was sure she was lying. That shrug was one of the stiffest he'd ever seen and she hadn't looked him in the eye. Instead she'd suddenly become interested in the last crumbs of her dessert and was following them around the plate with her fork. "And did chasing down Lang alleviate that boredom?"

Bernadette frowned into her coffee. The wine was making her groggy and she was afraid she might suddenly blurt out everything and, even worse, begin to cry. "It made me tired. I'd like to go home now."

She did look exhausted, he thought as he waved the waiter over and asked for their check.

When the bill came, Bernadette snatched it up before Max could even open it. "You got us in here, this will be my treat," she said, taking out her credit card.

Max rebelled at the thought of her spending her hard-earned money on him. After all, he'd been the one to invite himself along. "I insist we, at least, go Dutch," he argued, reaching for the black folder.

He looked so uncomfortable, Bernadette suddenly grinned. She had rattled the unrattleable Max Laird. Even more, she was enjoying playing the part of a totally liberated female. "I've never bought a man dinner before. I really want to do this."

Max saw the mischievous gleam in her eyes. This change of mood was so unexpected he was startled. "All right, sure," he heard himself saying, then silently promised himself he'd find a way to pay her back.

Bernadette enjoyed the slightly raised eyebrow the waiter cast in Max's direction when he returned with the credit card slip to be signed. From exchanges during the meal, she knew Max and the man were long-time acquaintances. Suddenly worried Max would be embarrassed, she glanced at him. Instead she saw an impish smile playing at one corner of his mouth.

"Obviously the lady enjoys my company," he said in response to the look from the waiter.

The waiter rewarded this with a skeptical grimace. "It's my guess she lost a bet." Then turning to Bernadette, he said with a warm smile, "I hope you enjoyed your meal in spite of the company."

"Yes, very much," she replied, then couldn't stop herself from adding, "And the company wasn't as bad as I expected."

The waiter tossed Max an "I knew it" look and went off to take care of his other diners.

Max had never minded a bit of teasing. He'd done enough of it in his time, he knew he deserved a payback. But the honesty he'd heard in her voice when she'd said his company wasn't as bad as she'd expected left him feeling piqued. "The next time I want my reputation trampled into the ground we can do this again," he said dryly as they left the restaurant.

"I'm sorry," Bernadette apologized quickly, upset she'd hurt his feelings. "I was only trying to follow through on the teasing."

Max groaned mentally. He'd sounded like a bruised teenager. "No, I should be apologizing to you and thanking you for a very nice dinner," he said. They'd reached his car and he opened the door for her.

Bernadette was surprised by the sincerity in his voice. She'd been sure that behind his polite facade, he'd been bored with her company. "You're welcome," she replied, sliding into the passenger seat.

As he rounded the vehicle and climbed in behind the wheel, the parting scene at the restaurant repeated itself in Max's mind. Putting aside his ego, he viewed it with a reporter's eye. A not very flattering but intriguing element emerged. Determined to pursue it, he said, "Of course, you didn't have to sound quite so honest when you implied you'd considered the possibility you might not enjoy my companionship."

Bernadette flushed. "That just sort of slipped out."

Max congratulated himself on reading her correctly. "Then you were concerned you might not have a good time with me?"

Bernadette scowled at herself. She'd put her foot in her mouth and now she was shoving it in further with every word. The full truth seemed to be the only recourse. "Yes, that thought did cross my mind. In all the time we spent together chasing Lang we'd never had what anyone could call a really friendly conversation. We talked about business and that was all."

"So even thinking I might prove to be unpleasant company, you went out with me anyway?" Max prodded.

Bernadette frowned impatiently at him. "Yes. I've just admitted that. I figured any company tonight would be better than none." As she realized what she'd said, she gave a mental gasp. Well, he asked for the truth, she reminded herself. Suddenly tired of being on the defensive, she added curtly. "Besides you didn't give me much of a chance to refuse and I was curious as to why you'd invited yourself to join me."

Max frowned at the road ahead. This was one investigative assignment he'd failed at miserably. Being blunt appeared to be the only course of action left. "I insisted on inviting myself along to find out what's bothering you so much, and any company, including mine, would be preferable to being alone."

This time, Bernadette considered telling him. Maybe talking about it would help, she reasoned. But the words formed a huge lump in her throat and refused to be spoken. "This is something I have to work out on my own," she managed levelly.

"Sometimes problems seem less unsolvable when you share them with someone else," Max coaxed.

"No one can help with this one," she replied. "And I'm really too tired to talk about this anymore."

And I shouldn't even have asked, Max grumbled at himself as a silence fell between them. This was obviously a very personal problem and rule number five on his list was to avoid other people's personal problems whenever possible.

She's a clever, determined woman. She'll work out whatever is bothering her just fine on her own, he assured himself as he drove away from her house a little later. He had his own agenda to take care of.

Easing the living-room curtains apart enough to allow her to look outside, Bernadette watched Max's car disappear down the dark street. The thought of being alone had caused so strong a rush of fear, she'd almost begged him to stay.

"I've got to get a grip on myself," she growled, releasing the curtain and pacing into the center of the room. "In the first place, everyone dies sooner or later. In the second, the doctor couldn't tell me for certain when it was going to happen. It could be tonight or a year from tonight. I need to forget about my possible demise and get back to living my life on an even keel." Her jaw set in a determined line, she decided she'd start with a soothing shower.

Chapter Five

Max drew a relieved breath when Bernadette stepped out of the elevator the next morning. Whatever the problem, she'd obviously solved it. Her hair was back in its usual severe, businesslike style. She was dressed in one of her tailored business suits, her makeup was demure and her carriage that of a woman in control of her world.

"Congratulations," Gordon Hedley called out to her. "Great story."

"Thanks," Bernadette replied as several other shouts from well-wishers echoed Gordon's greeting.

She saw Grace rise from her desk and pick up a stack of newspapers. Worry that she might have alienated the secretary suddenly swept through her. It was strengthened when she saw the stern look on the woman's face. An apology formed in her mind as Grace approached. They met at Bernadette's desk.

"Guess I'll have to be more careful who I leak a tip to," Grace said in lowered tones for her and Bernadette's ears only.

"I'm really sorry. I don't know what came over me," Bernadette apologized.

The reprimand in Grace's eyes vanished and she smiled warmly. "You're forgiven. You did a great job." She extended the stack of front pages to Bernadette. "I got you a few extra copies. Seeing this is your first front-page byline, I thought you might like a copy for your scrapbook and some to send to relatives."

"Thanks," Bernadette replied, relieved Grace wasn't holding a grudge.

As the secretary headed back to her desk, Bernadette glanced down at the front page. She'd been circling her desk. Abruptly she stopped. Her name was the only one in the byline!

She turned to Max to see him leaning back in his chair reading the comics. Crossing the short distance between their desks in two strides, she frowned down at him. "You took your name off the story."

He peered at her over his paper. "You got the tip first. You climbed the fences and scared off the dog. And, by the time I got back to the office you had the story in close to printable order. I figured you deserved the single byline."

"You did as much work as I did," she protested, her pride refusing to allow her to take full credit when it wasn't due her.

Looking up at her from his seated position, Max suddenly found himself recalling how nicely she'd filled out those tight jeans and how cute she'd looked with her hair hanging loose. Startled by these unexpected flashes of memory, he curtly reminded himself she was the home and family type. "What's done is done," he replied, pointedly returning his attention to the comics.

His patronizing manner grated on her nerves. Still, she'd always avoided confrontations when possible and there was no sense in pursuing this, she told herself. But instead of simply going to her desk and putting Max Laird out of her mind, she pushed the newspaper down from in front of his face and glared at him. "I don't need or want any favors from you. Just stay out of my way from now on."

As she turned and stalked to her desk, she was aware of others in the room watching her and Max, some covertly and others with quizzical expressions. A flush began to build and she quickly seated herself behind her word processor. She'd been sure she had herself under control this morning. Obviously her nerves were still on edge. Maybe I should call that psychologist, she thought. But as she started to look in her purse for the card, Roger Reynolds strode up to her desk.

"Guess you've been a little too excited to look at the assignment board. We've only got half an hour to get to the mayor's office," he said. "My award-winning photographs won't see their way into print if they don't have a story to go with them."

Bernadette looked at the photographer. He was close to the same build as Max and she knew he was the same age but that was where the resemblance ended. His face was boyishly handsome. His eyes were a deep brown and so was his hair, which hung well past his shoulders. He kept the thick brown locks bound in a ponytail when he worked and his usual office attire was old jeans and a sweatshirt in the winter. In the summer the sweatshirt was replaced with a T-shirt. Whichever style top he wore, it usually had a joke inscribed on it or a picture of a rock band. A hippie stuck in the wrong time period, was how she classified him. But he was pleasant company.

"We're doing the mayor giving medals of bravery to those two teenage boys who saw the fire at their neighbor's house and woke the people up then went in and helped save the children on the second floor," he elaborated.

"Right." She nodded, recalling she had written that down on her calendar two days ago.

Roger's grin broadened and, leaning closer, he said in a mock hushed voice loud enough to carry to Max's desk, "And don't let Max get to you. He wasn't being generous. He just didn't want to blow his reputation for being a lone wolf."

"You know me too well," Max shot back.

Ignoring him, Roger leaned closer to Bernadette. "Now, as for me, I wouldn't mind sharing a byline with you—or anything else, for that matter."

For a moment Bernadette considered his obvious offer. The thought that there were a lot of things in life she hadn't experienced taunted her. But the thought of experiencing them with Roger left her cold. "Then we'll take your car to the mayor's office," she returned. "I hate driving in city traffic."

Behind his newspaper, Max frowned as Bernadette left. He'd heard Roger make a play for her a hundred times before and it had never bothered him. But before, she'd always been quick to refuse the photographer's advances. This time, he was sure he'd detected a hesitation. Didn't she know the man was a womanizer who couldn't stop himself from coming on to anything in a skirt? he thought, fuming.

In the next instant, he was scowling at himself. Bernadette Dowd wasn't his problem!

He was again telling himself the same thing later that afternoon but the reporter part of him was refusing to listen.

During the day, her arrival at work had nagged him. Her surprise at the byline made it obvious she hadn't stopped to purchase a paper before coming in. Most reporters couldn't wait to see their first front-page story. He remembered the excitement he'd felt. He'd been waiting when the first copy had rolled off the presses. But she hadn't been interested enough to stop at a newsstand to pick up her own copy.

Then there was her return to the office with Roger. She'd actually been laughing at one of the photographer's jokes and from their conversation, Max gathered she'd gone out to lunch with the man. Dryly he wondered if she'd paid for that meal, too. Then he'd found himself thinking that if she hung around with Roger she would be paying a price beyond money. Again he'd berated himself for letting her occupy his thoughts. Her life was her own and he didn't want any part of it.

But then there had been the story she'd written about the boys who'd received the medals. In the past, her writing style had been very factual, concise, almost dry. Max had been in Ben's office when she'd brought the copy in. Ben's expression had turned to one of surprise when he'd begun to read the piece. "Not your usual style," he'd remarked to her.

Bernadette had looked a little uncomfortable. "Maybe I put in a little too much sap," she admitted.

Unable to quell his curiosity, Max had gone behind Ben's chair and read over his shoulder. Not her style at all, he'd thought.

"This should bring a few tears to people's eyes," Ben had said when he'd finished. Then he nodded with approval. "Maybe it'll even bring our circulation up. Nowadays it seems people like a bit more of the human side."

Bernadette, still looking a bit uneasy, had made a quick exit.

And now she was getting ready to leave for the day. It was only near midafternoon but Max had heard her telling Grace she had an appointment she had to keep. Sitting at his desk, he covertly watched her turn off her machine and get her purse out of her drawer. She should have had a glow of pleasure on her face, he thought. After all, she'd had a front-page story in today's edition and Ben had been so pleased with her article about the boys, he was thinking of giving it space on the front page of tomorrow's edition. Instead she looked tense.

She's probably just going through one of those inexplicable moody phases women go through, he reasoned, angry at not being able to put her out of his mind. Curtly he reminded himself he had a much more important task he should be concentrating on.

With a determined set to his jaw, he started to turn his full attention to his computer. But as she rose from her desk, a momentary flash of intense emotion played across her features. He knew fear when he saw it and he'd just seen it once again on Bernadette Dowd's face. The woman was scared of something, really scared. And he wasn't going to have any peace until he knew what it was. "There are times when my reporter's instinct is a curse," he muttered under his breath as he switched off his machine.

Max glanced at his watch. It was more than an hour since he'd pulled into the multistoried hospital parking lot two cars behind Ms. Dowd. Staying far enough behind she wouldn't see him, he'd followed her into the building. He'd waited a couple of minutes after she'd checked in at the registration desk, then he'd approached the nurse in charge.

Claiming to be a friend of Ms. Dowd's who had promised to meet her here but had forgotten exactly where, he found out she'd gone to radiology. Going there, he'd managed to discover she was having a brain scan. Not wanting her to spot him, he'd gone back to his car.

There, he'd held a long debate with himself. Obviously Bernadette had a health problem, one that required some serious tests. The situation was definitely none of his business. "This is a matter for her to work out with her doctor, her clergy or her family," he'd informed the empty space around. But as he put his key into the ignition, he couldn't stop remembering the look of fear he'd seen on her face.

"I'll just stick around and see that she gets home all right," he'd grumbled, impatient with himself for letting his reporter's instinct get him involved in Bernadette Dowd's private life.

Now he sat with his portable computer on in front of him while he kept an eye on her car.

It was getting onto early evening when she did finally emerge. She looked pale. "As soon as I see she's home safe and sound, I leave her on her own," Max bargained with himself as he pulled out of the garage behind her.

But Bernadette didn't go directly home. Instead she drove to the zoo.

"Damn!" he cursed under his breath. His conscience wouldn't allow him to let her go wandering around there alone this late in the day, especially with her behaving so out of character. Parking near her car, he followed her inside the gates. "I'm only going to make sure she doesn't get mugged," he told himself. But as he stood watching her staring at the seals with a lost look on her face, he knew he couldn't just walk away from her without trying to help.

"I've never been very good at this Good Samaritan stuff," he grumbled to himself as he approached her. Reaching her, he said casually, "Nice evening for a stroll through the zoo."

Bernadette jumped at the sound of Max's voice. Startled, she jerked around to see him there. "Yes," she managed to reply.

"I've been following you," he said bluntly, tired of playing this cat-and-mouse game. "I know you've made it clear you want me to butt out of your life and, the truth is, I'd like to do just that. But my reporter's instinct has refused to let me."

Bernadette saw the discomfort on his face and knew he meant exactly what he'd said. Well, it was time for her to say the words aloud anyway, she told herself. That would free him from his quest and maybe allow her to begin to live with the reality of her situation. "I was doing an article on Dr. Harold Riley and his research on cures for migraines. He asked me if I wanted to be a control subject to provide him with a little more data and to get a feel for the kind of tests his patients undergo. I said sure. He found an inoperable aneurysm."

Max studied her narrowly, as the word "inoperable" sent a chill along his spine. "And what kind of prognosis did he give you?" he coaxed when she remained silent.

"I'm going to die." There, she'd said it! The words left a bitter taste in her mouth but at least she'd said them.

Max felt as if he'd received a blow to the stomach. "When?"

A wry smile tilted one corner of her mouth. "That's the million-dollar question. It could burst in the next minute or five years from now. Most likely, however, because of the size, the doctor estimates it'll happen sometime in the next few months."

"Life is always a gamble. You could get hit by a truck tomorrow," he pointed out, searching for a way to make her situation less terrifying for her.

She nodded. "I know. But at least I'd have a chance of getting out of the way if I saw the truck coming." She wanted to shut up but, now that she was talking, the thoughts that had been plaguing her for the past two days insisted on flowing out. "It's like having a sword hanging over my head by a slender thread. And I've been thinking about all the things I've never done." She grimaced with apology. "That's why I robbed you of your story. I just wanted to do something important before my life was over."

"I didn't mind you working on the story," he replied, wanting to say something comforting but not being able to think of anything. "Have you talked to your family about this?"

Bernadette gave a small shrug. "I've never been close to any of them. We exchange Christmas cards and pictures once in a while. My aunt and uncle in Montana invited me to come for Christmas last year and we got along just fine but they're more like friendly acquaintances than close family. Besides, they can't do anything.''

Max regarded her worriedly. "You should have someone to talk to, someone to lend you support."

She saw the nervousness in his eyes and knew he really didn't want to volunteer. "Dr. Riley gave me the name of a psychologist who is supposed to be very good at working with people in my situation. He recommends the woman highly. I figured I'd give her a call and set up an appointment."

Max breathed a sigh of relief. "Professional help sounds like the way to go." Noticing people moving toward the exits, he added, "Looks as if they're closing. I'll walk you to your car."

"I guess it was a little late in the day to come here," she said as they joined the smattering of other people heading for the parking area. A wistful expression spread over her face. "My grandmother used to bring me here when I was a child but I hadn't been back in years. I just suddenly had the urge to see it again."

Max nodded with understanding. He remembered a time when he'd felt compelled to revisit places he hadn't been since he'd been a kid. The memories his travels had stirred had been bittersweet, but they'd helped him set a course for his life.

As they neared her car, Max began to worry about where her wanderlust might take her next. Surely an elderly woman and a child would not have gone anyplace really dangerous, he told himself. Still he heard himself saying, "You look tired. I'd suggest you go straight home."

Going home did not particularly appeal to her but she really didn't have anyplace else to go. "Yes, I will," she replied.

Pulling out of the parking lot behind her, Max was determined to go his own way. But instead he found himself following her. "I'm just going to make sure she goes home," he told himself.

Glancing in her rearview mirror as she turned out of the park, Bernadette saw Max behind her. That didn't surprise her. They both lived in the same general direction. But when she glanced in the rearview mirror a few miles down the road and saw he was still there, she frowned. Obviously he'd appointed himself her guardian angel and was seeing that she got home. She admitted she wouldn't have minded this, in fact she would have been flattered, if she'd thought he honestly cared about her. But his uneasiness had been obvious and she knew he was following her out of a misguided sense of duty, not because he wanted to.

After pulling into her driveway and climbing out of her car, she stood waiting for him.

Seeing her, Max knew she'd seen him. He considered simply waving as he drove by and then continuing on his way. Instead, he pulled in behind her. "Just thought I'd see you home," he said as she stood watching him impatiently.

"There's no reason for you to feel you have to hover over me," she returned tersely. "I'm not your responsibility. I can handle this just fine on my own."

That's what I wanted to hear, Max told himself. "Have a nice night. Get some rest," he said, climbing back into his car. Backing out of her driveway, his words echoed in his ears. He was talking in platitudes! At the corner stop sign, he glanced in his rearview mirror at her house. She was home. She was safe and she wanted to deal with this on her own, he repeated to himself as he jerked his attention back to the road.

"But discovering you have a fatal condition isn't something a person should face alone," he muttered. He wished he knew of someone to call to come stay with her, but he didn't. "So I guess it'll have to be me," he growled, making an abrupt U-turn.

Following Max's departure, Bernadette had entered the house, tossed her purse aside, kicked off her shoes and slumped down into her grandmother's rocking chair. When a knock sounded on the door, she groaned at the thought of getting up. And why should she answer it? she mused. Whoever was there was probably trying to sell something she didn't want. Besides, she didn't feel like talking to anyone just now.

"Bernadette! Are you all right?" Max's worried voice sounded from the other side followed by more knocking.

She frowned at the door in surprise. He'd taken off so fast she was sure he'd be halfway across town by now.

Abruptly the door opened and he came in. Seeing her sitting in the chair, he paled. "Should I call an ambulance?"

"For goodness sake, I just didn't feel like answering the door," she returned curtly. "I figured it was a salesman."

Max continued to study her worriedly. "I decided you shouldn't be alone right now."

Bernadette's frown deepened. "I don't need a baby-sitter and I most certainly don't want your pity. I only told you the truth because I figured it was the only way to get rid of you."

"Well it didn't work. You've still got me," he replied, shoving the door closed, then sitting down in a chair facing hers.

He reminded her of a person caught between a rock and a hard place. He didn't want to be there but he couldn't make himself leave.

The thought of them sitting there all evening staring at each other was wearing on Max's nerves. "How about some dinner? I know a great little Chinese place," he suggested, thinking that having others around might ease the tension he was feeling.

Bernadette had always hated feeling like a nuisance and that was exactly how Max was making her feel. "It's Thursday. Don't you have a poker game you're supposed to be at?" she said with dismissal.

Max couldn't believe he'd totally forgotten about the game. However, now that she'd reminded him, a solution to his dilemma presented itself. "Yes, I do," he said rising.

Bernadette breathed a mental sigh of relief. He was leaving. The sacred male bonding ritual of playing poker was too strong for him to resist. But instead of heading to the door, he was coming toward her. She tensed as he reached out and caught her by the hand. In the next instant she was being jerked to her feet.

"You're coming with me," he said without compromise.

She stared at him in stunned surprise. "I thought females weren't allowed."

"From now on you're Berny, just one of the guys," he replied. "Now go change into something comfortable and let your hair down while I call in an order for some pizza to pick up on our way. We can't arrive without food and drink."

A protest formed on the tip of Bernadette's tongue. She was sure he didn't really want her going with him. But the words refused to come out. She didn't want to be alone. Besides, this was an adventure she couldn't pass up. "I've never stormed a male bastion before," she said, mischievous amusement glistening in her eyes. "I'll be dressed in a flash."

A sense of elation at having brought a smile to her face, filled Max. "What kind of toppings do you want on the pizza," he called out to her as she hurried down the hall.

"Whatever you like," she called back. Then the desire to make this a night filled with different experiences, she paused and looked back at him. "Get one with everything, including anchovies."

He made a mock grimace. "Even anchovies?"

"*Even* anchovies," she replied firmly.

"It's your stomach," he said. Then with a shooing motion of his hands, he waved her toward her bedroom. "Get changed."

Chapter Six

Forty-five minutes later, with three pizzas, one with the works, one pepperoni and one plain cheese along with a six-pack of beer and a two-liter bottle of soda, they were pulling into the driveway of a two-story house on the south of town.

"I guess I should mention this is Molly and George Pace's place," Max said as he turned off the car. "Molly was married to my older brother."

Bernadette looked at him questioningly. "You never mentioned an older brother."

"He was a policeman, killed in the line of duty."

Bernadette noted the sudden tightening of Max's jaw and knew just saying the words had been difficult for him. Obviously he'd cared for his brother a great deal. "I'm sorry," she said gently.

"It happens." His jaw relaxed and he frowned thoughtfully at the house. "I still find it hard to believe Molly married another policeman. She was really shaken by Barry's death. But George is a good man. He's been a terrific husband to her and a great father to my niece and nephew. Guess she knows what she's doing."

Bernadette didn't doubt Max liked George but it was also clear he thought Molly might have been wiser to marry a man in a safer profession. Uncertain of how to respond, to her relief she was saved from having to say anything by the sight of two children, a boy and a girl, running out of the house to the car.

The boy looked to be around eight or nine, Bernadette judged, and had the same color blond hair and blue eyes as his uncle. The girl was younger by at least a couple of years and was a brunette with brown eyes and finely cut features.

Both children came to abrupt stops when they saw Bernadette getting out of the car.

"You brought a girl," the boy said in surprise.

"Wow! You're observant enough to be a reporter," Max teased.

"I thought women weren't allowed at the game," the girl spoke up, continuing to study Bernadette with interest. Her mouth formed a thoughtful pout. "I suppose she's going to have to sit in the kitchen or the living room with Mom?"

"I've christened her Berny and I'm making her one of the guys," Max said firmly.

The boy grinned mischievously. "She doesn't look at all like one of the guys. And I don't think George or any of the others will be fooled."

Max ruffled the child's hair. "This observant, humorous fellow is Kurt," he informed Bernadette. "And this lovely young lady is Paula. Kids, I'd like you to meet Berny."

Both continued to watch Bernadette dubiously as they said polite hellos and she returned their greetings. Then as Max lifted the pizzas out of the back seat, she was forgotten.

"What kind did you bring?" Kurt demanded, taking the pizzas from his uncle so that Max could get the drinks.

"One plain cheese, one pepperoni and one with the works including anchovies," Max replied.

"The works!" the boy echoed with delight.

"I've always wanted to try the works with anchovies," Paula squealed.

"Dibs on the first piece," Kurt called out as he headed to the house.

"They've always wanted the works with anchovies?" Max muttered at their departing backs.

"There's an excitement in trying something new, even if it doesn't work out as well you expect," Bernadette said.

Max saw the wistfulness in her eyes and guessed she was thinking of all the things she might never have a chance to do. On the other hand, she might have plenty of time, he reminded himself. Right now, she simply needed to learn to live with the uncertainty of her situation. "Looks like you've made me a hero," he joked, starting to follow the children.

"I'd wait until they've tasted the anchovies before I'd take any bows," she cautioned.

"You're right," he agreed again making a grimace at the thought of the salty little fish.

Bernadette eyed him covertly as they walked to the house. She'd never pictured Max Laird as a family man but the easy way he conversed with the children and the obvious love he felt for them caused her to see him in a new light. She found herself even able to imagine him with children of his own. "I'm surprised by how good you are with kids," she said, then flushed when she realized she'd spoken aloud.

"I like *other people's* kids fine," he replied. "I can play with them, even spoil them, then leave. I don't have to deal with their illnesses or their problems."

There was a resolve on his face that let her know he never intended to have children of his own. That was more like the Max Laird she thought she knew . . . a man who didn't want any ties binding him down. "The ultimate uncle," she mused.

"He can definitely be considered that," a small brunette said, coming out the door to greet them. After giving Max a hug, she turned to Bernadette. "I'm Molly Pace and I can vouch for Max being terrific uncle material."

"Molly, this is Bernadette Dowd," Max said as Molly paused to smile warmly at him.

Molly nodded. "The kids told me. She's Berny...just one of the guys." She extended her hand to Bernadette. "Welcome."

Accepting the handshake, Bernadette read the curiosity in the woman's eyes. Obviously Max bringing her here was very much out of the ordinary. "Thanks. I hope I'm not intruding."

"Not as far as I'm concerned," Molly replied. Casting Max an "I can't speak for the others" look, her tone became businesslike. "House rules are you wait on yourself. The food gets set out in the kitchen. There's ice in the ice bucket and when that's empty, there's ice in the freezer. The beers and cold drinks are in the refrigerator." Her smile returned. "And if you get bored with the chauvinistic company in the den, you're welcome to join me in the living room."

Bernadette again thanked the woman then followed Max into the kitchen where he put the beer and soda into the refrigerator with what was already there. The pizzas she noticed were opened and set on the counter side by side with two pieces missing from the one with the anchovies.

"Yuck!" a young voice sounded from behind them.

Turning, Bernadette saw Paula standing there with her nose wrinkled in disgust.

"There's something real salty and fishy tasting in this," the child complained, frowning at the slice of pizza on the plate she was holding.

"That's the anchovies," Max informed her.

"I'll pick it out for you," Bernadette offered, taking the girl's plate and using a fork to remove the offending topping.

"I think they're great," Kurt declared, coming into the kitchen to get another piece.

"You just like them because I don't," Paula retorted.

"It's one of those macho man things," Bernadette informed her. "It's the same as when they have contests to see who can eat a jalapeño pepper without having to drink water."

Max regarded her dryly. "A lot you know. Water wouldn't help even if it was legal. Only beer will ease the pain from one of those peppers."

Seeing the laughter in his eyes, Bernadette had the urge to laugh aloud.

"George has a jar of jalapeños. Could we try the beer thing?" Kurt spoke up excitedly.

"No, you may not try 'the beer thing,'" Molly snapped, an amused glitter in her eyes belying the sternness in her voice. "Now you two run along to the porch and enjoy this pleasant evening before you have to go to bed."

Kurt looked at Max pleadingly. "Another time?"

Max winked at the boy. "Another time."

"Men," Molly muttered good-naturedly, continuing through the kitchen, physically shooing the children out onto the screened porch.

Bernadette regarded Max with mock disapproval. "You're obviously a questionable influence on those children."

"I try my best to open their eyes to the world around them," he replied with a grin.

This time, Bernadette couldn't stop herself from laughing.

She looked kissable, Max thought, then was immediately angry with himself. Bernadette Dowd was a complication he didn't need in his life. He'd see her through the next few days until she had time to see that psychologist the doctor had recommended and begin to regain an emotional balance, then he'd get back to taking care of his own business. "Grab some food and come on," he instructed.

Accompanying him down the hall with a paper plate full of pizza, Bernadette felt it was only fair to warn him. "I've never played poker before."

Max groaned silently. Bringing a woman in was going to put a strain on his friendship with his fellow players. Bringing a woman in who didn't know the game was likely to get him blackballed. But he'd chosen this road and now he was forced to follow it. "You can watch the first couple of hands and I'll explain what's going on."

Entering the room, Bernadette noted the surprised expressions on the men's faces. She recognized Ben, Roger and Gordon from the newspaper. The other two were strangers.

"Bernadette?" Roger said her name questioningly as if he wasn't certain he was seeing correctly.

"For tonight she's Berny, just one of the guys," Max informed them. "Berny, you know Ben, Roger and Gordon. These other two are some of our cities' finest. George Pace..." Max nodded toward a clean-shaven, pleasant-looking brown-haired man in his late thirties with a stocky, muscular build. Shifting his attention to an older man, lean with a craggy face and gray hair forming a fringe around a large center of bald scalp, he finished, "And Patrick O'Malley."

"Good evening, gentlemen," Bernadette said, acknowledging the introductions. She saw skepticism on Patrick's and Gordon's faces while Roger looked curious and Ben looked puzzled. And although they all attempted to greet her politely, she sensed they were not pleased to have her invading their sanctuary. Having an adventure had sounded like fun but she didn't want to get Max into trouble with his friends. "I'm not a player," she said. "Just thought I'd have a peek at one of the last bastions of male sovereignty."

Having said this, Bernadette quickly slipped out of the room.

Max followed. He felt like a heel. Mentally he kicked himself. He shouldn't have brought her here. The men in there didn't know what was going on. He should have known they couldn't entirely hide the fact that they felt their privacy was being invaded. Obviously she'd sensed their rejection. Hell, she'd have had to have the hide of an elephant not to, he admitted. "Look, why don't we go to a movie. I'm not feeling particularly lucky tonight. If I stay, I'll probably lose my shirt."

Bernadette felt like an albatross around his neck. "I didn't ask you to be my baby-sitter but since you've obviously appointed yourself, I insist on setting a few of the rules. The first one is that you go play poker with your buddies and let me fend for myself." The sudden worry that he might try to enlist the aid of the men in the room by telling them about her situation, caused her to add in a lowered voice, "And I want my private life kept a secret."

Max raked a hand agitatedly through his hair. "I brought you here because I didn't think you should be alone tonight. You've had a shock."

She met his gaze levelly. "And I do appreciate your concern. But I've been on my own for a long time. I don't need or want you hovering over me. Now go play poker with your buddies and leave me to entertain myself."

His hand closed around her arm as she headed for the kitchen. "If you should decide you want to leave, you come get me," he ordered.

"Sure," she lied, having no intention of doing that. What she did intend to do was to call a cab and leave as soon as he was sequestered with his friends.

"I'm sure I can keep Bernadette entertained just fine."

Bernadette turned to see Molly coming down the hall. The woman made a shooing motion at Max. "Go play."

Relief spread through Max. Molly was a better companion for Bernadette than he could ever be. "If you insist," he said.

Bernadette saw the relief on his face. She wanted to be angry with him for making her feel like a duty to be attended to but she couldn't. Right now she needed a friend and he was determined to be one. For that she knew she should be grateful. "We both insist," she stated firmly. Then turning to Molly, she said, "I'm starving. Could we go someplace where I can sit and eat?"

Molly placed an arm around Bernadette's shoulders. "Come on."

As they started down the hall, Bernadette could feel Max watching them. "Go play!" she ordered over her shoulder.

Max frowned at their departing backs. He didn't trust Ms. Dowd. She had too strong a streak of independence. A part of him argued that if she wanted to sneak out on him, he should let her. After all, he couldn't baby-sit her forever. But another part refused to let her go out on her own so quickly. "Molly, can I talk to you a moment?" he requested, catching up with them and pulling his former sister-in-law away from Bernadette and back down the hall.

Bernadette scowled a warning to him, reminding him she wanted her privacy maintained, then continued into the kitchen.

She was pouring herself a soda when Molly entered. "Max is afraid you'll leave without telling him," the woman said forthrightly, studying Bernadette thoughtfully. "I'm supposed to report to him if you do."

"I wish you wouldn't," Bernadette replied.

"He wouldn't tell me what was going on but I recognized the look in his eyes. He's appointed himself your guardian angel."

Bernadette nodded. "But it isn't necessary. I can take care of myself." Feeling more and more embarrassed by the moment, she reached for the phone hanging on the wall. "I'll just call a cab and go home. I should never have agreed to come here in the first place.''

Molly gently touched her hand. "Trying to get away from Max won't do any good. When he makes up his mind to do something, he can be tenacious."

"So I've noticed," Bernadette admitted. "But I've never felt comfortable being where I wasn't invited. I appreciate your hospitality but I really have to be going." With a resigned scowl, she added, "And I'll tell Max before I go. I'll make sure he understands I don't need him trailing around after me."

"He won't listen to you. I know. When his brother Barry was killed, Max appointed himself the protector of me and the children. He insisted on sitting up through the night with the kids whenever one of them was sick and when I needed a shoulder to lean on, he was always here. Until I married George, I don't think Max even allowed himself a private life other than looking after us. If you leave, he'll just follow you."

A coaxing entered Molly's voice. "Why don't you, at least, stay for a while and eat your pizza."

Bernadette was sure the woman was right about Max. "I hate feeling like a burden," she said as she hung up the phone.

"I'd enjoy the company," Molly assured her, motioning for Bernadette to follow her into the dining room. As they sat down at the table, she sighed deeply. "When you arrived with Max I was hoping you were someone he was becoming romantically involved with."

"We worked together on a story. But we're not romantically involved," Bernadette assured her but even as she made this declaration an idea that had been nagging at the back of her mind again surfaced. Forget it! He wouldn't be interested! she ordered herself. Still the thought persisted.

"I blame myself."

Molly's words snapped Bernadette's attention back to her companion. "Blame yourself for what?"

"For Max not allowing himself to get romantically involved," Molly elaborated. "I know it's because of how I behaved when Barry died. I went to pieces. But that's the way I am. I screamed and cried and got all my grief out. But I could never make Max understand that was part of my healing process."

The frown on Molly's face deepened. "Once I'd gotten myself over the shock of my loss and begun to get on with my life, I told him he needed to get on with his...find a wife and have a family of his own. He's terrific with kids. But he told me he'd decided to remain a bachelor. He said he never wanted to put a wife and kids through what me and my children had gone through. I tried to convince him he was making a mistake...that loving and being loved were worth the pain. But he refused to listen."

"I have noticed that once Max makes up his mind, his decision seems to be carved in stone," Bernadette said, intrigued by this further insight into Max Laird's thinking. He was a great deal more sensitive than she'd ever have imagined. She frowned musingly at the wall that separated this room from the den where the men were playing cards.

Or maybe he was using his brother's death as an excuse to avoid a lifelong commitment. Maybe he was one of those men who would feel trapped in a long-term arrangement, she added skeptically. She gave a mental shrug. Either way, it made no difference to her. Her life and Max's were only going to touch briefly.

And the more briefly, the better, she thought. He'd brought her here because he felt sorry for her and she didn't like being the object of pity. She also didn't feel comfortable having her company forced on Molly. She forced the last bite of pizza down, then rose from the table. "I really appreciate your hospitality, but it's been a long day and I'm exhausted. I'm going to call a cab and go home."

Molly watched her worriedly. "You do look tired but Max must have some reason for wanting you to stay. Why don't you go up to my guest room and nap?"

Bernadette was sure the woman was only being so persistent because of orders from Max. "Thanks for the offer but I'll rest better in my own bed," she replied. Seeing Molly beginning to rise from the table, she added pointedly, "And, like I promised, I'll tell Max I'm leaving."

For a moment Molly looked as if she was going to protest, then she breathed a resigned sigh. "I won't even pretend to understand what's going on between you and Max," she said. "And I won't ask. Living with a policeman, I've learned not to pry." A sudden self-conscious grin tilted one corner of her mouth. "Well, at least I try not to pry too often."

The grin disappeared and her expression became motherly. "Anyway, this is obviously something you and Max need to work out on your own. I've enjoyed meeting you and you're always welcome here. Now, I'll go check on the children and let you get on with your life."

Getting on with her life was exactly what she needed to do, Bernadette thought as she dialed for a cab. She just wasn't exactly sure how to do that. But sitting around in this kitchen wasn't the way.

She waited until the cab had arrived, then knocked on the door of the den and stuck her head inside. "Just wanted to say good night," she said with forced cheerfulness, then quickly closed the door and strode out of the house.

Max caught up with her halfway down the walk. "I told you I'd take you home when you were ready to leave," he growled impatiently.

"And I told you I didn't need a baby-sitter," she returned curtly. "I'm tired and I'm going home. *Alone.*"

"Hey, lady, do you want me to call a cop," the cabdriver yelled holding his radio up to the window for Max to see.

"No," she called back. Then facing Max levelly, she said, "Go enjoy your poker game and let me go home and get some rest."

"Rest would be good," he conceded. He just wished he could trust her. "I'm going to call your place in half an hour. If you aren't there, I'm coming looking for you," he warned.

Bernadette shook her head at his stubbornness. "You can call. I'll be there."

As the cab pulled away, Max jotted down its number. If she wasn't at home, he'd find out from the driver where she went. "And once I know she's home safely in bed, then I can relax," he told himself. Tomorrow, he'd make sure she had an appointment with that psychologist and then he'd be free of this nagging need to protect her.

Chapter Seven

Bernadette sat at her desk the next afternoon typing out her story about a pancake breakfast the Shriners had given to raise funds for their charitable activities. Normally she enjoyed this kind of event. Today she'd been bored stiff.

"You're going to have to stop by the poker games with Max more often," Roger Reynolds said, moving a magazine so he could rest his hip on the corner of her desk. "He normally wins but last night, he was so distracted, I got back all the money I've lost to him this year."

Bernadette's immediate reaction was to feel guilty. Then she reminded herself that Max had been the one to harass her until she'd told him about her condition.

"Is something going on between you and Max?" Roger asked, continuing to study her with interest.

"Nothing," she assured him, typing in the last word of her story then pressing the keys to call up the spell checker.

"Glad to hear that. I wouldn't want to tread on another man's toes." He ran his finger from the hollow behind her ear to the chignon at her nape. "Your hair looked real nice last night. You should wear it loose more often. I never realized it had so much red in it."

Bernadette's first reaction was to brush his hand away but as she reached up to do this, she stopped herself. Again thoughts of things she'd never done nagged her.

"How about coming out and playing with me tonight," Roger coaxed. "I can promise you, I won't desert you for a game of cards. We can start with dinner and go from there."

Bernadette could feel him beginning to slip a pin out of her hair. She wanted to feel a sensual excitement but all she felt was a cold chill and a mild sense of irritation.

For the major part of this day, Max had been attempting to ignore Bernadette. He had, first thing this morning, spoken to her and made certain she called the psychologist and made an appointment. Then telling himself his duty was done, he'd ordered himself to concentrate on his own work. But watching Roger make a play for her was getting on his nerves.

She's a big girl. She can take of herself, he reasoned curtly. But instead of sending Roger on his way as she normally did, he noticed that she was doing nothing to discourage the photographer's advances. When Roger started playing with her hair, Max rose from his chair. She's still in a state of shock and I can't allow him to take advantage of her, he grumbled mentally, approaching her desk.

"Berny and I have a dinner date," he said, his gaze threatening Roger as the man removed the pin from Bernadette's hair.

Bernadette jerked around at the sound of Max's voice. She saw the impatient protectiveness in his eyes. He was playing big brother again. "We do not," she said, glaring up at him.

Roger held his hands up in front of him. "I make it a practice never to get mixed up in a lovers' quarrel."

"There is no lovers' quarrel between me and Max," Bernadette assured him.

"Well, as soon as you and Max work out whatever *is* going on between you, let me know," he replied, slipping off her desk and backing away. With a wink, he added, "I'm always available to you."

Bernadette smiled back willing herself to feel something. All she experienced was another chill.

"Sounds like some juicy office gossip over here. Care to fill me in?" Sabrina purred, leaving her desk and moving toward Bernadette's.

Behind the woman's smile, Bernadette saw a glint of malice in those blue eyes. During the time she'd been working here, she'd made it a point not to make an enemy of Sabrina. She didn't like the woman but she preferred to remain on neutral ground. "Max is just playing big brother," she said.

The malice in Sabrina's eyes faded and she smiled. "I knew I couldn't be that wrong. I'd never have paired the two of you in a million years."

Rebellion bubbled inside Bernadette. There had been a subtle but, nevertheless, underlying insinuation in the woman's tone that she considered Bernadette a toad no man could be interested in. "I've always found it difficult to pair you with anyone, too."

Anger flashed in Sabrina's eyes once again.

Max didn't like this turn of events at all. "You and I are going for a walk," he interjected curtly, catching Bernadette by the arm and forcefully pulling her from her chair.

"I need to turn my story in," she protested, attempting to jerk free.

"Grace, get Bernadette's story off her computer," Max called out, determined to get her away from Sabrina as quickly as possible.

Bernadette glanced at the secretary to discover Grace and everyone else still in the newsroom watching her, Max and

Sabrina. After all this time of maintaining a low profile and not causing any strife between herself and her coworkers, in one impetuous moment she'd made herself the center of attention and alienated Sabrina. "A walk in the fresh air might be a good idea," she admitted, allowing Max to guide her out from behind her desk.

He was still holding on to her arm when they reached the elevators. She seethed up at him. "I can exit on my own."

He simply scowled at her and held on. To her chagrin, she noticed that instead of the chill Roger's touch had left, beneath Max's hand her skin felt warm. The man doesn't want to have anything to do with me, she reminded herself curtly. As if to prove her point, he abruptly released her as soon as the doors were closed and they were on their way down.

Continuing to scowl at her, he said, "I'm taking you to see that psychologist now."

"There's no reason to bother her. I'm seeing her Monday. That's soon enough," Bernadette replied, forcing a calmness into her voice.

Max cursed under his breath. "It's not safe to leave you on your own."

She tossed him a haughty look. "I'm simply coming out of my shell. I realize now, I've been sort of hiding away in a safe little haven of my own making. I've decided to face the real world more fully." Before she'd actually said this aloud, she'd never realized these thoughts were floating around in her mind. But now that they had been said, she knew they were the truth.

They had reached the lobby level. Again catching her by the arm, Max guided her outside. "And you think insulting Sabrina and flirting with Roger is a good start?" he demanded dryly as he practically dragged her along beside him.

"Maybe insulting Sabrina wasn't such a good idea but it felt great," she returned. She was being forced to jog to keep up with him and her legs were wearing out. "Slow down," she ordered.

Max slowed his pace just enough so they could both walk. "Making an enemy of Sabrina is not a good move," he warned curtly.

"I've already said insulting her wasn't such a bright idea," she replied.

One down and one to go, Max calculated. "And what about Roger?" he demanded. "In the past, if he tried to flirt with you, you refused to give him the time of day. But just now you were ready to let him literally take down your hair."

Bernadette flushed, then her back stiffened. "I've led a very sheltered life. Maybe *too* sheltered."

Max's gut knotted at the implication behind her words. Coming to an abrupt halt, he stared down at her. "You need to exercise some caution. You don't want to take this 'coming out from your sheltered existence' too far, too fast."

His hold on her arm was causing an unnervingly heated sensation to travel through her and making it difficult for her to think clearly. With a sharp jerk, she broke free. "I might not have a lot of time to do it slowly."

Max's gut knotted more tightly. "I hope you're not considering what I think you're considering. At least, not with Roger."

"Let's just say I'd like to find out what all the shouting is about before I go," she replied.

The reproving look in Max's eyes deepened. "You'd actually go to bed with the man just to satisfy your curiosity?"

"Yes, I guess I would. Care to volunteer?" Bernadette's cheeks flamed scarlet. She couldn't believe she'd made that suggestion. But now that she had, she admitted she wouldn't mind if he did take her up on it. She could still feel the heat of his touch on her arm.

Max was tempted. He was shaken by how tempted. But he'd never taken advantage of a woman and he wouldn't start now. "You really aren't safe to be let out on your own," he growled.

His rejection stung but she refused to let him know. "Just because you aren't interested in spending some 'quality' time with me doesn't give you the right to insult me," she seethed.

"*Quality* time?" Max snapped, feeling panicked that she might actually act on this impulse of hers. "Haven't you heard of AIDS? You can't seriously be considering jumping into the sack with just anyone who's willing?"

"Not just anyone," she assured him with an impatient frown. "I'm not looking for another way to die." Feeling the need to prove she wasn't being totally unreasonable, she added haughtily, "I know how to use protection. I'm not that innocent."

"Great—I'm sure Roger will appreciate finding such a knowledgeable partner," Max shot back. "You do know that the man will go to bed with anything in a skirt?"

Bernadette knew Roger's reputation and knew it was deserved. She also knew Max had a strong point. "All right. I'll admit, Roger probably isn't a good choice."

Max raised an eyebrow. "Probably!"

"All right. All right. Roger is a bad choice," she conceded.

"I want you to promise me, you won't go having any more 'life' adventures until you've talked with that psychologist on Monday," Max demanded.

Bernadette started to point out that Monday might be too late, but stopped herself. She'd said too much already. The look on his face told her that if she didn't agree, he was going to dog her steps and again make her feel like a nuisance. "All right. Have it your way," she said.

Max's gaze narrowed on her. "I want your word."

Bernadette moved her left hand behind her and crossed her fingers. It was a childish gesture but it made her feel less like a liar as she raised her right hand and said, "I promise to behave."

Max wasn't convinced but he'd done his best, he told himself.

"And now if you don't mind, I'm going back to the office," Bernadette said, the last words issued over her shoulder as she put action to her words.

Max watched her go. Even as he was telling himself he'd done what he could and now it was time for him to get on with his own life, the swing of her hips was holding his attention. He recalled watching her at the All Night Saloon. If she did decide to try to attract a companion for a one-night stand, she wouldn't have any trouble. He suddenly found himself picturing her with a faceless stranger. The image angered him. "I just don't want to see her get hurt," he muttered, following her back inside.

Entering the newsroom, Bernadette headed for Grace's desk. As she moved down the aisles, she was aware of being covertly watched by a few of those who still remained and her already frayed nerves grew even more frayed. Once she'd determined that the secretary had gotten her story and handed it over to Ben, she decided it was time to leave.

Returning to her desk to straighten it and get her purse, she saw Sabrina in a far corner of the room. Her conservative side suggested she apologize to the woman and make some excuse for her outrageous behavior. But a stronger side rebelled. She knew Sabrina would never apologize in return. And maybe the woman deserved a bit of her own medicine, Bernadette reasoned.

As she covered her machine and put a couple of file folders away, she saw the blonde moving in her direction. Don't do any more damage, she ordered herself.

But Sabrina didn't approach Bernadette's desk. Instead she stopped at Max's. Placing a hand on his shoulder in a comradely fashion, she said in a honey-coated voice loud enough to carry to Bernadette, "Your little friend seems to be under a great deal of stress. I'd suggest you talk her into taking a vacation before she offends someone less forgiving than myself."

Bernadette had to bite her tongue to keep herself from asking Sabrina in the same honey-coated tone if there was anyone less forgiving than the blonde. I have got to get out of here, she moaned silently, unable to believe these urges to be combative.

To her relief, Sabrina moved on after delivering her snippet of advice. But as the blonde walked away, panic suddenly flowed through Bernadette. Maybe it was the aneurysm putting some kind of pressure on the portion of her brain that controlled her temper. She suddenly visualized herself going berserk. Grabbing the phone, she dialed Dr. Riley's office only to be informed that he was giving a lecture at Harvard Medical School.

It was only Sabrina who was provoking her, she reminded herself as she hung up. During the day she'd handled other irritations with her usual calm. I'm just tired and need to rest, she reasoned as she locked her desk, then headed to the elevators.

Max watched her go. He couldn't continue to constantly hover over her, he told himself. He had work to do and besides, she'd made it clear she didn't want him hanging around. But as the elevator's door closed on her, instead of putting her out of his mind, he kept remembering her flirting with Roger. She'd promised him she'd behave until Monday and he would have trusted the old Bernadette to do just that. But the current Bernadette was not so predictable.

I cannot spend my weekend baby-sitting that woman, he growled at himself. But the thought of her allowing herself to be picked up by some stranger caused a knot in the pit of his stomach.

An hour later he was parked a little ways down the block from her house. "I'm just going to keep an eye on her to make sure she stays home and out of trouble," he informed his image glaring back at him with an impatient expression from his rearview mirror.

Bernadette sat in her grandmother's rocker staring at the painting of the wooded landscape on the wall opposite her. She remembered when she was very young and her parents took her camping. For years she'd been promising herself she'd go again but she never had. Now she might never have the chance.

As she mentally began listing all the things she'd wanted to do and had put off, Max again entered her mind. Again a flush reddened her cheeks as she recalled her wanton invitation to him. "There have to be other men out there that I would feel as strong an attraction to," she muttered in frustration. But he was right. There were some experiences she should take a few precautions before seeking. On the other hand, she could almost feel time slipping away from her.

The walls of the house once again began to seem to close in on her. "It can't hurt to get dressed up and go out someplace nice for dinner," she said to the painting. "Maybe my Prince Charming will suddenly appear. He sure as heck isn't going to come to my door."

Max watched Bernadette come out of her house. Her pastel green summer dress was a conservative style. But with her hair left loose and flowing and the way she walked with a casual swing to her hips gave her an adventurous air. He groaned. The woman was a menace to his peace of mind. Starting his car, he pulled up and blocked her driveway.

Bernadette hit her brake as Max's Mustang suddenly filled her rearview mirror. She couldn't believe he was there. The thought that maybe he'd decided to take her up on her offer brought a rush of nervous excitement. But as she climbed out of her car, she saw the impatient anger in his face and knew that wasn't his reason for coming. "What are you doing here?" she asked coolly as he left his car and approached her.

"The real question is what are you doing?" he snapped back. "You promised me you'd behave."

"Behaving doesn't mean starving to death," she replied dryly. "I'm going out to get something to eat."

The frown on Max's face deepened. "You look more like you're going trolling."

Bernadette glared at him. "I suppose you want me to wear a dumpy housedress and wrap my hair around my head in a tight braid."

The impulse to say that was exactly how he wanted her to dress was strong. Instead he asked coolly, "Where were you planning to go for dinner?"

She named a small but expensive restaurant in Clayton. "And now if you'll get out of my way, I'd like to get going."

"Tonight dinner is on me," he heard himself saying. "And I'll drive."

"This really isn't necessary," she protested, not wanting to feel like a nuisance yet again.

"I think it is."

Bernadette knew she should be furious at him or at least irritated with him. Instead she found herself wanting to run her finger along the line of his jaw to test the texture of his skin. The sudden notion that maybe, if she tried, she might be able to seduce him played through her mind. After all, he did seem to be the only man she knew for whom she felt any real attraction. "If you insist."

Going back to her car to get her purse, she warned herself that he wouldn't be interested. Then I'll consider tonight practice, she told herself. She hadn't had much experience flirting. After she got home, she'd analyze her performance, note the rough spots and think of ways to improve. Smiling sweetly, she walked back to Max's car.

Max didn't like that smile. She looked like a woman with a plan that might involve him and that unnerved him. He'd never been one of those men who'd been fooled into thinking of women as the weaker sex. He knew they could be as tough as nails and when their mind was set on something they could be more tenacious than a hound on the scent of a fox.

Bernadette saw Max eyeing her suspiciously. This is not a good start, she warned herself. Her quick acquiescence had obviously put him on his guard. "This really isn't necessary," she said as she slid into the passenger seat. "If you want to change your mind, feel free."

Max looked over at her. There was only indifference on her face. Clearly she wasn't interested in pursuing him any longer. What an egotist, he chided himself as he put the car in gear and drove down the street.

A little later as she was being led to their table, Bernadette's gaze traveled around the restaurant. The dining area was small and furnished in dark woods with paintings of English country scenes hanging on the walls. Small bouquets of freshly cut flowers arranged in unique pottery vases and lighted candles in glass globes decorated each table. The tablecloths were black and the napkins shocking pink. The china was white with a single large pink lily painted on each dinner plate. She liked the decor, she decided, as the maître d' seated her, then handed her a menu.

Max looked at the prices and frowned. Obviously she'd decided that if she was going to die, she wasn't going with inexpensive food in her stomach.

When the waiter came to take their order and asked if they wanted a drink, Bernadette ordered coffee. She was nervous enough about what she planned to do. She didn't want anything that would cloud her judgment.

Max ordered coffee, too. He wanted a beer but considering Ms. Dowd's erratic behavior of the past couple of days, he decided he'd better remain completely sober.

"I understand the weather is supposed to be real nice for the weekend," she said as the waiter finished delivering their coffees and taking their orders. Hearing her words echoing in her brain, she couldn't believe she'd said something so mundane.

"So I heard," Max replied. Mentally he groaned. They'd been reduced to talking about the weather. This was going to be a long dinner.

Bernadette read the impatience on his face. So what else is new? she mused dryly. She wasn't good at flirting and his disinterest was not encouraging. This isn't going to work, she told herself. "Have you ever gone camping?" she blurted out the first thing that came into her mind.

Max was surprised by this sudden change in subject. But at least it was more interesting than the weather, he thought. "I've gone a couple of times," he replied.

"My parents took me once," she said, the memory again vivid. "I want to go again."

Max experienced a rush of relief. Now this was a safe adventure she could have. "That sounds like a great idea," he encouraged.

Bernadette breathed a frustrated sigh. "The problem is, I don't want to go alone."

Max found himself picturing her in those tight jeans out in the woods with her hair being lightly mussed by a fragrant breeze. Deep within he felt the embers of desire igniting. This was not as safe a topic as he'd thought. "Surely you must have a girlfriend you could ask to accompany you."

Bernadette shook her head. "Taking care of my grandmother took a lot of time and after she died, I concentrated on my job. All my high school friends are married or moved away or divorced with children. And, none of them has ever expressed any desire to go camping." Flirt, she ordered herself. "Actually I was thinking that the kind of companion I really need is a strong male to help carry the supplies and protect me from any wild animals." That wasn't flirting, that was a blatant proposition, she berated herself.

Again Max was strongly tempted but he had a code of honor he lived by and taking advantage of her in her present state of mind went against that code. "You promised me you wouldn't do anything rash until you'd talked to that psychologist," he reminded her.

Bernadette frowned into her coffee. She was proving to be a total failure at seducing him. She'd known she would be, she reminded herself. Obviously she simply wasn't his type. Or maybe he was afraid she'd die on him. That could be a real turnoff, she admitted.

Pushing that thought out of her mind, she lifted her head and looking past him, began scanning the other diners. Two tables away was a group of four men. She guessed they were having a business dinner. Beginning with the man she could see the easiest, she tried to visualize herself with him. The image left her cold. She shifted her gaze to the man beside him on his left.

Noticing the look of concentration on Bernadette's face, Max turned to see where her attention was focused and frowned at what he saw. "Sizing up the male patrons?" he asked dryly.

Bernadette flushed, then as a thought struck her, she grinned. "I'm sure Sabrina would have a great comeback for that but I wouldn't touch that remark with a ten-foot pole."

Max was surprised by this unexpected show of raunchy humor. But then Ms. Dowd had been surprising him for the past few days. And he wished she'd stop. That amused glimmer in those dark brown eyes of hers was much too enticing. As Bernadette's attention returned to the table beyond them, he found himself growing more and more irritated. "It's not polite to ogle men," he admonished.

"Men ogle women all the time," she returned, giving up on the businessmen and shifting her attention to one of the waiters.

"You look like a woman in the supermarket trying to pick out the freshest piece of meat," he scolded.

"I don't really care about the freshness but I do want it to be prime," she replied, surprised that she was beginning to enjoy this rakish banter.

Max glanced in the direction of her gaze and saw the tall, muscular waiter she was studying. His irritation grew. "Just because a man's body looks good doesn't mean he's a good lover."

Bernadette sighed. "The problem is experience is the only way to find out."

Max didn't like the way her mind was working. "Experience can be a very dangerous teacher."

"You're right," she admitted with a regretful grimace.

Their food arrived at that moment and she changed the subject to the meal. Still, while they ate, she discreetly continued her survey of the men in the room and any who entered. But her attention always came back to Max. As they ate dessert, she found herself watching his hands and wondering how they would feel if he were holding her. Touching her. A shiver of excitement raced through her. He isn't interested, she reminded herself.

"Now I know how a woman must feel when she's out on a date and the man she's with checks out every female who walks through the door," Max muttered.

Bernadette looked up at him quizzically.

"You've been subtle," he elaborated, "but I'm well aware that you've been looking over every man in this place."

Bernadette didn't bother to try to deny this accusation. Instead she said coolly, "It can't be dangerous just to look."

It might not be dangerous to her but it was wearing on his nerves, he retorted silently. Every time her eyes would linger longer than usual on one of the men, he'd feel a tightening in his stomach. He was not jealous, he assured himself. He was merely concerned. He had no designs on Ms. Bernadette Dowd. Still, the urge to drag her out of there, take her home and lock her in her room was close to overwhelming. Even worse, the thought of locking himself in that room with her kept taunting him.

Bernadette saw Max's hand go up and begin to massage his temple. He was so bored with her company he'd developed a headache, she fumed feeling like the toad Sabrina had insinuated she was. "I'd really like to go home now," she said.

Max saw the flash of anger in her eyes. She wanted to get rid of him was what she meant, he guessed. And he wouldn't mind getting away from her, he admitted as he signaled the waiter for the check. She was a strain on his control.

But as he drove her home he couldn't stop worrying about what she planned to do once he was gone. When they reached her house, he insisted on walking her to her door. He'd spent the drive home trying to think of something to say that would convince her to stay at home. Nothing had occurred to him. But he also couldn't make himself leave her alone without some reassurance that she would behave. "You could ask me in for a cup of coffee," he suggested as she unlocked the door.

Bernadette turned to look at him. The strain she saw on his face grated on her nerves. She hadn't asked him to play big brother. "I'm sure you have better ways of spending your time," she said levelly, opening the door and stepping inside.

Max knew when someone planned to slam a door in his face. And maybe he would be smart to let her, he thought. But he stepped inside before she could act. "I'm concerned about you," he said gruffly.

"I don't want you to be," she shot back.

Max cupped her face in his hands. "I can't stop myself."

She saw the frustration in his eyes. At the same time, the heat from his hands was traveling along her neck, warming her body and causing an ache deep inside. Hiding her own frustration, she said curtly, "I am well past the age of consent. I can choose my own destiny. Just because you don't find me sexually attractive doesn't mean there isn't some other nice guy out there. You have my word I won't go jumping into bed with just anyone. Now, will you please go away!" Jerking free from his hold, she started toward the kitchen.

Max ordered his legs to carry him out of the house, but they refused. Instead he reached her in two long strides. His hand closed around her arm and he forced her to turn and face him. "The real problem is that I do find you very attractive," he said huskily. "I don't want to even think of another man holding you but I don't want to take advantage of you, either."

The heat in his eyes sent a surge of excitement through her. "You wouldn't be taking advantage of me. You would be participating in my adventure."

"I wish I could see it that way," he replied, releasing her and taking a step back.

Bernadette stood looking at him. The moment of real decision had come. If she was truly serious about having an intimate relationship this was her opportunity. All she had to do was to convince him. The excitement grew more intense. She took a step toward him. Reaching up she began to remove his tie. "If you leave, I'll just have to find someone else," she threatened.

Even with the fabric of his shirt as a barrier, Max was acutely aware of the heat of her touch as her fingers brushed against him while she worked on loosening the knot of his tie. "I really don't think you've given this enough thought," he warned, catching her by the wrists and holding her hands away from him.

For a moment Bernadette was worried that, to throw her off guard, he'd lied about being attracted to her or that her amateur method of seduction had turned him off. But looking into his face she saw the passion in his eyes and her confidence returned. "I have given it all the thought I'm going to," she assured him. "My mind is made up."

Max was sure he'd never heard a woman sound more determined. And he was certainly a safer choice than anyone she was going to find using her methods of hunting, he reasoned. He'd also make her an offer he doubted she'd get from another man. "I'll be a part of your adventure," he said gruffly. "But we're going to take this slowly and if at any point you want to change your mind, you say so."

Bernadette smiled gratefully. "Thanks for the safety net."

I'm going to regret this, Max warned himself but he didn't see any way out. He couldn't allow her to go seeking someone else and possibly ending up with a man who would do her harm. "You're welcome," he replied.

The uneasiness she read on his face brought a frown. "This isn't going to be any fun if you don't relax and, at least, try to enjoy it."

"I've never had the pressure of being in the position of supplying a once in a lifetime romantic adventure," he returned.

Bernadette grinned at his disconcertedness. "Just think of this as a one-night stand. And don't worry, I won't be using a report card."

He frowned down at her. "You're not exactly one-night-stand material."

She saw his uneasiness increasing. "I hope that's a compliment," she bantered trying to lighten the mood.

His frown deepened. "It's an observation. I'd wager a year's salary that under any other circumstances you'd never consider intimacy with a man unless there was a firm commitment between the two of you."

"Under the current circumstances a commitment is the last thing I want," she said, pointedly. "I'm trying to experience the world, not be tied down."

She certainly knew how to argue her case, he conceded feeling his guilt slipping away. "Okay, so you really don't want a commitment." A mischievous glimmer entered his eyes. "But I'm under the impression that the nineties woman does keep a report card."

Bernadette grinned back. "Then you should feel lucky. Since I don't have anyone to compare you to, you have an advantage."

"I've always liked having an advantage," he returned. Realizing he was still holding her by the wrists, he released her.

Bernadette returned to unfastening his tie. "This isn't as easy as they make it look in the movies," she muttered, feeling awkward when the knot refused to come loose easily.

"Nothing's as easy as they make it look in the movies," Max replied, coming to her aid and loosening the tie himself.

When the knot was freed, she slipped the tie off and tossed it onto a chair. Next she removed his jacket and tossed it on top of the tie. Then she began unbuttoning his shirt. Excitement mingled with nervous uncertainty.

As her fingers brushed him, Max couldn't remember ever being so aware of any woman's touch. Already his blood was racing. He wanted her, that he couldn't deny. But he was also determined to live up to his word. He saw her hands shake slightly and forced himself to ask, "Do you want to change your mind?"

For one brief second, her conservative side almost said yes. Then she reminded herself that if she did, she might never have this opportunity again. "No," she replied firmly, then looking up into his face, she added, "but I could use a little encouragement. I thought this kind of experience was supposed to be a two-way street.''

"I'm just trying to live up to my side of the bargain. Once I fully enter the fray, turning back isn't going to be easy," he warned.

She frowned petulantly. "I wish you'd forget your cavalier side and concentrate on the lecherous portion of your nature."

Max didn't think he'd ever seen a pair of lips look more kissable. Leaning down he tested them. They were soft and the faint lingering taste of coffee remained on them. Stopping was going to be real hard now, he thought as his hands came up to rest on her hips and the curve of her body ignited a fire within him.

The touch of his lips and the feel of his hands caused any lingering doubts Bernadette might have had to vanish. She felt like a kid on her first roller-coaster ride. Excitement so strong she could barely breathe surged through her. "This is fun," she murmured against his mouth.

Max was shaken by the strength of the passion she'd awakened in him. He'd barely kissed her and the lengths of their bodies were still separated by inches. Still, he craved her like a thirsty man would crave water. He'd been a lot closer to other women and never had any trouble backing off. But if he got any closer to Bernadette, he knew it was going to take every ounce of control he had to stop. Lifting his head from hers, he let her work on the buttons of his shirt while he continued to keep that distance between them.

Bernadette freed his shirt. Like a child examining a new toy, she ran her fingers through the curled hairs on his chest. They tickled and stimulated her at the same time. Her palms flat against him, she moved her hands upward, then ran them along his shoulders pushing his shirt back. "You feel strong," she said with approval.

What I feel is like a man standing on a railroad track watching a runaway locomotive speeding toward him, he thought. His common sense told him he should move out of the way, but his legs refused to respond. Instead his hands traveled exploringly along the line of her hips. "You feel pretty good yourself," he returned.

Bernadette saw the blue of his eyes darken to the shade of midnight and a womanly satisfaction filled her. Relax and enjoy this, she ordered herself. Impulsively she fastened her hand around the buckle of his belt. "I think we should move this to the bedroom," she said, pulling him down the hall.

The heat of her hand and the swing of her hips frayed his control until it was as thin as a spider's thread. She's a consenting adult, he reminded himself. And she's determined to have this experience. I might as well relax and enjoy it. But relaxed was not how he felt as they entered her bedroom and she began unfastening his belt. "Maybe I should remove a few of your garments before we go any further with mine," he suggested as she slipped the belt off and tossed it onto the upholstered chair in the corner.

Just the thought of him undressing her caused a surge of delicious pleasure. "If you'd like."

What I'd like and what I should do are two very different things, he returned silently. What he should do is leave this room, lock her inside and sit outside with the key. But that wasn't going to stop her, he argued. She'd probably climb out one of the windows and head for the nearest bar. Forcing himself to work slowly, he began removing her clothing. By the time she was down to her lacy underthings, his palms were wet with sweat from the control he was exerting on himself.

"This is much more stimulating than I thought was possible," Bernadette said as his fingers brushed against her thighs. "I honestly thought people were exaggerating."

"Sometimes it can be a less stimulating experience," Max replied, amazed by how new this experience felt to him. It was almost like the first time except he knew more about what he was doing. My senses are simply enhanced because

I'm aware that this should be special for her, he reasoned. Again forcing himself to think only of her feelings, he looked hard into her face as he lightly followed the curves of her body with the tips of his fingers. He was looking for any signs she might be regretting her decision. All he saw was a reflection of his own passion in her eyes. A sense of male triumph sent a surge of power flowing through him.

Impatiently Bernadette turned and tossed back the covers of the bed. Then returning her attention to him, she began unfastening his pants. "I hope you don't think I'm hurrying this," she said, fascinated by the strength of his maleness.

"No problem. I'm having a little trouble with patience myself," he replied, reaching behind her and unfastening her bra.

A sudden self-consciousness swept through Bernadette. When she'd decided to have this experience, her practical side had insisted on having some say. Now it was yelling at her. "There is just one thing...." She nodded toward the dresser behind him.

Turning he saw a decorative bowl filled to the brim with an assortment of condoms. Max mentally slapped himself. Normally he would have thought of using protection on his own. And he should have this time. But Ms. Dowd had been throwing him totally off balance for the past few days. And he hadn't expected to end up in her bedroom.

"I wasn't sure what kind a man would prefer so I bought a variety," she said.

Max couldn't stop himself from laughing. "I've seen drug stores with less of a selection," he joked, releasing her and going over to choose one.

"I saw the bowl idea on one of those talk shows," she explained, his grin chasing away her embarrassment.

"Someone should package the idea. This could be the answer to that age-old question about what lovers should give to one another. Or if a woman is seriously interested in a man she could send him an assortment bowl to let him know. That would certainly take a lot of guesswork out of how to plan an evening.''

Bernadette laughed with him. ''You have a much better sense of humor than I used to give you credit for.''

''Let's just hope my sense of timing is as good,'' he replied, returning to her.

For a moment, she worried that this short interlude might have hampered her ardor but as he reached her and drew her to him, desire burned even more strongly than before.

''You taste delicious,'' Max murmured against her skin as he trailed kisses down her neck to her shoulder. He knew he couldn't wait much longer. As if she was reading his mind, she moved her hands to the waist band of her panties and helped him slip them off. Then she was pulling him down onto the bed.

The feel of his body against hers stroked the fire within her until it burned red hotter. A need more intense than any she'd ever experienced caused a tremor to sweep through her.

Max felt her tremble and silently groaned in frustration. It wouldn't be easy but he had promised her he would stop if she changed her mind. ''Are you getting frightened?'' he asked huskily. ''If you want to quit, we have to stop now,'' he added warningly. ''I only have so much control.''

''I'm not frightened,'' she assured him. ''A little nervous and excited,'' she elaborated, ''but not frightened.''

Max drew a relieved breath. ''I'm really glad to hear that.''

He dipped his head and kissed her shoulder as he spoke and she felt as if the fire was going to consume her.

''Max...'' her voice trailed off, but he understood the unspoken note of yearning. She was ready and eager for him, and the thought intensified his passion as he claimed her.

Startled by the sudden pain Bernadette tensed in his arms.

Concern again showed on Max's face. "It should only hurt a moment," he said soothingly. "I'll try to make it better," he promised, startled by how very deeply he did want to please her.

Easing back, drawing her with him as he went, he moved their bodies in a gentle rhythm, his hands massaging her hips as he held her to him.

The tension left her and pleasure rippled through her as the fires of passion once again began to burn hotly.

"You seem to be quite an expert at this," she said, her voice close to a purr as his touch became more erotic.

"Not really." Max couldn't believe the way her body was igniting in his hands. He experienced a sense of power he'd never felt before and it heightened his own pleasure until he wanted to roar with masculine satisfaction.

Bernadette breathed a sigh of ecstasy. "I'm so glad I didn't pass up this experience."

Max grinned crookedly. "Thanks for inviting me along to share it with you." A little voice deep inside warned him he might regret this later. Then he saw her eyes bright with desire and the knowledge that she was enjoying him as much as he was enjoying her brought a fresh surge of gratification. The warning grew louder. No woman had ever made him feel so alive. I've simply been without female companionship too long, he reasoned, and pushed the warnings from his mind. He would deal with the consequences later. Right now, the woman he was with was again claiming his full attention. Her breathing had become ragged, matching his.

Bernadette gasped in rapture as his possession became more forceful. Then with an instinct born deep within her, she began to move with him. Lost in a world of sensation, she was aware only of the two of them and the raging fire that threatened to consume them.

Suddenly, when she thought there could be no more, an explosion of pure ecstasy shook every fiber of her being. A small shriek of surprise mingled with joy escaped.

Max smiled with satisfaction, then allowed his body to join hers in the heights of rapture.

Even sated Max found himself not wanting to leave her. She'd been wonderful to make love to—so exciting and responsive. So guilelessly sexy, too. He hadn't expected that. Recalling the pleasure they'd just shared made him want to make love to her again. *I have definitely been neglecting certain aspects of life more than I should,* he chided himself.

"Thank you," Bernadette said, her breathing still coming in small gasps as he eased himself away from her.

"You're welcome," he returned, stretching out beside her. He gave himself a mental nod of approval. He had performed well. Then he grinned at this show of conceit as the image of a rooster strutting around a hen yard entered his mind. *I'm merely glad I was able to make this first time special for her,* he told himself.

As her breathing returned to normal, Bernadette lay with her eyes closed enjoying the sense of complete peace that was slowly weaving itself through her. Max had been the perfect choice, she thought drowsily.

Max stared at the ceiling. He was tired but invigorated at the same time. Feeling that he should attempt to make some sort of small talk, he turned toward her only to discover she'd fallen asleep. He brushed a stray lock of hair from her cheek. The smile on her face told him all he needed to know and he too drifted to sleep.

Chapter Eight

Bernadette groaned with displeasure at the ringing of the phone, which had woken her. But as she reached for the receiver a small smile played across her face. She was tired but she didn't regret the loss of sleep. She was also glad she'd had a whole bowl of protection.

I should be at least a little bored with him by now, she thought as her foot brushed against his leg. But instead of boredom, a fresh wave of desire washed through her. She was amazed to discover she was so insatiable. Then the phone rang again reminding her of why she was awake.

"Are you going to answer that?" a male voice grumbled. "Or shall I answer it and give whoever is calling something to talk about?"

"I'll get it," she replied, wondering as she picked up the receiver just what her caller would think if Max had been the one to answer the phone. My caller would have been very surprised, Bernadette answered her own question when she recognized Grace's voice.

"Sorry to bother you," Ben's secretary said. "I know this is your day off but you got a call that sounded pretty important. It was a woman. She said her name was Judy Karlson and she claimed to be the person who tipped us off to Lang. She left a number."

At the mention of Lang's name, the fog cleared from Bernadette's mind. Scrounging around in the drawer of her bedside table, she found a notepad and pen. "Give me the number."

As soon as she had the number, Bernadette thanked Grace, hung up and dialed.

"Hello." A woman's shaky voice answered on the third ring.

"Am I speaking to Judy Karlson?" Bernadette asked.

"Who wants to know?" the speaker demanded.

Bernadette heard the fear in the woman's voice. "This is Bernadette Dowd."

"Chuck figured I'd been the one to squeal on him," the woman said, her words coming in a rush. "I know it wasn't smart but he can be a little rough at times and I just wanted him put away for a while so I could get away and start a new life. But they didn't put him away. He made bail and he came here. He knocked me around a little but I didn't confess." The fear in the caller's voice grew stronger. "I'm scared he's going to come back. I need some money to leave town. I thought maybe your paper would pay a little reward to me for giving them that tip."

"We don't usually pay informants," Bernadette replied, uncertain of what to do.

The woman began to cry. "You've got to help me. I'm afraid he might kill me when he comes back. He's real mad."

Bernadette knew she had to do something. And the first thing was to get the woman someplace reasonably safe. "Is there a public place where you can wait for me?" she asked. "Someplace where he can't get you alone and hurt you."

"There's a small café on the corner." Judy gave the cross streets.

"I'll be there as soon as possible," Bernadette promised.

Max was on his way to the shower by the time she hung up. He wasn't sure who she'd called or why but from her end of the conversation, he knew there could be trouble. "Wherever you're going I'm coming with you," he said, over his shoulder.

Bernadette didn't argue. Chuck Lang was not someone she would choose to tangle with alone or with only another woman.

Tossing off the covers she experienced a wave of regret. They had reached for each other again and again throughout the night, yet she still wasn't tired of Max's lovemaking. In fact, she wished they had all day to lounge around and enjoy each other more. "But we don't," she reminded herself, recalling the fear in Judy Karlson's voice.

Half an hour later they were eating bagels with peanut butter as Max guided his car out of her driveway. "It's a good thing you found something for us to eat," he said. "After last night, I was starved."

"Me, too," she replied, then heard herself adding honestly, "I'm only sorry we didn't have more time."

Max had been worried she might be regretting her decision to experience intimacy. Now that worry vanished and he felt a sense of triumph. Apparently he'd performed just fine. "I'm glad you enjoyed yourself."

Bernadette smiled at the memories that flashed through her mind. "Yes, I did. Thank you very much."

Max grinned crookedly. "You're very welcome."

Bernadette knew he would leave the next move up to her. For one brief instant she considered showing some restraint and sending him home. In the next instant she was calling herself stupid. She had no future so why should she deprive herself here in the present? Aloud, she said, "I was wondering if you'd like to stay at my place again tonight."

It occurred to Max that maybe he should start putting some distance between himself and Ms. Dowd. But the thought of spending another night with her was too much of a temptation. "I'd enjoy that."

Bernadette breathed a relaxed sigh of satisfaction. This adventure into intimacy was working out very well.

But a few minutes later she was thinking that her adventure into investigative reporting was not working out so well for Judy Karlson. The woman had said she would be wearing a red scarf and sunglasses. Joining Judy Karlson in the booth she'd chosen at the rear of the café, Bernadette understood why. She could see the bruising below the rim of the dark glasses and the red scarf wasn't able to entirely hide the ugly darkening mark on Miss Karlson's neck.

"Nice shiner," Max said as he slid in beside Bernadette. "Lang give it to you?"

Judy lowered her glasses just enough to allow herself an unobstructed view of her two new companions. "And a few in places that don't show in public," she replied. "He was real angry."

While Judy Karlson was inspecting her and Max, Bernadette did her own inspection of the woman who'd asked for her help. Miss Karlson was, with the help of a bottle, a blonde. A formfitting tank top showed she was slender but with a full bust. Her makeup was dramatic and her nails were the long artificial kind. The way she was eyeing Max made it clear she liked men.

Bernadette couldn't stop herself from glancing at Max to see if he was responding in a masculine way to the curvaceous blonde. He wasn't. She experienced a rush of relief. In the next instant, self-directed anger swept through her. She shouldn't care if he did look at other women. After all, what she and Max had together was merely physical and with absolutely no strings attached. Keep your mind on business, she ordered herself.

"There's a battered women's shelter I can take you to," she offered.

Judy shook her head and slid her glasses back in place. "No way. If I stay in town, he'll find me."

"But won't you need to be here for the trial?" Bernadette asked. "Surely, because your Lang's girlfriend the prosecutor will want to put you on the stand and question you about what you know of his activities."

Judy shrugged a well-shaped shoulder. "What could I tell anyone? All I know is hearsay. I never saw him doing nothing. Besides, he tells me they're already offering him a deal. This is the first time he's ever got caught in one of his scams so, except for a few juvenile offenses, his record is clean. And—" she leaned toward them and lowered her voice "—he claims he has friends in high places who can help get him off easy." She sat back and her voice returned to normal as she finished. "He'll probably end up with a slap on the wrist . . . a fine maybe and a little probation time or community service."

Bernadette looked at Max for confirmation of what the woman was saying.

"Could be," he said.

Leaning across the table, Judy again lowered her glasses and focused her attention on Max. "But I may not be so lucky. He can do real damage when he gets going. He broke my arm last year and he wasn't nearly as angry as he is this time." Fear again filled her voice. "Look, I've got to get out of town."

"Let me make a phone call," Max said. Turning to Bernadette, he added, "Order me something to eat, I'm still hungry."

She caught the gleam in his eye and her heart beat a little faster. "I'll order something substantial."

"The eggs and breakfast steak is pretty good here," Judy recommended as Max strode way. "And he does look like a steak man to me."

Bernadette turned to the woman to find her watching Max walking away with something akin to a predatory expression on her face.

"Nice pair of shoulders," the blonde commented. "A woman could enjoy leaning on those. 'Course from this angle, I can't see anything that isn't nice."

Bernadette's stomach tightened as she fought back the urge to tell Miss Karlson to stay away from Max. She had no right to feel the least bit possessive of him, she chided herself.

Suddenly the blonde's expression became apologetic. "Sometimes I get a little carried away when I see a good-looking hunk. I didn't mean nothing. I don't have any designs on your man. I just want your help."

Embarrassed she'd let her feelings show, Bernadette said stiffly, "He's not my man."

Judy raised an eyebrow. "If I was you, I'd try to change that," she said.

If I had all the time in the world, I might, Bernadette admitted. But she didn't. "I'd better order that food," she said, signaling for the waitress.

"I've got a call in to a friend of mine on the police force. As soon as he confirms they don't need you, we'll see what we can do to help," Max informed Judy when he returned to the table.

She nodded and motioned for the waitress to bring her some more coffee.

Max had just finished eating when his call came. Returning to the table, he said, "Looks like you were right. You're not considered a good witness for either side."

Judy smiled brightly. "My code has always been to hear as little as possible and repeat even less." Abruptly she frowned. "And from now on, I plan to live by that even more closely." Her gaze leveled on Bernadette and Max. "My car's packed. If you can provide me with some cash, I'll be going."

"I can give you five hundred," Bernadette said, feeling guilty for the beating the woman had taken.

"I'm not sure Ben will spring for that much," Max cautioned.

"I'll work it out with him," Bernadette returned, determined to help the blonde get away from Lang even if the money came out of her own pocket. She certainly didn't need to worry about saving for her old age anymore. Turning to Judy, she said, "Can you guide us to the nearest bank machine?"

"You just follow me," Judy instructed, already scooting out of the booth.

Max waited until he and Bernadette were alone in his car trailing Judy Karlson in hers to the nearest machine, then he said, "I know this is going to sound callous, but you shouldn't feel guilty. Judy Karlson knew what kind of man Chuck Lang was when she called in the tip and she had to know the chance she was taking. Besides, it wasn't as if her motives were altruistic. They were, in fact, strictly for her benefit. She tried to use us to rid herself of Lang."

"Yes, but this beating was because of something I did and I'm going to help her," Bernadette insisted.

Max frowned impatiently. "I didn't say you shouldn't help her. I just said you shouldn't feel guilty. Even if Lang hadn't gotten caught, he'd have found some reason to knock her around anyway."

"I suppose," Bernadette agreed. They'd pulled into a shopping center and were heading for a bank. A few minutes later, Judy had her money and was waving goodbye.

"Maybe you ought to consider giving up investigative reporting," Max suggested as he and Bernadette climbed back into his car. "In your case it could prove to be expensive."

"Maybe," she conceded, already counting the five hundred as a loss. Still, she didn't regret giving it to Judy if it would help the woman begin a new life.

For his own peace of mind, Max hoped Bernadette would take his advice. In the meantime, they had the weekend. He'd checked the board on Friday and seen that neither of them was scheduled to work. Of course, so far nothing had gone the way he'd planned. He'd expected to spend today and tomorrow going over his own files and working on his private investigation.

But the bad guys weren't going anywhere, he reminded himself. And after last night he figured he owed Bernadette a couple of days of fun and games. Besides, it had been a long time since he'd taken any time off. Actually it had been four years, one month, two days, nine hours and eighteen minutes, he calculated quickly. That had been the moment when his brother had died in his arms. Shoving that hurtful memory from his mind, he glanced at Bernadette. "What would you like to do with the rest of this day?"

"Are you sure there isn't something you'd rather be doing than escorting me around?" she forced herself to ask.

"Nothing," he assured her. Then as a thought struck him, he added, "Unless you've changed your mind and you're getting tired of my company."

"No, I'm definitely not getting tired of your company," she replied honestly.

Max drew a relieved breath. If she had tried to send him on his way, he knew he wouldn't have been able to simply leave. Not after last night. He'd have been compelled to follow her around until she'd talked to that psychologist on Monday. Being by her side instead of having to tag along behind was going to make his life a whole lot easier.

But not comfortable, he thought as the urge to take her straight back to her bedroom grew strong. He would let her set their agenda, he ordered himself firmly. "Now that we've established we're not bored with each other, what would you like to do today?"

Mentally she ran through her list of things she'd never done. "I've never been to a really big amusement park," she said after a few moments.

"Like the one south of town?"

Bernadette nodded.

"Neither have I," Max admitted. He glanced down at his suit. "We'll swing by my place so I can change." Then he looked at her. She was dressed in a tailored pant suit. "And you'll be more comfortable if you change, too. We'll swing by your place after we've been to mine."

Excitement swept through Bernadette. She was going to get to see Max's place. *I shouldn't be so interested,* she warned herself. *He was only spending time with her because he felt sorry for her and he was worried she'd do something rash. By Monday he was going to want to get back to his own life. Besides, he probably won't even invite me in,* she added.

A few minutes later they pulled into an apartment complex.

"Hi, Max," a pretty brunette walking a terrier called and waved as they passed her.

Max waved back.

Keep quiet, Bernadette ordered herself as a curl of irritation twisted inside her. Instead she said dryly, "I guess you never get lonely here."

Max could have sworn he heard an edge of jealousy in her voice. Normally that would have caused a danger signal to go off in his brain. Today, however, he felt flattered. "She's very married to a cop who's a close friend of mine."

Bernadette did manage to stop herself before she said she was glad to hear that. *His private life was really none of her business,* she again told herself. *What was going on between them was merely an interlude. On Monday it would be over.*

"Do you want to come in and wait?" he offered, parking in front of one of the buildings.

If she was still her more conservative self, Bernadette knew she would have demurely chosen to wait in the car. But this new self was too interested to stay behind. "Sure," she said, starting to climb out the moment he turned off the engine.

His apartment was much neater than she'd expected from all the rumors she'd heard about bachelor pads.

As if he sensed her surprise, he said, "I have a maid service come in every couple of weeks. Yesterday was their day to be here. They're allowed to straighten as long as they don't touch anything on my desk."

She heard the warning in his voice and knew he meant that rule to apply to her, too. "Hands off the desk," she replied, holding her palms up toward him to let him know she'd gotten the message.

He grinned, then glanced toward his answering machine and saw it blinking. He pressed the Playback button.

"Henry, where did you get that silly Marx Brothers comic routine to answer your phone?" a female voice with a thick French accent demanded with amusement. "Oh, well, never mind. I know you are terribly reliable but I just had to call and remind you to feed my cat on Sunday. You promised, remember. She likes to eat at one sharp."

Bernadette looked at Max. "Maybe you should put in a message that let's people know whose answering machine they've contacted. I hope Henry is as reliable as she thinks and doesn't need that reminder."

"I'm sure Henry is very reliable," he replied nonchalantly. "I've gotten messages for him before. The woman must have a menagerie."

A second message from Molly reminding him that he was expected for Sunday dinner interrupted any further conversation about the first message. "And if you and Berny are still hanging around together, bring her," Molly finished.

"I'll call Molly and cancel," Max said as the machine switched off, then he headed into his bedroom to change.

He obviously didn't want her spending too much time with his family, Bernadette mused. Well, she couldn't blame him. Molly was bound to get the wrong idea about them.

Pushing the phone messages from her mind, she wandered around the room. On a table by the couch was a picture of Max and another man who bore a strong family resemblance. Another picture nearby showed Molly with a baby in her arms and the man from the first picture holding a toddler. Obviously these were photos of Max's brother. He had a nice smile, Bernadette thought. Returning her attention to the picture of him with Max, her gaze focused on Max. He looked more carefree than she'd ever seen him. In all the time she'd known him, even when he laughed, she'd sensed a guardedness about him, as if he refused to allow himself to totally enjoy anything.

Setting the picture down, she let her gaze again travel around the room. Max's desk was a gigantic old rolltop affair with rows of pigeonholes across the back of the interior. It looked like an antique, she thought. Moving toward it for a closer look, she suddenly stopped and stared. On the other side, shielded from her view earlier by the desk was an antique safe. Just like ones she'd seen in old Western movies, it was black and stood on legs that looked to be about four inches high. Gold leaf decorated the front and the handle used to open it was polished brass.

"It's fireproof but that's about all it's good for. It has the loudest tumblers you've ever heard. Any burglar could break into it in less than a minute."

Bernadette looked over her shoulder to see Max approaching. He was dressed in jeans and a T-shirt. He looked younger, less harsh and she had the most incredible urge to undress him. Behave, she ordered herself. She didn't want him tiring of her too soon. "Sounds interesting. Maybe you'll let me try breaking into it sometime," she said.

"Maybe."

She heard the hesitation in his voice. He was worried she might be thinking of becoming a fixture in his life, she guessed. "On the other hand, I can think of more interesting things to do than hang around your apartment," she said, to put his mind at ease.

"So can I," he replied, feeling the need to get her out of there before he tried to convince her that hanging around his apartment for the afternoon could be very enjoyable. He forced a smile. "Starting with amusement parks."

Bernadette was sure he was more tense than when they'd entered his place. As they drove toward her house, she noticed the grim set of his jaw and her nerves broke. "Look, if you're having second thoughts about the amusement park, I understand. If you're not interested in going there it won't be any fun for me," she said, then added stiffly, "you're obviously getting bored with my company. And I'm sure you can think of at least a hundred other places you'd rather be and a dozen other people you'd rather be with."

Max drew a terse breath. He didn't want another argument about his spending the weekend keeping an eye on her. "You're reading me wrong. I'm just uncomfortable because I'm trying real hard to concentrate on getting you to that amusement park when I'd rather get you back in bed."

His admission caused a rush of pleasure. "Going back to bed doesn't sound like such a terrible idea."

Maybe not, Max agreed silently. But how much he wanted to get her alone scared him. He was beginning to fear she could prove much more dangerous than he'd thought was possible. "We're going to the amusement park. I won't be accused of limiting your experiences."

Not wanting him to get bored with her too quickly, she decided not to argue with him. "All right. The amusement park if you insist."

Later as they entered the park, Max was glad to be in the midst of crowds of people. He'd taught himself to hold a tight rein on his emotions but the strength of his attraction to Bernadette threatened his control and made him uneasy. At her home, when she'd gone into her room to change, he'd almost gone in to help her . . . only dressing wasn't what he had in mind. Concentrate on the rides, cotton candy and popcorn, he ordered himself.

But that order was easier to issue than to follow. The antique cars proved to be safe but the river ride left her wet with her T-shirt and shorts clinging seductively to her curves. The carousel sounded like a good idea until he watched her hair blowing in the breeze. He was reminded of how she looked with the chestnut tresses spread over her pillow.

Determined to get thoughts of her out of his mind, he guided her toward the bumper cars. There, he figured, with each of them in their own cars, he could keep a lot of distance between them. Whatever end of the floor she headed for, he'd go in the opposite direction. But as they stood waiting their turn, he saw the way the drivers on the floor were being jostled as they ran into each other. The thought of her aneurysm bursting because of the jarring suddenly overwhelmed him. "I've changed my mind," he said, pulling her out of line.

He also vetoed the roller coaster. The Log Flume seemed safe, he decided. All it involved was riding a plastic fake hollowed-out log down a winding channel of water with a couple of steep downhill drops. But as he climbed in behind her and she braced herself against him, he realized he'd made another mistake. The feel of her was so enticing, he barely noticed the final drop that brought screams from the other riders.

"I'm hungry," Bernadette announced as they climbed out of the fake log. She'd been trying hard to enjoy the rides and she had. But mostly she was aware of Max. She'd never thought of herself as ever being lecherous but that was how she felt. What she wanted most was to get him alone.

Max breathed a silent sigh of relief. Eating sounded safe. "What would you like? From the various eateries we've passed, I'd say we should be able to satisfy any craving you have.''

Food was not the solution to the craving she was having at this moment, Bernadette thought. And hadn't she promised herself she was going to live for the moment. So what if he was tired of her by tomorrow. She might not even live to see the sunrise. ''I was thinking of Chinese carry-in at my place.''

Max read the invitation in her eyes. He'd always prided himself on his willpower but he wasn't made of steel. ''Sounds like a great idea to me.''

As they headed to his car, Bernadette studied him covertly. Three days ago, she would never have picked Max Laird as the person she would spend some of her last days with. Now she couldn't imagine anyone who would have been a better choice. Of course what was happening between them was more fantasy than reality, she reminded herself. It wouldn't last. It was never intended to last. But while it did, she was going to enjoy every moment.

Back at her place, she went in to take a shower while Max called in the order for their food. She was shampooing her hair when she heard the shower curtain move.

''It'll be forty-five minutes before our food is ready,'' Max's voice sounded above the water. He'd tried to stay away but his self-control had worn thin. As he'd walked down the hall to tell her dinner would be a little late in coming, he'd begun to strip even before he'd realized the idea had crossed his mind. ''Thought maybe you could use someone to soap your back,'' he said stepping in with her.

Bernadette smiled welcomingly as the sight of him brought a hot rush of passion.

When he took over working the shampoo into her hair, her toes actually curled from the delicious feel of his touch.

''My turn,'' she said as soon as her hair was rinsed. Again feeling like a child with a new toy, she picked up the bar of soap and began sudsing him.

"I haven't got enough control for this," he growled. Stopping her, he stepped under the water to rinse himself, then turned off the tap.

Bernadette grinned in anticipation as he wrapped a towel around her, then stepping out, picked her up and carried her into the guest bedroom. "No sense in getting your bed damp. We'll be needing it later," he said as he laid her down. "And I can't even wait long enough to dry us off."

"Waiting is definitely out of the question," she agreed huskily, discarding the towel and pulling him down into her arms.

Several hours later as she lay beside Max while he slept, she felt relaxed and happy. Both were emotions she'd been sure she'd never feel again after Dr. Riley had pronounced her death sentence. Max had proven to be the perfect companion to see her through her initial crisis.

A broad grin spread across her face as she recalled why they'd been half an hour late picking up their food. Showers, she mused, could be a great deal more fun than she'd ever thought.

And we still have tomorrow, she reminded herself. All she had to do was not let herself get any romantic notions. This was strictly a physical relationship entered into on both sides merely to satisfy her curiosity. On Monday they would both go back to their own lives. But Monday was a whole day away. Smiling softly, she drifted to sleep.

Chapter Nine

Bernadette studied Max over the rim of her coffee cup. They'd spent a lazy Sunday morning lying in bed, reading the newspaper and enjoying each other. Now it was nearly noon.

During the past days, she'd become more and more aware of Max's subtle mood shifts. Although she hadn't wanted to, she'd become more and more aware of him in general, she admitted. He was much kinder and more caring than she'd given him credit for being. He wasn't perfect. He had a cynical side but, considering some of the stories he'd covered, she couldn't blame him for developing a certain cynicism toward humanity.

However, it wasn't his views of humanity in general that was on her mind at the moment. It was his attitude toward her. For the past half hour, he'd seemed uneasy and she was becoming more and more certain he wanted to leave. She was also certain he wouldn't leave on his own. Time to shove him out, she told herself. She'd known this would come but she hadn't expected it to feel so painful. "There really isn't any néed for you to stick around until tomorrow. Honestly I'll be fine on my own," she said breaking the silence between them. "You've been a terrific baby-sitter but you can go home now. I'm sure you must have business of your own you need to get done before the weekend is over."

Max had been sitting there wondering how he was going to get away from her long enough to meet with an informant. The message on his answering machine had been playing through his mind for the past few minutes. Marlena had done an excellent job. Anyone other than him hearing the call about the cat would have been sure it was a wrong number instead of a coded request for a meeting. However, he experienced a prickling of irritation at Bernadette's words. "Are you trying to politely tell me you've grown tired of my company?" he asked dryly, then silently laughed at himself. He'd come close to sounding like a rejected lover.

Bernadette was tempted to say yes and make a clean break now. Waiting until tomorrow wasn't going to make parting any easier. But she couldn't make herself give up one last night with him if he honestly wanted to stay. "No. I just don't want you to feel trapped and right now you look like a man who feels caged," she replied bluntly.

Max experienced a wave of elation that she wasn't tired of him. It's just my ego, he told himself. "I do have an errand I should run," he said nonchalantly, his tone implying the errand was of no real consequence but a nuisance that had to be taken care of.

Bernadette gave him an impatient look. "Then I wish you'd take care of it."

Max nodded and rose. But as he headed for the door, the fear that something might happen to her while he was gone shook him. He strode back and stood in front of her. "I want your word you'll wait right here for me."

The protectiveness she saw in his eyes caused a warmth to spread through her. "I'll bake a cake."

"I like chocolate," he said over his shoulder as he again headed to the door.

"And I like you," she murmured as the door closed behind him. "Too much," she added, regretfully. If she didn't have this death warrant hanging over her head, she would try to court him, she admitted. But it seemed selfish to try to win someone's love when she knew she would not be around very much longer.

"So we'll both have to settle for some chocolate cake," she said, rising from her chair and moving to the counter.

A few minutes later while she was mixing the batter, the phone rang. Answering it, her stomach knotted when she heard Dr. Riley's voice coming over the line.

"I'm in my office," he said. "Could you come by?"

"Right now?" she managed to choke out.

"Right now," he replied.

"Yeah, sure," she said, unable to bring herself to ask if the brain scan had shown signs the aneurysm was enlarging.

"Good," came his businesslike reply. "I'll be expecting you."

Bernadette felt almost robotic as she hung up. Going into the kitchen, she put the unfinished batter into the refrigerator, turned off the oven and left Max a note saying an important errand had come up and she'd be back soon.

"Or maybe I won't be back at all," she murmured, voicing the fear that was tormenting her. "If I don't, it's been fun," she added, pressing a kiss on her finger then pressing the finger on his name.

She left the door unlocked so he could get in. As she pulled out of the driveway, her conservative side flashed to the forefront and for a brief moment she worried that a stranger might rob her. "If I'm dead, I won't care," she retorted to the image in the mirror and pushed the worry from her mind.

In the elevator on her way up to Dr. Riley's office her legs felt like jelly. She wasn't ready to die yet.

"Bernadette," he said, rising from his chair and coming around his desk to greet her as she entered.

The uneasy expression on his face caused her stomach to knot even tighter. He's probably amazed I'm still able to walk around, she thought. This thought was given substance as he took her by the arm and led her to a chair in front of his desk.

When she was seated, he rounded the desk and reseated himself. Then leaning toward her, he said, "A terrible mistake has been made." He shifted his shoulders as if they were uncomfortable. "I was away the past few days lecturing or I would have caught it sooner. Luckily I came in this afternoon to try to catch up on some work."

He tapped a folder on his desk. "I found your latest test results here." Apology spread over his face. "They show no aneurysm."

Bernadette was sure she'd heard him wrong. "They what?" she demanded.

"I called my assistant. He came in. We went back over the previous results and that's when we discovered the error. He admitted he'd dropped a couple of files. Apparently when he picked them up, he accidentally switched the results. A patient of mine who is suffering terrible migraines is the one with the aneurysm. She was just in yesterday for another battery of tests and a comparison of those with the ones in your file made the mistake obvious."

Bernadette wanted to shout for joy but instead she sat frozen, afraid to believe what he was telling her. "I *don't* have an aneurysm?" she said stiffly.

"No. You're one of the healthiest young women I know," he replied. "I'm really sorry about this mix-up."

"I thought you were going to tell me the aneurysm had enlarged and was going to burst at any moment," she muttered, anger mixing with her relief.

He looked disconcerted. "I suppose I should have told you about the mistake over the phone but I thought it would be best if I did it in person."

Bernadette stared at the man. "A mix-up. There was a mix-up," she repeated.

"I'm really sorry for everything you've been put through." He apologized again. Attempting to point out the bright side, he added, "But at least your worries are over and your life can go back to normal."

Bernadette was a muddle of emotions. This man's mix-up had turned her life topsy-turvy. And although he was obviously sorry, he could not possibly undo the damage he'd done. Afraid of what she might say if she stayed, she rose and strode out of the office. Standing at the elevator, she was tempted to return and ask him if he had any idea of the strain he'd put her under or the drastic change in her behavior, which had resulted from his prognosis. But instead she stood there until the elevator came, then stepped inside and rode down.

Walking to her car she realized the sun seemed warmer and the day brighter. She was going to live! True, her life had taken some shocking paths but they weren't anything she couldn't live with, nor would she regret them.

Max filled her mind as she drove home. Thinking she was going to die, she had not allowed herself to even consider the possibility of pursuing a relationship with him beyond this day. But she was going to live and she couldn't think of a better life than one spent with him. She grimaced at her reflection in the mirror as she faced the truth. She'd fallen in love with Max Laird. Now all she had to do was convince him to fall in love with her. She remembered the warmth and protectiveness she'd seen in his eyes. That gave her hope she might be successful.

Max was waiting for her when she returned. "Wherever you went must have agreed with you," he said, his gaze raking over her.

She saw the concern in his eyes and her hope grew. On the way home, she'd practiced several ways of telling Max what had happened. But now that the moment had arrived she simply heard herself blurting out, "Dr. Riley called. There was a mix-up. I don't have an aneurysm. I'm perfectly healthy."

For a moment Max stood staring at her in stunned silence. "A mix-up," he repeated finally finding his voice. Guilt flooded through him.

He looked as if he'd been punched in the stomach, Bernadette thought. Even worse, she saw the guilt on his face. Her hope vanished. "So it looks like you can get back to your life and I'll get back to mine," she said levelly, hiding her disappointment.

"I feel like I've taken advantage of you," he said gruffly.

Bernadette scowled at him. "You didn't take advantage of me and the last thing I want from you is an apology for what happened between us."

Max raked a hand agitatedly through his hair. "It should never have happened."

The regret she saw on his face made Bernadette want to scream at him in frustration. Instead she presented a calm front as she said dryly, "You don't have to look so remorseful. We were victims of circumstance. In a way what happened wasn't even real because it wasn't the real us participating. Ordinarily I'd never have chosen your company and you'd never have given me the time of day. So, the way I see it, we'd both be better off to forget the past few days and go back to being acquaintances."

She didn't have to make it sound as if, had she been in her right mind, he was the last man she'd have selected to have a liaison with, he thought irritably. In the next instant he was admonishing himself. He should be grateful she was taking this attitude. He didn't want to be tied down and she was definitely the tying-down type. "You're right," he agreed.

His words pierced like a knife and Bernadette realized she'd been hoping he might suddenly realize he'd begun to care for her and tell her she was wrong. Fool! she mocked herself. The urge to throw him out was close to overwhelming. "Now is as good a time as any to get back to our own lives," she said, motioning toward the door.

Max knew he was being told to leave and he ordered his feet to carry him out. But as he reached the door, he turned back to face her. "I hope you aren't going to let what happened between us have a lasting effect on your life. You're not really the type for affairs."

Ire rose in Bernadette. He didn't want to be a part of her life but he wanted to tell her how to live it. "Don't flatter yourself," she returned drolly. "You weren't so much fun that the thought of being without a man will cause me to rush out, looking for my next conquest."

He'd asked for that, Max told himself. Aloud he said, "Good," then, deciding it was definitely time for him to leave, he went.

"What now?" Bernadette murmured as he drove away. She felt totally off balance. A part of her was elated while another part felt hollow. She remembered the unfinished cake batter in the refrigerator. Her first impulse was to throw it away. But she'd always been able to work through her problems much better when she was cooking, she reminded herself. For some reason she had never been able to fathom, this domestic chore had a way of easing her tension and enabling her to think more clearly. Going into the kitchen, she continued making the cake.

When it was in the oven, she pulled out the ingredients for her meatless chili and got a pot of that started. She recalled she hadn't had any cornbread for a long time. Deciding that would go well with the chili, she got out the dry ingredients and combined them so they would be ready when the time came.

"The cake will need icing," she muttered, grabbing her cookbook off the shelf once again. But as she searched for the right page, her vision began to blur and she realized tears were filling her eyes. "Damn!" she growled at herself, then flushed when she realized she'd actually cursed. She never cursed.

"Max Laird isn't worth crying over," she berated herself. "I should be happy and relieved. I'm going to live. I can get back to my real life."

But instead of feeling better, her stomach seemed to knot tighter. Angrily she brushed the tears from her cheeks. For the first time since she'd sent him on his way, she let herself remember the time they'd spent together. She'd been afraid she would regret her behavior and she did, but not as intensely as she'd thought she would. She admitted that if she hadn't believed she was going to die at any moment, she wouldn't have seduced him. And she was totally responsible for the seduction. But what had happened had happened. She couldn't change it. "It's best if I just forget and get on with my life as if these past few days never happened," she ordered herself.

With that thought firmly in mind, she finished making the icing.

All during his drive home Max couldn't get Bernadette out of his mind. He should never have let that situation go as far as it had. He realized it was an old-fashioned notion, but the thought that he should volunteer to marry her tormented him. Marriage, however, wasn't in his plans.

Fighting down a fresh rush of guilt, he recalled that she hadn't seemed to mind getting rid of him. "She probably wouldn't have married me even if I had asked," he told himself as he pulled into his parking space in front of his apartment building. Obviously he wasn't her choice of a lifetime mate. "Which is just as well," he muttered, reminding himself he already had a commitment.

Entering his home, he pushed her out of his mind and went directly to his antique safe. Quickly he pulled out the files laying haphazardly inside. Reaching underneath, he twisted each of the corner screws half a turn. Returning his attention to the interior, he pressed on the backside of the safe flooring. A false bottom popped up revealing several files inside. He pulled these out and tossed them onto the desk. Then seating himself in front of them, he opened the top file and began making notes. His informant who could do the French accent so well had provided information that might prove very useful, he thought with satisfaction.

But as dedicated as he was to the task before him, he couldn't keep Bernadette's image from nagging at the back of his mind. He also couldn't shake off a feeling of uneasiness where she was concerned. Agitatedly, he slammed the files closed, returned them to their hiding place and left.

Bernadette was tempted not to answer the knock on her front door. She wasn't in the mood to talk to anyone.

"Bernadette," Max's gruff tones sounded through the barrier.

For a moment she stood frozen. Then the hope that he'd discovered he honestly cared for her bloomed. But when she opened the door and saw the impatience in his eyes, she knew that wasn't why he was there. "Did you forget something?" she asked coolly.

Max shifted uncomfortably. He couldn't stop remembering how she'd felt in his arms and along with that memory came guilt. "I just wanted to make certain you were all right. You've had several shocks over the past few days. I know the one today was a pleasant one but it was a shock nonetheless."

"I'm fine." She pronounced each word distinctly.

The guilt he was feeling grew stronger. "If I were the marrying kind, I'd marry you," he said bluntly, then heard himself offering, "And if it'd make you feel better we can go through the ceremony and then get a quick divorce."

Bernadette glowered at him. Did he think she had no pride? "I'm an adult. You don't have to treat me like some misguided adolescent. I can deal with my mistakes just fine and I most certainly do not need to marry you to be able to live with myself."

He was making a real mess of this, Max thought. "I didn't mean it that way." She raised a skeptical eyebrow and he knew lying wouldn't help. "Well, maybe I did," he admitted.

Her stomach knotted. Again, for a split second, she'd held the hope that he might say he really cared for her. Anger flared inside her. "Go home!" she growled. Then a sudden thought struck her and she said, "Wait one minute."

Quickly she went into the kitchen and got the chocolate cake. She'd been trying to decide how to get rid of it before she gave in to temptation and sat down with a fork and ate the whole thing. Carrying it back to the door, she fought down the urge to push it into Max's face. Reaching him, she shoved it toward him. "You wanted this."

Max started to tell her to keep it, but before he could speak he noticed the ire in her eyes. The thought that if he didn't take it, he might be wearing it struck him and he accepted the platter.

"Now go home," she ordered, picturing him with the chocolate icing and cake smashed over his face and half wishing she'd allowed herself this one last impulsive act.

Max knew danger when he saw it and he saw it now. "Thanks for the cake," he said then strode to his car.

He'd known she was trouble, he reminded himself as he drove home. But he didn't need to worry about her any longer. The cool, under-control Bernadette Dowd was back. And he should feel lucky about that, he added, a crooked smile tilting one corner of his mouth as he recalled how close he was sure he'd come to getting the cake pushed into his face.

Bernadette finished changing the sheets on her bed, then straightened and surveyed the room. "I don't regret what happened," she informed the emptiness, then with a sigh, amended, "Well, maybe a little." But what was done was done.

Her gaze came to rest on the bowl on top of her dresser. Although she'd acted irrationally, at least she'd behaved responsibly, she thought gratefully. "And now it's time to get on with the rest of my life," she said resolutely. She smiled.

She was going to live and that opened up a great many possibilities.

Chapter Ten

Bernadette stood surveying herself in the mirror. She was dressed in one of her most conservative gray linen suits. Her hair was pulled back into a chignon at her nape and her makeup was demurely applied. She looked the same as she had looked the day before Dr. Riley's mistake had sent her veering off the course she'd set for her life. "And I am the same," she assured herself, giving the image in the mirror an approving nod before picking up her purse and briefcase and heading for work.

Stepping out of the elevator and heading to her desk, she felt a prickling on the side of her neck. Glancing in the direction from which the uncomfortable sensation had come, she saw Max standing in the doorway of Ben's office. Seeing her look his way, he nodded a stiff good morning then turned and closed the door.

Deep within she felt a nudging of regret. If he wants to play the Lone Ranger, then I wish him a happy life, she assured herself, continuing to her desk.

"You and Max have a fight?"

Bernadette glanced over her shoulder to see that Roger had joined her. "No," she said with a quizzical look designed to make him think she didn't understand why he would ask.

Clearly not buying her innocent act, his gaze narrowed on her. "I could have sworn you two were an item. I expected to see you arrive arm in arm."

Bernadette had reached her desk. She tossed him a 'get real' glance as she seated herself. "Max Laird and I worked on a story together. That's all."

Beyond Roger she saw Max coming out of Ben's office. Again she experienced a pang of regret. Furious that she wasn't able to completely ignore the man, she added dryly, "Be honest, can you really picture me and Max together as a couple."

"No," Roger admitted.

Silently Bernadette thanked him. She'd needed to hear that. All last night and this morning, she'd assured herself she'd put the brief interlude with Max Laird into the back of her mind. She'd even convinced herself she hadn't really fallen in love with him, that what she'd felt was mere infatuation. But seeing him again was causing some fantasies she didn't want to have.

"What I can picture is you and me having dinner together," Roger continued coaxingly.

Now that was something she couldn't picture, Bernadette returned mentally. Aloud, she said, "I've vowed not to date the men I work with."

For a moment he looked as if he was going to argue, then he grimaced thoughtfully. "I can accept that. Guess it would be hard facing someone daily after a split."

Harder than you can imagine, Bernadette thought, seeing Max heading her way.

"Ben came up with the money for the informant," he said, dropping a check on her desk.

Roger whistled. "Must have been some important information. The boss rarely pays."

Bernadette was surprised, too.

"Guess I caught him in a mellow mood," Max tossed back, then continued on to his desk.

Roger glanced at his watch. "Duty calls," he announced. "The President's coming to town and I'm supposed to snap a few photos."

Bernadette forced a smile of goodbye, but her mind was still on the check. Picking it up, she headed to Ben's office.

"I need to see the chief," she told Grace. Listening to herself, she was shocked. Normally she would have asked politely. But this time she'd sounded more like she was issuing an order. She had, in fact, sounded a lot like Max. Grace, she noticed, also looked surprised.

"I'll just buzz and tell him you're here," the secretary replied, still watching Bernadette dubiously as she pressed the intercom.

A moment later, Bernadette was entering Ben's office flourishing the check in front of her. "Did you honestly issue this?" she demanded, shoving the door closed behind her.

He raised his hands in a gesture of surrender. "I don't know what's going on between you and Max. He tells me it has nothing to do with the paper so I don't want to know. You two are not public figures so your private lives are your own."

"Then this check isn't really from you," she said, voicing aloud what she was already sure of.

"Max seemed to think he should have paid the informant and knew you wouldn't take his money. He gave me cash and I wrote the check. But I'm not a money launderer. I warned him that if you asked, I'd tell you the truth," Ben replied.

"Thanks." Bernadette tore up the check. "I'd appreciate it if you'd return his money to him." Again her words came out more as an order than a request and, she admitted, she liked sounding more authoritative. It made her feel more in control of her destiny, she thought as she turned to leave.

"Just wait one minute," Ben growled.

Maybe she should have asked him a little more politely, she decided as she turned back and saw the reproving expression on his face. "I . . ." She started to apologize.

"Like I said, I don't want to know what's going on between you and Max but I'll tell you what I told him. It better not interfere with your work and I don't want it disrupting this newsroom."

"Yes, sir," she replied, this time showing the proper respect.

He relaxed then and waved her out.

She was going to have to control this more aggressive manner she seemed to have developed, she scolded herself as she passed the secretary's desk and gave the woman a smile only to be met with a dubious look.

Watching Bernadette return to her desk, Max knew she'd returned the check to Ben. Well, he'd tried, he told himself. He'd also seen Reynolds making a play for her and seen her send the photographer on his way. The real Ms. Dowd was definitely back.

But there did seem to be something different about her, he was forced to confess. I've seen her in some very revealing ways during the past few days, he reminded himself. Because of that, she would never look exactly like the old Bernadette Dowd again. Satisfied with this explanation, he returned his attention to his current assignment.

Bernadette frowned as she looked at the story assignment Grace had left on her desk. She was supposed to interview a young boy who'd been rescued from drowning by his faithful dog. She'd never minded this kind of story before. In fact, she'd usually have viewed it as a nice change from the political haggling she normally covered. But to-

day the assignment struck her as dull. People need uplift-
ing stories, she scolded herself, and made the call to the
boy's home to set up an appointment to interview him.

Returning to the newsroom later that afternoon, Bernadette was wondering if it would be ethical to add a little excitement to the story by hinting that there was a snake in the
water near the boy. I could simply mention that water moc-
casins are common in the state, she reasoned, then was appalled she'd even considered tainting her story with innu-
endos. She'd stick to the facts. That was what reporting was
all about.

Clearly my brush with death has had a few unexpected
side effects, she mused. Seeing Grace heading her way, she
smiled a friendly hello. After this morning, she was determined to be on her best behavior.

Reaching Bernadette, Grace's manner became confidential. "You received a call," she said in hushed tones. "The
woman refused to leave her name or a number where she
could be reached. She sounded nervous and said she would
call back."

Bernadette felt her adrenaline flowing. Was the caller
another informant with another story? she wondered.
"Thanks," she said to Grace.

"Just be sure you check with Ben before you go off to
meet anyone," the secretary warned. "We don't like our
reporters taking unnecessary chances."

Bernadette started to ask if Max was required to follow
that rule, but stopped herself. She was trying to smooth the
waters with the secretary, not cause more waves. "Sure
thing," she replied.

Grace smiled with approval, then returned to her desk.

Seating herself in front of her computer, Bernadette began to write her story. But she found it difficult to concentrate on the report of the rescue. Her heart continued to

pound at a more rapid rate as, impatiently, she listened for her phone to ring.

You're going to be real disappointed if it's someone trying to sell you something, she warned herself. Or it could be Lang's girlfriend, thinking she's found an open bank, looking for more money. With these possibilities in mind, her nerves calmed and she was able to direct her attention to the story about the boy and his dog.

Her first draft was finished and she'd begun the rewrite when her phone rang.

"Bernadette Dowd?" the woman caller asked nervously.

"Speaking," Bernadette replied, keeping her voice calm. Her caller wasn't Lang's girlfriend and it didn't sound like anyone trying to sell her anything.

"I need to talk to someone but I've been afraid. I read your story about the boys who got the award and I read your piece about Mr. Lang. You seem like a person with sensitivities and guts."

"Thank you," Bernadette replied, finding herself liking this description of herself, especially the part about the guts.

"Could we meet?" the caller asked.

"Sure." Bernadette couldn't believe she'd so readily agreed to meet with a stranger. "Would you mind telling me your name and could you give me some idea as to what you want to talk to me about?" she asked, feeling the need to behave at least somewhat practically.

"I can't over the phone," the woman replied.

Bernadette noticed the caller's voice had gotten shakier. Instinct warned her that at any moment the woman might change her mind about talking at all. "That's all right," she said quickly. "Where would you like to meet?"

"I suppose it would be best if you didn't come to my home," the caller said. "I live over near Shaw's Gardens." There was a sharp pause and she corrected herself. "They're called the Missouri Botanical Gardens now. Anyway, I go there a lot. It's a nice place to walk. We could meet at the bridge over the lake where people feed the fish. Do you know the place?"

"Yes," Bernadette replied.

"I can be there around five-thirty. It's pretty deserted then," the caller said.

Bernadette breathed easier. "And how will I recognize you?" she asked.

"I'm six-two and will be wearing blue slacks and a blue and pink blouse."

"And your name?" Bernadette coaxed.

"I'll tell you that when you get here." There was a moment's hesitation, then the woman added, "And please come alone."

"I'd..." Bernadette began, attempting to coerce the woman into revealing her name but a click sounded and the line went dead.

Bernadette looked at her watch. It was just four now. She had plenty of time.

Max frowned. He'd been eavesdropping and from what he heard, he was sure Bernadette had been contacted by an informant. When she headed to Ben's office, he was sure. He knew Ben wouldn't let her go without backup. And he told himself there were others who could keep an eye on her just fine. On the other hand, he hated to miss a good story, he argued. In the next instance, he was on his feet, heading to Ben's office, too.

Inside Ben's office, Bernadette had just finished telling the editor about her call.

"You can't go alone," he said without compromise.

"She might not talk if I arrive with someone else," Bernadette argued.

"You won't arrive with anyone else," Ben explained. "Another reporter will simply be there to keep an eye on you from a distance."

A knock sounded on the door and Max entered.

"I tried to stop him," Grace snapped from behind Max. "But that's about the same as trying to stop a runaway locomotive." She shook her head at Max. "The train would be easier."

"It's all right," Ben said, waving her out of the room.

Grace nodded knowingly and left.

"Thought I smelled a story in the works," Max said coolly.

"I'm sure it's nothing that would interest you," Bernadette returned with dismissal.

Ben frowned at the two of them. His gaze came to rest on Max. "Bernadette needs backup." He shifted his attention to her. "I trust Max to keep you from getting hurt. Your safety is all that matters to me. Like I said before, whatever is going on between you two personally, leave it at home. This is business."

"What's the deal?" Max asked.

Ben explained about the call while Bernadette stood silently by, working on keeping her temper under control. She was sure Max was there because he was still feeling guilty and trying to protect her.

"I'll play the tourist. That way I can use my video camera and get a shot of the woman," Max said when Ben finished.

Ben nodded in agreement. "Good." His gaze again raked over the two of them. "And you'd better arrive apart, in case she's watching the parking lot."

At least that's one battle I won't have to fight, Bernadette thought with relief. Just the thought of riding with Max had caused her to feel tense. She was trying to get on with her life, but she couldn't put what had happened between them out of her mind entirely. That was going to take a little more time.

"I want to get there ahead of you," Max said as they rode down in the elevator together. He'd been avoiding looking at her. Every time he did, he pictured her with her hair hanging loose and a great deal less clothing on. The image was thoroughly disturbing to his peace of mind.

But he had a point he needed to make. Keep her dressed, he ordered his eyes as he turned to her. "Investigative reporting can be dangerous," he said grimly. "I thought you were going to go back to doing the human interest stories and covering local politics. You're good at that."

Bernadette met his gaze levelly. "I realize now I was only existing as opposed to really living my life. I intend to follow whatever leads come my way." She tossed him a dry smile. "I've decided to be Berny from now on."

Mentally Max groaned. The meek Ms. Dowd had become a tigress. "Just be sure you use common sense," he warned. "Some of the people who turn informants are not particularly nice."

She glared at him. "I wasn't born yesterday."

He raised an eyebrow skeptically.

"Well, maybe in a way I was," she conceded, considering the difference in herself from just a few days ago. "But I'm a fast learner."

Max had to agree. She'd surprised him at every turn. "Just be careful," he ordered as they parted to find their individual cars.

Bernadette gave him a fifteen-minute head start, then pulled out. Her pride continued to rebel at the thought of Max watching over her. But her practical side felt a lot safer.

Reaching the Botanical Gardens, she parked and went inside. She and her grandmother had come here fairly regularly to enjoy the tranquil garden settings. The lake was large and to her right beyond the main entrance. She headed directly for it. Reaching the path that circled the elongated, irregular-shaped body of water, she glanced at her watch. It read 5:17. Choosing to approach the bridge from the far side, she began walking at a brisk rate. Passing a side path that wound upward to a small pagoda overlooking the lake, she saw Max. He was standing a short distance along the side path, playing the tourist and photographing the scenery with his video camera.

Remaining on the main path, she continued around the lake. Approaching the wooden bridge from which visitors fed the colorful carp populating the lake, she slowed. As her caller had predicted, at this time of day, the gardens were nearly deserted. There was only a single woman standing on the bridge dropping food pellets into the water.

Moving closer, Bernadette saw that the woman's hair was white and she was wearing blue slacks and a blue-and-pink blouse just as the caller had described. Controlling the urge to glance over her shoulder to see if Max was nearby, she continued to the bridge. The woman looked harmless enough, she thought as she drew nearer. Stopping at the food dispenser, she bought a handful of pellets then casually took a position beside the older female.

The late-afternoon sun glistened off the gold, yellow and white bodies of the huge carp vying for the food being dropped. Remembering she had not given the woman a description of herself, Bernadette said, "I'm Bernadette Dowd."

"I thought you'd be older," the woman replied, glancing at her dubiously, then returning her attention to the fish.

Watching her, Bernadette could see her companion was nervous. "You said you had something you wanted to tell me," she coaxed.

The older woman nodded. "My name is Martha Jude," she said slowly, as if not completely certain what she was doing was wise. "My husband was Philip Jude. He was not a good man." She glanced at Bernadette again. "I didn't mean he wasn't good to me. He was." Her gaze shifted back to the fish. "What I meant was, he wasn't an honest man."

Looking through his telescopic lens, Max immediately recognized the woman on the bridge as someone he should know. It took him a couple of moments to put a name to the face. When he did, he cursed under his breath. If Martha

Jude had any information, he wanted it. But he didn't want Bernadette mixed up in this. It was much too dangerous.

Bernadette covertly studied the woman beside her. As Martha Jude's pause lengthened into a silence, she said questioningly, "You said your husband *was* good to you?"

"He's been dead nearly four years now," Martha replied. "When he first died, I was too afraid to talk. Later, I figured it wouldn't do any good and it could be dangerous. But through the years it's been eating at me."

Her gaze leveled on Bernadette. "Like I said, he wasn't an honest man but he was good to me. His death was labeled an accident but I'm sure he was murdered. He probably deserved to die. I think he'd killed others. He had some very expensive, very high-tech guns he kept locked away. I don't think he ever knew I knew about them but I did. I also knew he'd been a marksman in the Marines and he'd handled explosives."

"Are you saying you think he was a serial killer?" Bernadette asked, beginning to question the woman's sanity.

"No." Martha looked at her then, her gaze hard and forthright. "He was a hit man . . . a hired killer."

Bernadette was now seriously worried about her companion's sanity. "Do you know the names of any of the people he killed," she asked, wagering the first one Mrs. Jude named would be John F. Kennedy.

"No. I could take a few educated guesses." Martha shrugged as if growing uncomfortable with this conversation. "I never saw him do it and he sure never confessed to me. I just know he did." A small smile tilted one corner of her mouth. "I suppose I liked the element of danger that secret gave to our relationship. I'm pretty sure he knew I'd guessed but we never talked about it. I had the feeling that if I ever openly said what I believed, he'd feel he had to kill me."

This woman was definitely not entirely rational, Bernadette decided. "You said he's been dead for nearly four years. Why talk about this now?"

Martha's jaw tensed. "Because I think the man he worked for might have had Philip killed and my conscience won't let me look the other way any longer."

Bernadette was having a hard time believing any of what the woman was telling her, but determined to carry out this interview in a professional manner, she hid her disbelief. "And do you know who hired him?"

"He worked for Merriweather Neily. He was officially a gardener and he did love to work with plants. But nobody pays gardeners the bonuses he got and I'll wager not too many gardeners can afford half a million dollars in insurance."

Bernadette was now certain the woman was living in a fantasy world. "You think Merriweather Neily paid your husband to kill people and then had him killed," she asked, wanting to be absolutely certain she hadn't misunderstood.

Martha scowled at her. "I knew no one would believe me."

Bernadette was now sure the woman wasn't sane. Still, she maintained a businesslike manner as she asked, "What kind of proof do you have to connect Mr. Neily to your husband's death?"

Martha Jude looked at her as if Bernadette was the crazy one. "If I had tangible proof, I'd be pushing up flowers just like Philip."

"Without proof, I don't think you should be spreading these stories," Bernadette cautioned, feeling a rush of sympathy for Merriweather Neily. Obviously this woman had a grudge against him and was willing to slander him to get even.

Martha snorted with disgust. "Well, I tried," she said, then tossing the remaining fish pellets into the water, she strode off the bridge.

Watching her leave, Bernadette considered warning Mr. Neily.

"What did Martha Jude have to say?"

Bernadette swung around to see Max standing close behind her.

"You know her?" she demanded. Embarrassment mingled with anger. "I suppose she's one of the crackpots you've dealt with before. Whenever she gets bored or paranoid, she calls a reporter and makes some wild accusation. And since I'm the new guy on the block where investigative reporting is concerned, I got the call this time?"

"What did she say to you?" Max asked, keeping his tone casual. If Bernadette was willing to label Martha Jude as a crackpot and forget about her, he was willing to let her. She'd be a lot safer that way.

"She claimed her husband was a hired killer." The rest seemed so preposterous, she stopped there.

Max's gut tightened. "Did she say who she thought might have hired him?"

"Would you believe Merriweather Neily?" Just saying this made her feel ridiculous. "What in the world would he have people killed for . . . bad manners? Or inviting someone from the B list to an A list party? Or maybe someone who promised a couple hundred thousand to his favorite charity and only came up with half?"

"I think you should go home and forget this meeting ever happened," Max suggested.

Bernadette's embarrassment returned. Not only did she feel like a fool but she'd had Max watching her being made a fool of. "That woman shouldn't be allowed to get away with making accusations like that," she huffed, glaring at the now empty path Martha Jude had taken. A sudden thought struck her. "She knows I didn't buy her story. She might try to convince someone else it's true. I think Mr. Neily should be warned."

Max cursed silently. Bernadette Dowd had to be one of the most difficult women in the world. As she started to walk away, his hand closed around her arm. Forcing her back around to face him, he said in a low growl, "Stay away from Merriweather Neily. Whatever you do never mention this meeting with Martha Jude to anyone, not even Ben. We'll tell him it was some old woman who insisted on remaining anonymous and who wanted to turn her neighbor in for having too many cats."

Bernadette stared at him. "You're acting as if you believe her story."

"Let's just say I know a little bit more about Merriweather Neily than most people in this town. Stay away from him. You could get hurt." The vision of his brother Barry lying on the slab in the morgue suddenly filled his mind. A chill raced through him. He couldn't let the same thing happen to Bernadette. He had to convince her to stay away from Neily. Ordering her would do no good. Of that he was convinced.

Another approach occurred to him. "Look, fair is fair. I gave you the Lang story because you had it first. I've been investigating Neily for a long time now. He's mine. Okay?"

The last thing Bernadette wanted was to be stumbling over Max every time she turned around and that was exactly what would happen if she insisted on pursuing this story, she pointed out to herself. "He's yours," she agreed.

Max breathed a mental sigh of relief. "All right. Now what exactly did Martha Jude tell you?"

Bernadette repeated, as closely as she could remember, word for word what the woman had said.

"What happened to the guns?" Max asked when she finished.

"She didn't say." Stupid! Bernadette berated herself silently. When she'd asked about evidence and the woman had said she didn't have any, she should have asked about the guns. If they'd been used in a killing they'd match bullets the police had from the bodies of the victims. "But finding the guns won't prove Neily had anything to do with the deaths. It will only verify Philip Jude's involvement," she reasoned.

"But it will prove a closer connection to Neily than I've been able to establish before," Max replied. "I'm going to have to try to convince Martha Jude to trust me and talk to me."

"I'm not so sure she'll talk to anyone but me," Bernadette said, recalling the woman's nervousness. "I'm not even sure if she'll talk to me again." She knew she'd just agreed to stay out of Max's investigation but he needed the information from Mrs. Jude. "However, it can't do any harm to try. I'll call her and ask about the guns."

Max didn't like the idea of Bernadette getting any more involved than she already was. On the other hand, he suspected she was right about Martha Jude. He'd tried to talk to the woman soon after Philip Jude's death and been greeted by silence. Today was the first time Mrs. Jude had broken down and talked to anyone. "The less you know the better. You call her and tell her I'm a friend she can trust. Set up a meeting for me to meet with her then forget you ever heard her name."

Fear for Max swept through Bernadette. She still had difficulty picturing Merriweather Neily as a bad guy, but if he was, then Max was in grave danger. "You should have a backup. I'll arrange the meeting but I'm watching from a distance."

The image of his brother's dead body again filled Max's mind. Then he saw Bernadette lying beside Barry. His hands closed around her upper arms. "No!" he growled. "I want you to go home as soon as you've set up the meeting. I won't have your blood on my hands."

Bernadette started to argue but the words stuck in her throat. There was a pain in his eyes so intense, it shook her. The thought that maybe he really did care for her brought a renewed surge of hope. "Max?" she said his name questioningly.

Max drew a shaky breath. He didn't like exposing his emotions so openly and he didn't want to give her the wrong impression. "I don't like feeling responsible for anyone other than myself," he said gruffly.

Fool! Bernadette screamed at herself. He cared but not the way she wanted him to care. I thought you'd given up on this guy, she scolded herself. I have, came the response. Her jaw tensed as she faced him coolly, "Fine. Have it your way. I'll make the call and then disappear."

But as they made their way back to the entrance of the gardens, she knew she wasn't going to leave him on his own. Company policy is no one goes to meet a snitch without a backup and Max is going to have a backup, she promised herself. She'd just make sure Max didn't see her.

Spotting a public phone in the main building on their way out, Bernadette changed direction and headed to it. "We might as well try to call her now," she said, remembering Mrs. Jude had said she lived near the gardens.

Max looked the number up in the phone book and Bernadette dialed. Martha Jude answered on the fifth ring.

"I want to apologize for not giving more credence to your story," Bernadette said only to be greeted by a silence from the other end of the line. "I have a friend who'd like to talk to you," she continued, her voice taking on a coaxing quality.

"I shouldn't have even talked to you," the woman snapped back.

Bernadette sensed Martha's intent to hang up. "Please, wait a minute," she said quickly. "What happened to the guns you mentioned?"

For a moment there was silence, then Martha said stiffly, "I don't know. When I came back from the funeral, I felt like there was something different about my house. I looked around. Everything seemed to be in place. But I was sure it had been searched. I went into the closet and opened the secret compartment Philip had constructed. The guns were gone. I've told you everything I can tell. Don't call me again."

A click on the other end let Bernadette know the woman had hung up.

Max glanced around to be certain they were still alone. Then wanting to be as cautious as possible, he grabbed her by the arm and guided her out to the parking area before he even spoke. "You're lucky no one was around when you mentioned the word 'guns,'" he growled. "That's the kind of thing that can bring attention to you."

"I kept my voice low," she reminded him curtly.

He knew she had, still he didn't like her being involved in this at all. "What'd Martha say?"

"She said she shouldn't have talked to me in the first place. She's real scared and I don't think she's going to talk again. She also says she's told me everything she knows," Bernadette replied apologetically.

"What about the guns?" he demanded.

"She claims they disappeared while she was at her husband's funeral."

Max issued a disgusted snort. "I knew it was too good to be true." His gaze narrowed on Bernadette. "Go home and forget this afternoon ever happened," he ordered.

She studied him. "Are you going to try to talk to Mrs. Jude yourself?"

He shook his head. "No. I tried to talk to her right after her husband died. I used every persuasive ploy I knew. Nothing worked. When that lady decides not to talk, nothing's going to drag a word out of her. Besides, Neily knows I'm keeping an eye on him. If he finds out I've looked her up again, he'll wonder why. I don't want to put her in jeopardy unnecessarily."

"If it makes any difference, I think she really has told us everything she knows," Bernadette said honestly.

"My guess is you're right," Max replied. "If Neily thought she knew more, she wouldn't have been around to tell us anything."

Bernadette continued to study him dubiously. "You're honestly convinced the man is dangerous."

Max glowered down at her. "I know he's dangerous. Now go home and stay out of this."

Bernadette's back stiffened with pride. He was making it very clear once again he wanted her out of his life. Well, that was fine with her. Aloud, she said coolly, "Sure." Then without a backward glance, she unlocked her car, climbed in and drove away.

Chapter Eleven

Sitting at her kitchen table eating reheated chili, Bernadette visualized Merriweather Neily. She'd only seen him a couple of times but he was the kind of man a woman would remember. He was in his mid-forties, around six feet tall and slender. His eyes were brown and he had an intense way of looking at whoever was speaking, making them believe he'd forgotten everyone else in the room. His hair was still mostly hickory in color but some graying around the temples gave him a distinguished air.

Pauline Neily, his wife of fifteen years, could only be described as elegant. She was from one of the most socially prominent families in St. Louis, had been a debutante and one of the most sought after women in her set. She was ten years younger than Merriweather. Tall, slender with blue eyes and naturally blond hair, she could wear the latest fashions as well as any of the highest priced fashion models.

The Neilys had three children, two boys and a girl. All three spent the school year away at the best boarding schools money could buy. All were good-looking children and appeared to possess the same well-cultured social graces as their parents. There were rumors of the older boy getting into a few ruckuses but nothing serious.

All in all, the Neilys seemed like the ideal American upper-class family, she concluded. On the other hand, although she found Max Laird to be totally frustrating and certainly overbearing, he was an excellent investigative reporter and not a man to jump to irrational conclusions. If he thought Merriweather was involved with murder then he must have some reason for believing that. Still, the thought of the very distinguished Merriweather Neily keeping a full-time hit man in his employ was a bit hard to accept.

The urge to learn more nagged at her. Swallowing a bite of chili, she reminded herself she'd promised Max to leave this story alone.

"However, it can't do any harm if I just go through the newspaper's archives and see what articles I can find about the Neilys," she reasoned as she finished her chili and put the bowl into the dishwasher. She wouldn't do anything with the information. Her research would be merely to satisfy her own curiosity.

An hour and half later she was seated in front of the microfilm machine, reading an article about a charity function organized by the teenage Merriweather Neily, when Herbert Greenich brought her a fresh stack of films. Herbert was, Bernadette knew, in his eighties. He'd officially retired years ago but after only a few months away, he'd come back asking for his old job back. At first he'd been told the newspaper couldn't afford to hire him back. So he'd volunteered his time. All the reporters sought him out when they needed back articles for research. Finally the publisher had broken down and put him back on the payroll on a part-time basis.

But while he was only paid for twelve hours a week, Bernadette had rarely gone down to the archives room when he wasn't there. "My apartment feels so empty since my wife died," he'd told her once. "This place is like an old friend." And so she'd grown to think of the long, lank elderly man as part of the fixtures.

"So you're doing a story on the upper crust of St. Louis society," he said with a chuckle as he piled the fresh stack of boxes by the machine and took away the stack she'd finished going through.

"I'm considering it," she replied. She'd needed a pretext for going through the files and claiming an interest in prominent St. Louisans in general had seemed like a safe ploy.

Lowering himself into a nearby chair, Herbert grinned. "These new ones aren't nearly as interesting as their ancestors," he said.

Bernadette's eyes were getting tired. Besides, she was well aware that Herbert was a walking encyclopedia of St. Louis history. She simply hadn't wanted to make him suspicious by asking any direct questions. However, since he seemed in the mood to talk, she decided this might work to her advantage. "How so?"

Herbert's eyes sparkled with mischief. "Well, little lady, let's just say some of these law-abiding, highfalutin, good friends of our police and upstanding members of society came from families who weren't too particular how they accumulated their wealth."

"Oh, really?" Bernadette gave the man her most encouraging smile.

"Course you won't find nothing about that in those papers," the old man said, tilting his chair back against the wall and grinning even broader.

"I won't?" she asked innocently.

"Nope." His manner became sage. "You're young. But as you see more of the world, you're going to find out that money can buy friends in even the highest places."

Bernadette was tempted to tell him she wasn't totally naive. But she knew she would learn more from him if she played dumb. "That's very disheartening."

The old man grinned patronizingly. "That's life."

"I was reading about the Valences," she said, deciding it would not be prudent to begin with the Neilys.

Herbert grimaced with disinterest. "They came by their money the old-fashioned way. The grandfather, Bert Valence, married into it. He was a simple laborer for a lumber company. Seems the owner had a daughter who was as plain as a door and as difficult to get along with as a mule. But she was an only child. Bert married her and brought her here to St. Louis. Turned out she was one heck of a businesswoman. She took her money, invested it and tripled it within five years. It was as if she had the Midas touch."

"Sounds like that might make a great romance story," Bernadette said.

Herbert shook his head. "Inez, that was her name, got herself two children by Bert, then barred him from their bedroom. After that, he kept a mistress on the side. Everyone knew but nothing was ever publicly said. He died first and Inez wore black the rest of her life, playing out the part of the grieving widow. Most people think she loved money more than life itself but she did dote on those kids. She made sure to buy them a place in the upper crust."

Herbert shifted in his chair just enough to allow himself to see the screen in front of her. Then setting back against the wall once again, the mischievousness returned to his eyes. "I see you were reading about Merriweather Neily. Now that's an interesting family."

Bernadette schooled her face into an expression of surprise. "I thought they'd be one of the most boring but they are among the most prominent so I thought I should read a little about them.''

"Well now, it's true this current generation is pretty dull and Merriweather's father, that'd be Findley Neily, was nothing more than a wastrel," Herbert agreed. The mischievousness in his eyes grew brighter. "But the grandfather, Clarence Neily, and the great-grandfather, Burton Neily, now there were men you wouldn't want to turn your back on.''

"Which reels should I look through to find information about them?'' she asked, letting her interest show.

Herbert shook his head. "You won't find nothing in print except for an obituary about how Burton was gunned down in a gunfight. According to my granddaddy, Burton had come to St. Louis with bags of money. Claimed he'd struck a rich vein in California. He set himself up in the banking business and started buying real estate. He was doing real good. Been here for maybe ten years. Then one day this drifter came to town, saw Burton and swore Burton was the highwayman who'd robbed a bunch of stages out in the territories and killed maybe a dozen people. Burton claimed the man was a liar and called him out. Both of them ended up getting shot and dying.''

A chill ran along Bernadette's spine but she was determined to remain objective. The story was interesting but didn't actually prove the Neilys had larceny in their blood, she cautioned herself. The drifter could have been mistaken.

"That was around 1915," Herbert continued. "Clarence Neily was twelve at the time. His mother wasn't very good at managing the family business and it began to go downhill. Then came Prohibition. Clarence set up a still, actually it was almost large enough to call a brewery, right on the grounds of their estate. I know because my daddy worked for him. Clarence bought himself a judge or two and a few cops. His brew was the best around. Wanting to keep as much profit for himself as he could, he even set up his own speakeasies.''

Herbert laughed lightly. ''At first his momma didn't approve but when the money started rolling in, she shut up. His nightclubs became the place to be for the socially prominent and his position in high society grew stronger. By the time Prohibition was repealed, he was a very wealthy man. He turned his clubs into legitimate enterprises, donated to charities and furthered his place among the elite by marrying the daughter of one of the oldest families.''

Herbert shrugged and rose. ''That's when the family gets boring. They went completely legit. They managed to survive the depression without a dent in their money. Of course, there was Findley Neily, Clarence's son. The man was a drunkard and a wastrel but he died before he could go through the family fortune. Merriweather was twenty when his father drowned. From what I've seen, he's rebuilt the family's wealth and some.'' Herbert nodded his head with approval. ''Nice man. Bet you didn't know it's his donations that keep two of the homeless shelters in this town running and every Christmas he gives thousands of dollars for food and toys to needy children. But he don't like none of that getting printed so it doesn't. Guess maybe he's trying to make up for any misdeeds his ancestors might have done.''

''Sounds like he's got a good heart,'' Bernadette agreed, finding it more and more difficult to reconcile Max's suspicions of the man with the information Herbert had just provided. Sure there was some larceny in the Neily blood but it didn't seem to have been inherited by Merriweather or his father.

For another hour, she scanned old newspapers then gave up. She'd read dozens of articles and there was nothing anywhere to indicate that Merriweather Neily was anything other than a humanitarian willing to give of his time and money to help charities he felt were deserving. Admittedly he also savored his position as a prominent member of the upper crust but everyone, she reasoned, had their small vanities.

Driving home, she thought of Martha Jude. The woman clearly lived in a fantasy world. She'd probably been bored with the idea of being married to a gardener so she'd invented a sinister side to her husband to add a little excitement to their existence.

But it was Max who really concerned Bernadette. She'd always thought of him as someone who was reliable, someone whose opinion could be trusted. But he honestly believed Merriweather was a criminal. She began to wonder if maybe he had a personal grudge against the man that was tainting his judgment. That seemed the most reasonable answer, she concluded.

Tomorrow she was going to have a talk with Max. This vendetta could jeopardize his career. He'd helped her when she'd needed someone to lean on. She'd try to straighten him out now and then they'd be even.

Turning down her street, she frowned. "Looks like I won't have to wait until tomorrow," she muttered, spotting Max's car parked in front of her house.

As she pulled into her driveway, she saw him getting out and coming toward her.

"Where in the hell have you been?" he growled, reaching her as she rounded her car to meet him.

"I was at the newspaper going through old issues," she replied. "I've read everything I could find about Merriweather Neily and nothing, absolutely nothing indicates he's anything other than what he presents himself to be. Even Herbert says the man's on the up-and-up."

Max fought the urge to take her over his knee and spank her. Instead he took her by the arm and guided her forcefully to her door. "We will continue this conversation inside."

Now was as good a time as any to try to set him straight, she decided, offering no protest.

Max waited until they were inside and the door was securely closed, then with his jaw taut from his attempt to hold his temper, he said, "You talked to Herbert? You let him know you were interested in Neily?"

She frowned impatiently. "No, I didn't let him know I was interested in Neily. I told you I wouldn't. He thinks I'm doing an article on St. Louis high society in general. You know how he is. He likes to talk. He got to telling me stories about people's backgrounds I wouldn't find in the newspaper."

"I asked you to leave this alone," Max snarled, his fear for her growing.

Bernadette's frown deepened. "Surely you're not so paranoid you think Herbert is spying on us at the newspaper for Merriweather Neily."

"No." Max raked a hand agitatedly through his hair. "I don't know," he corrected himself gruffly. "He could be. There's no way to know who owes Neily a favor."

Bernadette was having a hard time believing her ears. "I've always thought of you as being levelheaded but I wish you could listen to yourself. Are you sure you haven't built up this suspicion of Neily simply because of some personal grudge?"

Her question brought back a rush of harsh memories. "I asked my brother that same thing two days before he died."

The anguish she saw on his face tore at her. "Your brother?"

Max studied her in silence while he held a mental debate with himself. If he told her what he knew, he could be putting her in danger. But if he didn't convince her there was danger, then she was going to put herself in jeopardy. "Damn!" he cursed in frustration.

His gaze leveled on her. "I've never told anyone what I'm about to tell you and once I've told you, you'd be wise to forget everything I've said. I'm only doing this to convince you I'm not on a personal vendetta nor am I a paranoid who sees conspiracies around every corner.''

''Whatever you tell me, I'll keep in the strictest confidence,'' she promised.

''Barry was a detective with homicide. A couple of years before his death, he was in charge of investigating the death of a young woman by the name of Jacquline DuBrye who appeared to have accidentally died from a fall in her home. He was ready to close the case when the woman's sister, Carolene DuBrye, came to see him. She claimed Jacquline had been involved with a very influential politician. Carolene named the man. As far as my brother had ever heard, this man was a loving father and faithful husband. Even more, his popularity was strongly based on this unblemished family-man image. But Carolene swore Jacquline had had an affair with the man. Her sister, Carolene explained, was a naive innocent who had only entered into the affair because she was desperately in love with the man and he'd promised to divorce his wife and marry her. Then a few months later, the man had simply informed Jacquline he was tired of her. At first, according to Carolene, Jacquline had been despondent, then the despondency had turned to anger. Jacquline swore she'd get even. She felt the man had ruined her, now she was going to ruin him. The next day Jacquline was dead.''

''So the woman thought the man had killed Jacquline and made it look like an accident?'' Bernadette said.

''That was her theory,'' Max confirmed. ''But Barry determined it couldn't have been him. Very discreetly, because he had no evidence other than the sister's story that this man had even known Jacquline DuBrye, my brother investigated the man's activities the day of the death. Turned out he was speaking in front of a few hundred people five hundred miles away at the time of the death. The death was officially listed as an accident. But the sister wasn't happy.

She told Barry she was going to pursue her suspicion that the man had something to do with her sister's death. Less than a week later she was dead, killed by a rattlesnake bite while on a camping trip with friends. Again it looked like an accident and there was not one shred of evidence to prove differently. But the two deaths so close together nagged at my brother.''

"I know it was tragic," Bernadette said, attempting to be the voice of reason. "But coincidences like that do happen."

Max regarded her grimly. "Then came the accident that killed the husband of a prominent judge. The husband had been caught embezzling from his company. Before there could be a trial that would have embarrassed the judge and possibly seriously harmed her career, he was killed by a burglar who was never found."

"Those deaths could still have been coincidences," Bernadette argued.

Max nodded. "Yes, but my brother's gut instinct was bothering him. He went back over files of accidental deaths and unsolved murders that had occurred during the preceding five years. A pattern of what he termed 'advantageous deaths' began to emerge."

An uneasy feeling crept along Bernadette's spine. "You can't be implying what I think you're implying," she gasped. "If you're connecting Merriweather Neily and Philip Jude with these deaths then you're talking about a murder-for-hire scheme."

"One where the clients are either very wealthy or very influential or both," Max confirmed. His frown deepened. "But my brother couldn't prove anything and he didn't have a clue as to who was running the show. Then came George Krutz's death. He was found drowned in his swimming pool with a blood alcohol level high enough to stun an elephant."

"Ophilia Krutz's husband?" Bernadette asked. Ophilia she knew from several of the charity functions she'd covered. She didn't particularly like her but she had to admit that although Ophilia seemed as cold as ice, the woman had a good heart or at least an open pocketbook.

"The man was a drunkard and a bore. He was also going through his inheritance like water through a sieve. Then there were his mistresses. All in all, his death bode well for his wife but she wasn't even in the country at the time. However, in this case, my brother got a break. He found a pack of matches in Krutz's coat pocket from a bar downtown.

"When he questioned the bartender, the man remembered Krutz. He was also able to confirm that Krutz had been in the night he died. According to the bartender, Krutz was fairly intoxicated when he came into the establishment and the bartender had, at first, refused to serve him. The bartender had expected an argument, but instead Krutz had laughed. 'How about just one for the road?' he'd coaxed. 'I'll drink it while you call me a cab.' Then Krutz had produced a fifty-dollar bill and told the bartender to keep the change for his trouble.

"The bartender decided if Krutz was going home in a cab, then one more drink couldn't hurt. So he'd called for a taxi then served Krutz. When he placed the drink on the bar, Krutz had leaned closer and in a conspiratorial whisper said, 'I'm giving the man with the green thumb a merry chase.'

"Worried Krutz wasn't right in the head, the bartender decided it might be prudent not to serve him after all. 'Maybe you've had one too many already,' he said, starting to remove the drink.

"Krutz had laughed again and placed a friendly hand on the bartender's wrist. 'He doesn't have a real green thumb. That's just an expression. He's Merriweather's gardener. I saw him watching me a couple of days ago when he was trimming the high hedge between our properties. Then last night I saw him again. He was right behind me when I stopped at a light. Either he's taken a fancy to me or my wife has hired him to keep an eye on me and make sure I don't do anything that's going to embarrass her too much.'

"Krutz had laughed again and admitted he'd been a little indiscreet about his last affair. At this point the cab had arrived and honked. 'Guess it's time for me to go home and let the gardener get his rest. He has to be at work at the crack of dawn. Those weeds wait for no man,' Krutz had joked, then left."

Max paused for a moment after relaying this conversation, then continued grimly, "Next, Barry went to talk to the widow and asked her point-blank if she'd hired anyone to keep an eye on her husband. She admitted she'd considered it. She explained that her religion forbade her getting a divorce but she had considered having someone watch over her husband with the hope that anything he did that might cause her some embarrassment could be prevented or at least kept quiet. But she swore she hadn't acted on that impulse. Not wanting to tip his hand too quickly, my brother didn't mention the gardener.

"At that time, Jude was Merriweather's chief gardener but there were also a couple of other men who worked part-time. Barry ran checks on all of them. He discovered Jude had been a marksman in the Marines. Further checking revealed Jude had hired out as a mercenary after he'd left the service. But the man was also an expert gardener and seemed to really enjoy his work. My brother had to admit to the possibility that Jude had tired of killing and was now merely a peace-loving citizen. Barry also couldn't prove Krutz was being followed by anyone. Neither the bartender nor the cabdriver who took Krutz home saw anyone. And as drunk as Krutz was he could have been seeing pink elephants and thought they were real.

"But my brother kept investigating very quietly. As you know, Merriweather Neily has his own charitable foundation of which he is primary administrator. And while on the record, his salary is modest, on closer inspection he receives bonuses for all monies donated and his expense account pays for most of his travel and his parties. Barry also discovered that many of the people he had listed as beneficiaries in his 'advantageous deaths' file contributed heavily to this foundation.''

"Murder in the name of charity?" Bernadette said frowning dubiously.

"It works. Merriweather gets paid and the people who hired him even get to deduct the cost of his service from their taxes."

The picture of murder and greed Max was painting was making Bernadette more and more uneasy. "But what about proof?" she asked, realizing that so far all he'd been able to provide was speculation and supposition.

The frustration Max was feeling was mirrored on his face. "I knew my brother was worried about something but he wouldn't talk about it. Then a week before he died, he told me about Merriweather and Jude and what he suspected. He said he was hoping to uncover some proof soon. He'd found one of Merriweather's customers who was having conscience problems. This person had told him that Merriweather had video tapes of all the deals he'd cut and used those to keep his customers from talking. Barry's informant also said Merriweather had friends in high places. He said Merriweather would know about anyone who had turned informant before the report could be typed up."

Max gave a disgusted snort. "The man was right. The day after Barry told me this, a very prominent banker was found to have committed suicide. Turns out he was Barry's informant. I respected my brother but I was still having trouble believing him until that happened. Then a week later, Barry died trying to break up a robbery in a liquor store. The murderer got away without a trace. I was sure it was a setup and Merriweather was behind it but remembering

Barry's warning, I kept my suspicions to myself. I couldn't prove anything and I didn't want to tip Merriweather off that I knew about my brother's investigation. I knew where Barry kept his secret files. I copied them and left the originals. When Molly and I got back from the wake, I checked and the originals were gone. That was when I was absolutely certain my bother's theory was rock solid and I started keeping an eye on Merriweather and Jude.''

As incredible as his story was, Bernadette found herself believing him. ''Martha Jude said she thought Merriweather had her husband killed. Do you think Jude had begun to be haunted by the ghosts of his victims and decided to turn informant?''

Max shook his head. ''No. I think Jude was killed because he'd gotten clumsy and been seen so Merriweather had him killed as a warning to his other shooters to be more careful. The death might also have been to mock me, to take away the one lead I had to tie Merriweather to Krutz's death. By that time, I'm sure Merriweather at least suspected I knew everything Barry had known and that I was continuing my brother's investigation.''

Bernadette studied Max narrowly as a flaw in his story nagged at her. ''If Merriweather is so keen on tying up loose ends, why aren't you dead?''

Max's expression grew grimmer. ''I think he enjoys the game. He knows how frustrated I am. And he knows I know I can't trust anyone. There's no way for me to be sure who he owns or doesn't own. And he knows I don't have any hard evidence.''

Again a chill ran along Bernadette's spine. ''You think Neily is that cold-blooded.''

Max frowned at her impatiently. ''The man arranges murders for profit and he looks to me like a person who's very satisfied, even pleased with his world.''

Bernadette had to agree that Merriweather Neily did seem to enjoy his life. ''But surely some of the people he's ar-

ranged murders for are remorseful,'' she said, wondering
how a person would go about finding another one who
might be experiencing a guilty conscience.

"If they are, they aren't talking,'' Max replied. "They
could be afraid of being bumped off like my brother's informant. But I think it's more likely that they see Merriweather as a sort of high-class pest exterminator.''

"I guess anyone on his list of donators is suspect,'' Bernadette mused.

"Not just that list." Unable to remain immobile, Max
paced across the room. Just talking about Merriweather
caused his frustration to multiply. Stopping abruptly, he
turned to face her. "I think sometimes he does murders as
favors. Say for instance a young, promising politician has a
mistress or an opponent who could damage or interrupt his
rise to power. I think Merriweather might take care of the
'problem' figuring he can call up the debt later, perhaps in
the form of a favor that could prove more valuable than
mere money.''

"If everything you suspect is true then Merriweather
Neily might be untouchable,'' Bernadette said.

"I like to believe that no one is totally untouchable,'' Max
replied. He looked hard at her. "However, he is extremely
dangerous and I don't want your death on my conscience.
So I want you never to repeat what I've told you and to go
on with your life as if, as far as you're concerned, Mr. Neily
is just another wealthy, community-minded citizen.''

Bernadette met his gaze levelly. "The old me, who preferred safety and convention to rocking anyone's boat,
would probably agree. She might even be able to convince
herself that you're loony. After all, you don't have a shred
of solid evidence. But I believe you're telling the truth and
I want to help.''

Reaching her in two long strides, Max's hands closed
around her upper arms and he pulled her to her feet. "If you
really want to help, then you'll do as I've asked.''

The imprint of his hands was hot against her skin and a weakening heat raced through her. She was furious with herself for being so susceptible to him. She had to get rid of him before he realized how strong an effect he had on her. "All right. Have it your way," she said.

Max drew a relieved breath and released her. "It'd be best if we became unfriendly acquaintances again," he said.

"That can be easily arranged," she assured him.

"Good," he replied, then quickly left. Walking to his car, he felt a load lifted off his shoulders. Keeping a hostile atmosphere between them was the best way to protect her. And, he added, it would also make it easier for him to put their weekend affair out of his mind.

Still, he wasn't happy with himself for telling her about Neily. But the only way to stop her from meddling was to prove to her just how dangerous the man was. Glancing back at the house, he saw her at the window. Against his will, he recalled how good she'd felt in his arms. "She's more trouble than a dozen women combined," he grumbled, shoving his key into the ignition.

Bernadette watched as he drove away. Again he'd been blunt about wanting her to stay out of his life and this time she would! "And he'd better stay out of mine from now on, too," she added.

A little later as she climbed into bed and memories of time spent with him there abruptly filled her mind, she pushed them out. From this moment forward, there was no place for Max Laird in her life, she vowed. Merriweather Neily was another matter, though. She'd keep her ears and eyes open where he was concerned.

Chapter Twelve

Bernadette frowned at the phone receiver in her hand. She'd spent a restless night. Several times, she'd woken and lay wondering if maybe Martha Jude might know something she didn't know she knew. Finally she'd decided it wouldn't hurt to try to meet with the woman again for a little chat. But it was midafternoon now and this was the fourth time today she'd tried calling the woman and again all she'd gotten was an answering machine.

Dropping the receiver back into its cradle, she glanced at Max's desk. He wasn't there. He hadn't been there all day. She wondered if he was the reason Martha Jude wasn't at home. Maybe the woman had agreed to meet with him.

This is his story, she told herself. If she meddled she could get him hurt. Grudgingly she returned her attention to writing her story about a dispute between a student and school board in one of the more prestigious school districts. The student was in the process of having the entire upper portion of his body tattooed. Proud of the artwork, he was insisting on going shirtless to school and the school board was taking the position that his appearance was disturbing to the rest of the student body and therefore they were requiring him to wear a shirt.

Finishing the article, Bernadette turned it in and prepared to leave for the day. As she drove home, she was tempted to change direction and go by Martha Jude's home. But the worry that she might put the woman in jeopardy kept her from acting on that impulse.

When she arrived home, she noticed that her living-room rug needed vacuuming. This new life she was making for herself was good, she reaffirmed, but there were a few old habits such as cleaning house she decided she should keep. For the next few hours she cleaned, took a break to eat and then finished cleaning.

By the time she climbed out of her shower, she felt more normal than she had for days. She was drying her hair when a knock sounded on her door.

Glancing at the clock she saw that it was nearly ten. She wondered who would be at her door this late and she peeked out the peephole. It was Max. He looked tired and the urge to comfort him was strong. Then she remembered that he was the one who was so insistent about the two of them keeping their distance. Anger flared. Making certain her robe was fastened, she opened the door and glared at him. "You keep telling me to stay out of your life, but that's a little hard when you keep showing up in mine."

Meeting her anger with a look of irritation, he brushed past her, pushing the door closed behind him.

Being forced to flatten herself against the wall to avoid a collision caused Bernadette's anger to grow. "And I don't remember inviting you in."

"I wasn't going to stand on your porch while I gave you this," he returned with a growl. Reaching into his pocket, he pulled out a small tape cassette and held it up for her to see. Then he strode into her kitchen, pulled a lighter out of his pocket and set the cassette on fire.

Bernadette stood watching him with a dry scowl. "And what was that all about?" she asked when he'd put out the fire and tossed the destroyed tape into the trash.

"That's about being careful and covering your tracks," he retorted.

Impatience flashed in her eyes. "What are you talking about?"

"That was the cassette from Martha Jude's answering machine. You're just lucky I was the one who retrieved it instead of one of Merriweather's men."

"I didn't leave my name," she pointed out defensively.

"Someone could have recognized your voice," he growled back. "I warned you to stay away from her."

Knowing he was right, she chose not to continue this debate. Instead the fact that he'd had the tape caused her to realize he must have seen Martha. "So you met with Martha Jude," she said, wondering if he'd discovered anything.

"In a way," he replied, his expression becoming grimmer. "I drove past her place last night after I left here. I was going to stake it out and try to talk to her when I didn't think anyone would see me. But I discovered someone else was already watching her so I watched the watcher. This morning, she came out and drove to a nearby grocery store. Her watcher followed. There she went inside and came out a few minutes later with a bag of groceries. She went to her car, opened the trunk and set the bag inside. I noticed there was already another grocery bag there. Then I saw a heavily bearded man wearing sunglasses approaching carrying a third bag. He stopped at her car. She lifted the second bag out of the trunk and exchanged it for the one he was carrying. Then he walked on."

"A switch," Bernadette said, her adrenaline pumping. "Drugs?" she asked, jumping at the obvious.

"Turned out to be guns," Max replied.

"Guns?" The truth struck her like a bolt of lightning. "*The* guns? Her husband's guns?"

Max nodded. "I wasn't certain at the time of the exchange what was going down. The moment the man had looked into the bag to confirm its contents, he quickly cut through between Martha's car and the next, then suddenly the car that I'd been following came toward her. I guessed they were either going to grab her or hit her. Either way she was going to be joining her husband fairly soon. But she was faster than they thought and luckier. She ran in my direction. I pulled out, she flung open my passenger door, hopped in, pointed a gun at me and ordered me to drive."

Bernadette found the image of the white-haired woman holding a gun on anyone incredulous. "Martha Jude pulled a gun on you?"

Max frowned introspectively. "I seem to be attracting more than my fair share of unpredictable women these days."

Bernadette knew he was including her. "Well, at least you're obviously not suffering any permanent harm," she remarked frostily, recalling how easily he seemed to have put the time spent with her out of his mind. Furious with herself for even caring, she said, "You were telling me about Martha pointing a gun at you."

Max had been thinking that his encounter with Ms. Dowd had left more of a permanent mark on him than anyone had left in a long time. Impatiently he pushed that thought out of his mind. "Right," he said, concentrating on his experience with Martha Jude. "While I wove through the parking lot, then out onto the street and lost our pursuers, I told her who I was. Once I'd refreshed her memory, she remembered me from when I'd come to talk to her about her husband after his death. I told her I'd take her someplace safe if she'd tell me what she was up to."

"When I asked her about the guns, she must have realized they were valuable and she tried to sell them to Merriweather," Bernadette said, wanting him to know she was clever enough to figure out the woman's motives.

"Close," he replied. "She knew the guns were valuable. Some of the 'accidental' deaths were made to look like robberies in which the victim was killed because he surprised the robber. Ballistics could tie her husband to the deaths and she could tie Neily to her husband. She'd been biding her time, keeping the guns hidden away until she needed cash. Recently she'd begun to get bored with her life and decided it was time for a change."

"Changing one's life can take some unexpected turns," Bernadette muttered.

"And innocent bystanders who get caught in those turns can be in for some nasty surprises," Max returned.

Feeling the sharp sting of insult, Bernadette glared at him. "It wasn't that bad!"

Realizing she'd thought he was referring to him and her as well as Martha Jude, Max frowned impatiently. Being with her hadn't been bad at all, he admitted silently. In fact, it had been too enjoyable. "I was talking about Martha Jude," he said. "And you were the innocent bystander I was referring to."

Bernadette's face flushed. Ignoring this show of embarrassment, she faced him with an air of restored calm. "How do I fall into the category of the innocent bystander?"

"Her meeting with you yesterday was part of her plan," he explained. "Martha wanted some added insurance. That was why she contacted you. She figured if she told Merriweather she'd talked to a reporter and hinted that she could be in danger from Merriweather, then he wouldn't try to kill her."

Bernadette felt shaky. "So Merriweather knows I know about him."

Max shook his head. "I fixed it. She hadn't given Merriweather a name so I had her call him and say she'd talked to me."

Fear for her own safety turned to terror for Max. "You set yourself up to be hit?" she demanded angrily. "Are you crazy?"

Max saw the concern in her eyes. It pleased him to know she didn't completely detest him. "He knows that without the guns I don't have any proof. And Martha swore she wouldn't talk to me again. She also swore she'd forget he tried to have her killed if he'd leave her alone and just let her leave town."

"And what'd he say?" Bernadette asked, feeling a little more calm but still afraid for Max.

"He said he would."

"And you and she believed him?" she asked hopefully.

Max frowned at her naiveté. "Neither she nor I was born yesterday. Of course neither of us believed him. But she'd been planning her getaway for a while. She had fake papers and she'd kept hold of the grocery bag from the exchange. Inside was the full two hundred thousand she'd asked for. I guess Neily didn't want to take a chance she might want to count it before she produced the guns. She had me drop her off at the airport where she had packed bags and a disguise waiting in a locker. Since the guns were gone and she refused to talk to the police and even if she had been willing to tell them what she knew, they'd still have had no hard evidence they could take to court, I figured I might as well let her go. I didn't want her blood on my hands."

"I'm sorry," Bernadette said, feeling his disappointment as deeply as if it was her own. Then the smell of burned plastic reminded her of the cassette and she asked, "How'd you get the tape from her answering machine."

"To show her gratitude to me for helping her, she told me she'd packed her husband's things away and stuck them in the attic. Then she gave me her keys and a note saying I had permission to take whatever I wanted from the house. I was there searching through her husband's stuff when you called. I figured Merriweather's men would show up tonight to make a thorough search and I didn't want them listening to the tape and connecting you to Martha.''

Bernadette couldn't shake the fear she felt for him. ''I know I should thank you but I don't like the idea of you putting yourself in danger because of me.''

''I've been on Merriweather's list since Barry's death,'' he replied. ''I'm used to it.''

He was certainly the most aggravating man she knew and she assured herself she no longer held any deep feelings for him. But she couldn't bear the thought of him being harmed. ''I still don't like it.''

Max scowled at her. ''Well, that's the way it is and that's the way it's going to be. Now, I'm going to tell you for the last time, stay out of this.''

If he'd asked her nicely, she would have agreed to his demand. But she wasn't going to be ordered around by anyone. ''You are not my master!'' she snapped back.

''You,'' Max growled, ''are going to make some man a very trying wife.'' He couldn't believe he'd brought up marriage. He also didn't like the taste the mention of her getting married left in his mouth.

''Well, at least you won't have to worry about being that man,'' she returned, vowing that if he was the last man on earth, she wouldn't marry him.

For one brief moment, Max experienced something that felt like regret. Even if he was the marrying kind, Bernadette Dowd would not be his choice, he assured himself. She'd become totally impossible to reason with. ''Women,'' he stated, seething under his breath.

''Men!'' she snapped, letting him know she thought he was as difficult and unreasonable as he thought she was.

"Either you give me your word you'll stay out of this, or I become your shadow and believe me I can be a real nuisance," he threatened.

"That I'm already aware of," she tossed back. She also knew he meant to keep that threat. She breathed a disgusted breath. "I'll stay as far away from Merriweather Neily as possible and I'll forget I ever met Martha Jude."

"Good," Max replied, then strode out of her house. But leaving hadn't been as easy as he'd made it look. As infuriated as she made him, he'd still wanted to kiss her. "And a heck of a lot more," he admitted grudgingly as he drove away.

Bernadette fought back the urge to scream. "That has got to be the most..." she said as she fumed, unable to think of an adjective to adequately describe Max Laird. How could she ever have thought she was in love with him, she mocked herself. Suddenly she remembered how gentle he could be and how much fun. *"No!"* she screamed at herself and pushed those memories to the dark recesses of her mind.

Still, she couldn't stop worrying about him. And lying in bed that night, the worry that he might meet with an "accident" plagued her. When she slept she dreamed of him being killed and awoke in a cold sweat.

"How can I care so much about a man who wishes he'd never even said hello to me?" she berated herself as she fixed her breakfast the next morning.

Because, as angry as he made her now, he'd been there for her when she'd needed someone to lean on, she reminded herself. Even more, she had to admire his dedication to bringing his brother's killer to justice.

All the way in to work, she was tense. Only when she entered the newsroom and saw him seated at his desk, did she relax.

But her relief didn't last long. Almost immediately she had to leave to cover a story on the opening of a new neighborhood park in the north county. And the moment Max was out of her sight, her nerves again tensed. He's a big boy. He can take care of himself, she silently assured herself as she rode with Roger to the assignment.

But her mind remained only half on her interviews. The other half worried about Max. When she returned to the newsroom and discovered him gone, her anxiety increased.

Making herself sound as if she was annoyed by something Max had done and wanted to confront him about it, she asked Grace where he'd been sent. When she learned he was covering a murder in Forest Park, her nervousness increased. There were sure to be a zillion police around, she reasoned and again ordered herself to relax. But that proved impossible.

Her story was done and handed in before he returned. But instead of going home, she lingered around the newsroom wanting to make certain he got back all right. When he did finally step off the elevator and passed her desk without even looking her way, she felt like a fool. Go home! she ordered herself and this time she followed her command.

But as soon as she walked through her door, she knew she wasn't going to stay. Quickly she changed into jeans and a light shirt, made herself a thermos of coffee, packed a bag of food and took off for the newspaper. Driving through the parking lot, she spotted Max's car.

"This will be good experience for when I'm tailing some crook," she joked, again feeling like a fool but unable to make herself go back home. Then as her words echoed in her ears, she realized how much she'd enjoyed tailing Lang and knew that if the opportunity to tail another crook ever arose again, she'd jump at it.

However, tailing Lang had been very different from tailing Max. Lang had been an exciting game. Max, on the other hand, was a thorn in her side that she couldn't get rid of. "I can't follow him around forever," she muttered as she sat parked across the street from the exit of the parking garage waiting for him. "I'll just do this for a few days to make certain Merriweather doesn't decide Max has become too much of a thorn in his side. After all, Max is partially out on this limb because of me and I can't just walk away and leave him stranded.''

She was halfway through a crossword puzzle when she saw him pulling out onto the street. She followed a couple of cars behind. He stopped first at a newsstand she knew carried papers from all over the United States and the world. His second stop was a Chinese restaurant. Memories of the meal they'd shared played through her mind. "That was another lifetime," she chided herself, angry she'd experienced a spasm of regret that they'd have no more meals like that. "What we had was merely physical. It would have burned out in time, anyway.''

She'd started to reach for a sandwich when he came back out carrying a bag of food with him. It was a large bag and the thought that he was on his way to share it with someone caused her stomach to knot. "If he wants to spend time with a woman, that's none of my concern," she grumbled at herself.

But she did admit to a feeling of relief when, a few minutes later, he pulled into his apartment complex and went into his own place. "I just didn't want to feel like a voyeur and I would have if he'd been on his way to a date," she muttered under her breath.

She was sitting watching the front of his apartment wondering how long she should stay and knowing her nerves were going to make her remain there most of the night, when she caught a movement out of the corner of her eye. She jerked around to discover Max frowning at her through the open window of her car door.

"I told you to stay away from me," he growled.

Pride hid the pain his bluntness caused. "I'd like to do just that," she returned honestly. "But I'm your backup whether you want me to be or not. My conscience won't let me get any rest until I know I haven't put you in danger.''

"It's like I told you. I'm not in any more danger than I was before. Merriweather seems to get a kick out of keeping me dangling. By not killing me, he blows holes in my theory that he's a cold-blooded murderer. As long as I don't have any evidence on him, he's not going to touch me."

"You have no idea how much I'd like to believe that," she groaned in frustration.

"What's it going to take to convince you?" he demanded.

Looking up into his cool gaze, she was finding it hard to believe she couldn't simply walk away from him. It was obvious he didn't want her there. Still, she couldn't make herself leave. "I figure if Merriweather doesn't make a move on you for the next couple of days we're back to the status quo."

For a long moment Max studied her in silence. He'd never met a woman as determined as Bernadette Dowd. Abruptly he opened her door and began rolling up her window. "You might as well come inside. I saw you following me and on the off chance I couldn't get rid of you, I bought enough dinner for two."

"I brought my own dinner," she informed him haughtily. "And I'm perfectly happy right where I am."

"Well, I'm not. My neighbors are bound to wonder why you're here and there's no telling what their fertile imaginations will come up with. And someone will probably call the police." His hand closed around her arm as he spoke and he gently but firmly pulled her out of her car.

"I suppose I can keep a closer eye on you in your apartment," she conceded, not liking the idea of explaining her presence here to a policeman.

But keeping a closer eye on Max could be a mistake, she admitted a little later as she sat at his table sharing dinner with him. He'd remembered she liked the sweet tasting sesame chicken. For himself, he'd gotten curried beef and she knew it would be extra hot. She remembered how he'd had her taste it and she'd claimed it made it feel as if she could breathe fire. He'd laughed and kissed her. That was a fantasy, she reminded herself curtly and forced the pictures from her mind.

Max had been studying her covertly. This was definitely a different atmosphere than the last time they'd shared Chinese, he thought. But he didn't want to think about that time. It was never going to happen again. The problem was, as irritating as she'd become, she still had that cute way of pursing her mouth when she was thinking. Time to get rid of her, he ordered himself. "Are you ready to go home now?" he asked coolly. "As you can see, I'm safely in for the night."

She frowned in frustration. The urge to go home was strong. Being here alone with him was not easy. Pride would not allow her to wish they were once again lovers but she could not stop herself from remembering how good being in his arms had felt. The man is making me crazy! she wailed silently.

She frowned at the door, mentally walking out. In her mind she made it all the way to her car but she couldn't make herself get in and drive away. Her gaze shifted to him. "How do I know you won't go out again?"

"You have my word," he returned. A shock raced through him. He'd always considered it a nuisance when anyone worried about him. But there was a small part of him that enjoyed having this woman concerned about his welfare. However, her being there not only gave him someone else whose safety he had to worry about, but it also was a strain on his self-control. After all he was a man and he couldn't entirely forget how it'd felt to hold her.

Leave, she ordered herself. Instead she heard herself saying, "Merriweather could send someone here."

Max scowled impatiently. "I appreciate your concern but it's unnecessary. I'm a big boy, I can take care of myself."

"I keep telling myself that," she returned, frustration mingling with impatience in her voice. "Then I find myself arguing that your brother probably thought the same thing himself."

The sudden shadow that passed over Max's face told her she was right.

Then his scowl was back. "I've had more practice looking over my shoulder."

"If you're always having to look over your shoulder, you could walk into trouble you don't see ahead of you," she rebutted.

Her argument was difficult to counter, he admitted. He'd certainly walked straight into her life without considering the consequences. Deciding to try another tact to get rid of her, he said, "What would your grandmother think of you becoming my shadow?"

"My grandmother would be appalled by my new lifestyle," she admitted. An impish grin abruptly played across her face. "But my parents would love it. They were true adventurers. They did free-lance reporting for nature magazines. My mother was the photographer and my father wrote the text. They died in a plane crash on their way to a glacier in Alaska."

Max was about to point out that he didn't want her following her parents' example and dying young. But before he could speak, her smile faded and she said, "My grandmother was good to me and she was afraid of losing me the way she lost my mother. Because of that she raised me to be cautious. But it's as if I was only half-alive until now."

Max knew when he was fighting a losing battle. "You can have the bed. I'll sleep on the couch."

Bernadette blinked. She'd become so absorbed in thinking about her parents, she'd momentarily forgotten she'd been arguing with Max. "What?"

"I surrender. You can sleep on the bed," he said, beginning to clean up the cartons left from their dinner.

"I don't want to take your bed," she protested, relieved he had capitulated but now feeling like a total bother.

"I insist," he returned, wanting her behind a closed door when he got into his files.

"I really don't mind sleeping on the couch," she persisted.

Pausing as he picked up the cartons he'd stacked, he scowled at her. "Take the bed or leave."

She caught the added emphasis he'd put on "leave." Again the urge to head for the door was strong but instead, she said with schooled indifference, "All right I'll take the bed."

The image of him lying beside her suddenly flashed into her mind and she found herself wishing for his company again. Wanton wench! she berated herself and quickly turned her attention to helping him clear away the dinner dishes.

As she walked toward the kitchen, Max watched the easy swing of her hips. Not only was having her here an annoyance because he had to worry about her getting caught in the crossfire if Merriweather did send someone after him, but she was also definitely a threat to his self-control. However, the fact that she didn't want to be there any more than he wanted her there was having close to the same effect as a cold shower.

Bernadette glanced at her watch as they finished cleaning up after dinner. It was too early for bed. "Do you mind if I watch the news channel?" she asked.

Max caught the edge of boredom in her voice. "If you're going to start doing surveillance, you should learn to bring along something to work on," he instructed, then mentally kicked himself. He'd sounded as if he was encouraging her and he didn't want to do that. The thought of her getting that pretty little neck wrung by a criminal type caused a chill to race along his spine.

"I'll remember that for future reference," she replied, not adding that her decision to follow him had been an impulse not something she'd thought out and planned. Turning on the television, she concentrated on the news and attempted to ignore him. But against her will, she found herself watching him out of the corner of her eye as he seated himself in a clearly much-used, upholstered armchair and began reading through the stack of newspapers he'd picked up on his way home.

He looked rather domestic with his jacket and tie discarded, the top button of his shirt unbuttoned, his shoes kicked off and his stocking feet propped up on the coffee table, she thought. But Max Laird was not the domestic kind! she quickly reminded herself.

Max shifted uncomfortably. As he switched newspapers, he glanced covertly toward her and saw her studying him. Normally he could ignore anyone watching him, but with her he found himself wondering what she was thinking. Probably nothing good, he decided. "Help yourself," he said coolly, indicating the newspapers with a nod of his head.

"Thanks," she replied, picking one of the discarded ones just to have something to do with her hands other than resting them idling in her lap.

For the next few minutes she concentrated on glancing through articles. But always in the back of her mind, she was aware of Max's presence and her nerves grew more tense.

"I suppose you'll need a toothbrush."

Startled by this unexpected observation, Bernadette glanced around the side of her newspaper.

Max had ordered himself not to think about her but that's all he'd been thinking about for the past half hour. Disgusted with his lack of self-control, he said stiffly, "I figured you didn't think about bringing a toothbrush."

"You're right, I didn't," she replied. As a thought struck her, she added, "And if you're considering suggesting I go home and get one so you can give me the slip, forget it. I'll just suffer through and pick up one tomorrow."

"That could have been a good ploy. I wish I'd thought of it," he returned honestly as he rose from his chair and headed into the bathroom.

Bernadette returned her attention to the newspaper but her mind refused to focus on the story in front of her. Instead she wondered what had caused Max to ask about toothbrushes. He'd probably done it to further emphasize what a novice she was, she decided. When he'd spent the night at her place, she'd learned he carried a shaving kit with the basic essentials in the trunk of his car. And that's another thing a good investigative reporter should have, she silently mimicked him lecturing her again.

Unexpectedly the paper was pushed a little aside and she looked up to see him standing there with five cellophane wrapped toothbrushes of various colors held like a bouquet in his hand.

"Choose one," he instructed.

"Do you always keep such an ample supply handy for unexpected company?" she asked. The sudden thought of him offering this same choice to other women he'd actually invited to his place caused a pang of jealousy.

"My mother's a dentist. Every Christmas she gives everyone in the family a stocking stuffed with toothbrushes and dental floss."

In spite of her tenseness, the image of Max standing in front of a Christmas tree holding a stocking stuffed with toothbrushes caused a smile to tickle the corners of her mouth. "Your mother's a dentist?"

The way she was fighting to hold back that quirky little grin was sort of endearing, he thought. It's not endearing; it's hazardous, he corrected, reminding himself this was a woman who would want a commitment. "I was seven when

Mom decided to go to dental school. She used to practice on all of us." He flashed a humorless, bare-toothed smile.

"I suppose you could always use free dental coverage as a selling point if you ever decided to ask a woman to marry you." Bernadette flushed the moment she realized she'd brought up him and marriage in the same sentence. Those two words don't belong in the same paragraph, she scolded herself.

"My mother has suggested that." Unexpectedly Max saw himself on Bernadette's doorstep with a huge bouquet of toothbrushes. The woman is a definite strain on my sanity, he chided himself, pushing the image from his mind. Aloud he said, "However, I doubt any woman has been swayed by that kind of offer."

The thought that she could be swayed by *any* offer from him shook Bernadette. He's one weakness I'm not going to indulge in again, she assured herself. "You're right. The green one will do," she said, making sure she didn't touch his hand as she plucked the chosen toothbrush from the assortment. Still, even the heat his hand had given to the cellophane caused her stomach to knot with regret. I will find someone twice... a hundred times better than him, she assured herself.

When he came back into the living room a few moments later after having returned the unwanted toothbrushes to their box, she decided she'd had as much of his company as she could stand for the night. "Unless you want the *New York Times* crossword puzzle, I'll just take it and go to bed," she said.

"Crossword puzzles have never been my forte," he replied. "You're welcome to it."

She saw the relief on his face and knew he was glad to be rid of her. Well, she'd be glad to be rid of him and if no one had made any attempts on his life by the end of the next forty-eight hours she would gladly walk away and never look back.

Max waited until he heard Bernadette in the shower, then he quickly retrieved the black appointment books he'd stashed earlier in the false bottom of his safe.

He'd lied to Bernadette when he'd said he hadn't found anything at the Jude house. He'd, in fact, found something that could prove important. In the small black appointment books was Jude's record of the dates and places he'd traveled. Max had long suspected that Merriweather's operation might extend farther than the boundaries of St. Louis county. Tomorrow, he'd start checking to see if he could discover advantageous deaths which had occurred in those places Jude had been during the periods of time the "gardener" was there.

For the next two hours, Max went through the books making a list of places and dates. Finally deciding he had enough information to begin his search, he rose and stretched. His gaze went to the bedroom door and he wondered if Bernadette was asleep. Telling himself he was only checking to make certain she wasn't going to walk in on him while he was returning the books to his secret compartment, he went over to the door and quietly opened it a crack to peek in.

She'd fallen asleep with the light on and the crossword and pencil in hand. Approaching the bed, he saw her bare shoulders and realized that she was naked beneath the covers. The image of her standing unclothed before him filled his mind and a heat raced through him. He kicked himself for not giving her a shirt to wear. Reaching the bed, he eased the crossword and pencil out of her hands and laid them on the bedside table. Then looking down at her, he frowned. She was a temptation. He could almost feel her in his arms.

The frown on his face deepened. He was trying real hard to treat her fairly. She wanted a man who'd give her a lifetime commitment and he wasn't that man. Even after Merriweather was exposed, and he'd sworn a solemn vow that would happen, there would be other dangerous people he would go after. He didn't want anyone in his life to worry about or to cause complications and at the moment she was doing both. Admittedly she was a very cute pain in the neck, but she was a pain in the neck nonetheless and the sooner she was out of his life, the better.

Bernadette had heard Max at the door. In spite of all the strong talks she'd had with herself, lying alone in his bed and knowing he was in the next room had caused a painful loneliness within her. She knew it was cowardly but she hadn't wanted to see or speak to him so she'd feigned sleep. She'd expected him to peek in and then quickly leave. Instead, he was still there. The heat of his fingers where they'd brushed her hand when he'd removed the newspaper lingered. Unable to resist, she opened her eyes.

Big mistake! her inner voice screamed. Just seeing him brought a flood of memories of their lovemaking. Heat raced through her and a yearning so strong it was an ache shook her. I've got to get this man out of my system, she groaned silently. A sudden inspiration came to her. Maybe all she needed was one last night with him. When they'd been together before, she'd believed she had a death sentence hanging over her head. Maybe that was what had caused their lovemaking to seem so memorable.

"I didn't mean to wake you," he apologized gruffly.

"It's lonely in here by myself." Inwardly Bernadette gasped. She'd planned to be a little more subtle.

Max was strongly tempted to accept her obvious invitation. She's one dangerous woman, he thought, stunned by how easily she'd shaken his vow to stay away from her. "Feel free to leave the light on," he returned aloud, ordering himself to leave.

Bernadette considered dropping her attempt to seduce him but her longing for his touch caused the aching inside to increase. You've got to get this man out of your system once and for all, she told herself. "Stay with me, Max. Just one last time?'' she coaxed. ''I know the rules. No commitments.''

He'd seen that look in her eyes before and knew it meant trouble. Again he ordered himself to get out of there fast. Instead, he heard himself saying, ''I'm not so sure that's such a good idea.''

Neither am I, Bernadette returned silently but the need to be with him was growing stronger by the moment. Impulsively, she tossed off the covers. Rising so near him that the action caused her body to brush against his, she then stood facing him. ''I promise not to start thinking of you as a wanton man,'' she teased seductively.

For an amateur, Bernadette Dowd was damned persuasive, Max thought, his resistance fading fast.

''We could both use a little relaxation,'' she coaxed, beginning to unbutton his shirt.

Relaxed was not at all how he felt, Max observed silently, but his hands had found her hips and the curve of them was soft and inviting to his touch. The warning that he might regret accepting her invitation flashed through his mind. She knows the rules, he argued back as he moved his hands along the lines of her body and the fire within him grew stronger.

Bernadette had unfastened his shirt and as she eased it off him, she leaned against him, kissing him lightly on the neck. She'd expected to feel at least a little shy or uneasy. Instead being here with him like this seemed natural. Well, we have done this before, she reminded herself dryly.

His touch was playing havoc with her senses. Tremors of pleasure raced through her and her legs began to feel weak. Running her hands downward over his chest to the buckle of his belt, she felt his breathing growing ragged and a womanly delight caused her to smile crookedly.

Max wanted to give in to the urges she was awakening. But his conscience forced him to make one final effort to stop her. ''I think we'd both be smart to stop now,'' he said,

his voice carrying a husky edge as she slipped his belt out of
the loops.

Even if she'd wanted to, Bernadette couldn't make herself turn back now. Her craving for him had grown too
strong for reason or sanity to control it. I'm sure being with
him this one last time will cure me, she assured herself again.
Looking up into his face, she said firmly, "I want to be with
you tonight, Max."

She'd loosened his pants and was slipping them down over
his hips. There was no sense trying to deny he wanted to be
with her, he thought wryly. The desire she'd woken in him
was obvious. "When it's possible, I try to accommodate a
lady's request," he said gruffly, helping her finish undressing him. But as she began to pull him down to the bed, he
stopped her. "And I always try to make certain I treat a lady
safely." Easing away from her, he opened the drawer of the
bedside table.

Lying on the bed watching him, Bernadette wondered
what it was about this man that made her want him so
much. She was impatient to feel him in her arms again.

Joining her on the bed, Max trailed kisses over her pausing at the spots he knew gave her the most pleasure. When
she moaned with delight his own passion was aroused even
more. "You do have a body that can please a man," he
murmured against her skin as he sought out the hardened
nipples of her breasts for a taste.

"You've got a very pleasing body yourself," she replied,
arching against him. Being with him seemed like more of a
need than a want, she thought as remembered ways of exciting him further played through her mind and she began
to employ them.

Max knew he couldn't wait too long. She had him nearly
crazy with desire. Looking into her face he saw his own
passion mirrored in her eyes. Knowing it was unnecessary to
hold back any longer, he claimed her.

Bernadette gasped with joy as he possessed her. Her hopes that this time would be different; that this time she might even feel a little bored died. As he caressed her and they moved to the age old rhythm of lovers, she again found herself soaring to heights of ecstasy.

Max felt her body responding to his and a sense of power came over him. The thought that he would like to have lengthened this moment until it lasted the night, entered his mind. Then silently, he laughed at himself. They'd both have to sleep around the clock to regain their strength, he quipped back at this foolishness. "Max," Bernadette gasped his name.

He knew she'd reached her zenith and with both regret and relief, he joined her.

A little later as she lay beside Max, Bernadette wanted to scream in frustration. Her plan hadn't worked at all. His lovemaking had been even more exciting than before and her hunger for him was as strong as ever.

A new hope suddenly emerged. He had enjoyed her company as much as she'd enjoyed his. Of that she was certain. Maybe he'd decide that they made a good pair after all.

Max lay frowning up at the ceiling. He'd enjoyed this tryst with Berny too much. She could very easily become a habit and habits could lead to commitments. He had to get out of bed. If he stayed, he'd want to make love to her again. "Berny," he said, shifting onto his side to face her.

She turned to him and the hope that he might be reconsidering his stand on being a lone wolf faded when she saw the hard set of his jaw.

"We've got to stop meeting this way," he continued. His attempt to add a light edge to his voice failed. His expression grim, he said, "I know you. No matter what you say, in the end, you're going to want a commitment and I can't give you that."

"You're right," she admitted.

"You're a terrific lady. You'll find someone who can give you the life you deserve." His words caused an acid taste in his mouth. He knew he sounded like a cad. She had to despise him. Maybe that'd be for the best, he reasoned, then quickly climbed out of the bed.

Silently, she watched him take some fresh clothes from the drawers and closet, then leave the room. She wanted to hate him, but she couldn't. She'd been the one to seduce him and she'd known this would be strictly a one-night stand for him.

"You're right, Max, I will find someone," she promised under her breath as the door clicked closed behind him. "Someone really wonderful," she added firmly. Then throwing the pillow he'd rested his head on off the bed, she snapped off the light and ordered herself to sleep.

Chapter Thirteen

Bernadette was seated in the back seat of Max's car working at not staring at the back of Max's head. He was driving and Roger was riding in the front passenger seat. All three were on their way to cover a speech being given at one of the local colleges by the current Secretary of the Interior. Several environmental groups were planning protests against various policies being enacted by the administration and there had been threats of violence. Not wanting the paper to miss anything, Ben had decided to send two reporters as well as a photographer. Bernadette was to cover the speech while Max talked with the protesters and Roger wandered among all the groups taking pictures.

Bernadette's mind flashed back to earlier that morning at Max's apartment. The scent of his after-shave had lingered in the bathroom and in spite of knowing he didn't want her there and assuring herself she didn't really want to be there, she'd felt as if she was right where she belonged. *I only felt that way because I've appointed myself his guardian for the* next couple of days, she reasoned, forcing her mind back to the present.

And Max did seem to accept the fact she was going to be his shadow for a while, she added with relief. When Ben had sent the assignments around and given Bruce Jenkins the job of covering the speech, Bruce had protested saying he'd listened to one too many politicians in his day and would rather cover a kindergarten opening than another political speech. Grabbing the opportunity, Bernadette had immediately volunteered to take his place. Ben had shown some surprise that she'd ask to go on assignment with Max, but Max had merely shrugged as if he didn't care who accompanied him and Ben had let her go.

Guiding the car through traffic, Max felt the prickling on the back of his neck. He'd hoped to have a respite from Bernadette's guardianship. This morning at breakfast, he'd kept remembering how good her lips could taste.

Admittedly, he'd had one break. While he'd gone straight into the office, she'd been forced to go home and change into more suitable attire. But when she'd stepped off the elevator, he'd discovered that she was beginning to look sexy to him even in her tailored suit and with her hair pulled tightly back.

I'll bet Sir Galahad didn't have anyone like Bernadette Dowd following him around, he mused dryly, admitting that his determined gallantry was growing more and more difficult. Of course, after last night, she'd probably slap him hard if he tried anything anyway, he reminded himself.

By the time they arrived at the college grounds, Max was glad to be going in one direction while Bernadette went in another.

Glancing over her shoulder as she and Max parted company, Bernadette saw his expression relax and felt a nudge of irritation. On the other hand, she couldn't blame him. She hadn't liked him appointing himself her guardian, either. Well, it's only for a day and a half more, she reasoned. Trying not to think about him for at least a few minutes, she concentrated on the people entering the auditorium to listen to the speech. But the thought of joining them made her feel restless. She confessed that, like Bruce, she'd rather be attending a kindergarten opening.

Her gaze shifted to the protesters. She saw Max interviewing a couple of very pretty young women. He looked absorbed in the conversation and something that felt like a jab of jealousy pierced her. He can have a bevy of college beauties, she assured herself and mentally set the hour she would feel comfortable freeing herself from her guardianship.

Pulling her gaze away from him, she slowly surveyed the other protesters. A bearded man dressed in jeans and a T-shirt and a well-worn corduroy jacket was sitting on the brick wall by the steps. She noticed he was watching Max and wondered if one of the girls was his girlfriend and he was worried about competition. Then the man's gaze shifted to the rest of the crowd and she decided she'd been mistaken when she'd thought he was actually watching Max.

But a couple of minutes later as her scanning of the gathering brought her attention back to the jacketed man, she again saw him looking in Max's direction. But Max wasn't talking to the girls any longer. Now he was speaking to an intense-looking couple wearing Greenpeace shirts. Bernadette's gaze narrowed on Max's observer.

Her first impression was that he was relaxed, simply watching the show. Now she noticed that the relaxed attitude was actually studied. There was an alertness in his gaze. When Max left the couple he'd been talking to and moved farther into the crowd, the man casually rose and stood on the brick wall. Watching him, Bernadette was certain he'd taken this higher perch simply because he didn't want to lose track of Max. A warning light went off in her brain. A light breeze whipped the man's jacket and her breath locked in her lungs. In that one brief moment, she was sure she'd seen a gun tucked into the back of his jeans. As if to confirm her suspicion, his hands were now shoved into the pockets of his jacket to prevent the garment from blowing again.

Ignoring the fact that the speech was to begin at any moment, she began to make her way toward Max. He was conversing with a group wearing Save Our Wetlands T-shirts now. To her relief they were clustered around him providing him protection.

"Aren't you supposed to be inside observing and taking notes about what's going on?" a familiar male voice asked from her left.

Glancing in that direction, she saw Roger. "No one takes notes anymore," she returned, fumbling in her pocket for her tape recorder. Shoving it toward him, she said, "Be a pal. Go in and tape it for me."

Seeing the protest on his face, she added pleadingly, "Please. It's really important."

Grinning sheepishly, he shook his head as if to call himself a sucker. "I've never been able to say no to a pretty woman." Taking the recorder, he headed inside.

Turning back to Max, Bernadette noticed he was moving away from the cluster of people. It was difficult, but she forced herself to walk, not run toward him. On her way she glanced around for anything that could be used as a shield. There was a large old oak near where he was headed. Reaching him, she hooked her arm through his. "Come with me," she ordered in hushed tones, pulling him in the direction of the tree.

Max read the fear in her eyes. "What's wrong?" he demanded, allowing her to maneuver him into a position behind the tree away from the crowd.

"There's a man here. He's wearing jeans and a brown corduroy jacket. He's been watching you and he's got a gun," she explained succinctly.

Max regarded her thoughtfully. She was a good watch-dog and if he ever needed anyone to guard his back, he would trust her.

Bernadette stiffened as she caught a glimpse of the man she'd just described coming their way. "He's coming toward us," she said, moving closer to Max as if to shield him with her body.

The feel of her as she brushed against him was inviting. She was becoming more of a threat to his peace of mind than Merriweather, he admitted. Scowling impatiently he said, "That's Fred Conley. He's an undercover cop."

"I can't believe you spotted me so easily," Fred said to her as he joined them.

The way Max was looking at her made Bernadette feel like a pest. Quickly she took a large step back and turned her attention to the new arrival. "You're a policeman?"

"Undercover assigned to security today," he replied. "Max and I have an arrangement. On occasions like this, when he's interviewing the crowd, I keep an eye on him and if he thinks anyone he talks to might be crazy enough to pose a real threat he gives me a nod so I know to keep a closer eye on them."

Bernadette felt like a fool. "Sorry I interfered," she said stiffly, then quickly started toward the auditorium.

Max knew he'd made her feel uncomfortable and the urge to apologize was strong. But his own reaction held him back. Her protectiveness had caused a surge of satisfaction and pleasure. Immediately it had been followed by a rush of fear. If he had been in danger, she would have been in the line of fire and that was the one thing he didn't want. Letting her remain uncomfortable was for the best, he reasoned. Maybe now she'd keep as far away from him as possible. They'd both be safer that way.

"Something going on between you and the lady?" Fred asked, pulling Max's attention back to him.

"No, nothing," Max replied.

"Too bad." A gleam of approval showed in the police-man's eyes. "She's not only cute, she's sharp. She spotted me almost immediately. If I ever needed my back covered, I'd feel safe with her."

"I'd worry too much about her getting herself hurt," Max returned gruffly.

"Yeah, that could be a problem," Fred admitted. Then with a nod, he slipped back into character and slowly saun-tered back into the crowd of protesters.

Bernadette couldn't believe she'd made such a fool of herself. Again seated in the back seat of Max's car, she tried to ignore the two men up front while she listened to the part of the speech she'd missed and took notes.

When they reached the paper, she went directly to her desk and began typing copy.

Watching her, Max knew she was embarrassed. A ripple of guilt ran through him. Again he reminded himself she'd be safer if she stayed away from him and the guilt sub-sided.

"She might feel foolish but she's still sticking like glue," he muttered disgruntledly to himself, later as he drove home with her following.

At every street along the way, Bernadette was tempted to turn away and head home but when Max pulled into his apartment complex, she was right behind him. "I'm defi-nitely a glutton for punishment," she grumbled under her breath.

Watching as she joined him, he recalled the way she'd tried to shield him in the park. Again fear swept through him, this time so intense a cold sweat broke out on his palms. If Merriweather did send someone for him and Ber-nadette got caught in the cross fire, he'd never be able to live with himself. He had to get rid of her. A solution came to mind.

As they entered his apartment, he shoved the door shut and captured her by the upper arms. "I keep warning you, Berny, that you're a threat to my control." He hadn't meant to kiss her, he'd only intended to threaten her but he couldn't resist one last taste. A kiss will add some reality, he reasoned. What he hadn't counted on was just how enticing her lips felt.

As his mouth found hers, Bernadette stood frozen. Had he reconsidered his feelings after last night? Was he actually going to admit he'd learned to care for her? Her heart pounded as he lifted his head away and she saw the passion mingled with impatience in his eyes.

Max was furious with himself. Every time he touched her, he wanted her. He'd never let a woman get under his skin this way before. I should have yelled at her from across the room, he berated himself. But it was too late now to change tactics. His hands closed tighter around her upper arms as he fought to maintain control. "I'm trying to be fair to you," he growled. "I can't offer you what you want. But I'm only human and, after last night, your inviting yourself to spend another night here is making keeping my hands off of you too much of a strain."

Bernadette was crushed. He was talking about lust, nothing more.

"Either you leave now or I won't be responsible for my actions," he finished gruffly.

A shiver of fear raced through her. This wasn't the Max she knew. He was actually threatening to take her against her will. But she couldn't make herself believe he was really a Jekyll and Hyde personality. Her shoulders squared defiantly. "If you're trying to scare me, you're doing a pretty good job. But I refuse to believe you would force yourself on me."

Max hated the fear he saw in her eyes. "I'm merely being honest," he growled. "You're a temptation and things could go too far again if you stay around here."

Bernadette had to admit, as determined as she was to have a husband and family, Max tempted her, too. But she also knew he was right. They would both regret giving in to this attraction again. She shook free from his hold. "You've made your point. And you're right, I should go home. If Merriweather was going to do anything he would have done it by now or he'll wait until I'm gone. Either way, my staying here is serving no purpose." Suddenly remembering what day it was, she added, "Besides, tonight is your poker game. You'll be well looked after."

Max breathed a mental sigh of relief. At least she was being reasonable.

Bernadette had meant to merely turn and leave but instead, she glared at him. "If you weren't so determined to be a lone wolf, we would be a good match." Her cheeks flushed as she realized she'd spoken aloud what had been going through her mind.

Max's jaw tensed. "I saw the pain Molly suffered when Barry died. And I know how much his death hurt my parents. I don't want to add anyone else to the list of people who might grieve for me. I guess, what I'm saying is I don't want to feel responsible to anyone but myself."

"Then I wish you well," she replied stiffly. With her hand on the doorknob, she added, "I'm not stupid enough to spend my time hoping you'll change. If you do, you know where you can find me, but don't expect me to be there forever." Then turning abruptly away, she left.

Striding back to her car, she couldn't believe she'd come to within a hair of actually proposing to him. Modern women speak their minds all the time, she told herself as she climbed in behind the wheel. They know what they want and they go for it. And she did consider herself a modern woman . . . just not quite that modern.

Still, she admitted as she drove away, she wasn't sorry about anything she'd said. "I'm glad I didn't just walk away and leave myself to wonder what might have been," she informed the image in the mirror. Now that she knew how absolutely determined Max was to remain on his own, she would put him out of her mind for good and get on with her life.

But late that night as she lay unable to sleep the thought that modern women didn't take no for an answer taunted her. "Maybe I could change his thinking. I know he has a sensitive side. Maybe I could win him over, and make him fall in love with me," she murmured to the emptiness.

His grim image as he'd told her about his brother abruptly filled her mind and doubt about her success assailed her. She frowned darkly. Max was a man dedicated to a goal. And, one thing she'd learned about him was that when he set his mind to something, he allowed nothing and nobody to deter him. She groaned. No woman could compete with that kind of dedication. She admired him for his tenacity in doing what he knew was right, but at the same time she felt totally frustrated.

Still, even as she assured herself she would be facing a losing battle, the memory of how secure and happy she'd been when he'd been there with her flowed through her. Forcefully, she pushed her doubts to the far recesses of her mind. She wasn't sure how to proceed but he was worth the effort. She had to, at least, try.

"However, bags under my eyes isn't going to help," she admonished herself, and finally drifted off to sleep.

Chapter Fourteen

Bernadette stood speechless.

"This'll be great publicity for the paper and a nice citation for you to hang on your wall," Ben was saying. "Not to mention the thousand-dollar public service reward."

"Merriweather Neily wants to give me a plaque and a monetary reward for the Lang investigation?" she asked, finding this turn of events a little hard to believe.

Ben frowned impatiently. "Neily's always been very civic minded. He feels that by presenting this reward, he'll be encouraging others to report on criminal activities they see occurring and thus help lower the crime rate." He glanced at his watch. "We're expected at Neily's estate at ten. He's invited the mayor and a few other locally influential politicians in addition to the television stations. And he's serving a brunch afterward. My guess is that everyone will show. No one passes up an opportunity to go to his estate. I'll have Roger and Gordon cover it."

Recovering from her shock, Bernadette wondered what Neily's game was. "Isn't this awfully sudden?"

Ben shrugged. "He said his kid came up with the idea last night during dinner and he wanted to carry through on it while your story is still on people's minds." Ben regarded her patronizingly. "You know how fast people forget. Lang is old news already."

Bernadette couldn't fault this reasoning. Even more, her curiosity was peaked. She'd never met Merriweather Neily up close and personal. This was her opportunity. And Max couldn't accuse her of breaking her word not to pursue the Neily investigation. After all she hadn't initiated this invitation. Besides, if she didn't go, her refusal would be suspicious. "I'll go freshen my makeup," she said without further hesitation and, giving Ben a wide smile, she strode out of his office.

As she headed for the ladies' room, Max strolled toward her. He seemed to be concentrating on reading whatever was written on the sheet of paper he was carrying but as he passed her, he said in hushed tones, "Meet me on the roof."

She managed to keep from looking at him as she continued on to the elevator. A grin played across her face as she pressed the button for the top floor. This cloak and dagger stuff was fun, she admitted. She was smart enough to be a little scared but still she liked the sense of excitement. And she liked the opportunity to meet with Max in private. "If only I'd had more practice in flirting, I'd feel more confident," she murmured under her breath as the elevator stopped on the top floor.

Finding the stairs, she made her way to the roof and waited. The day was warm and the sky clear. Glancing around, she wished they could have found a more romantic place to meet. But any port will do in a storm, she reasoned.

Five minutes later, she was glancing at her watch impatiently. The thought that maybe he'd simply lured her up here and then locked the exit door to keep her from going to Neily's crossed her mind. Quickly she strode to the door and tried the knob. It opened.

"He only gets two more minutes," she muttered as she again glanced at her watch. She wasn't going to Neily's without at least checking her makeup. Restless, she walked back to where she had a view of the city and the silver arch shimmering in the sunlight.

The sound of the door opening caused her to turn around.

"Come over here," Max ordered, slipping around behind one of the air-conditioning units dotting the roof.

"You do choose the most romantic places," she said coquettishly as she joined him.

He frowned impatiently. He was scared for her and she was making jokes. The urge to give her a shake was strong but, recalling the last time he'd touched her, he didn't trust himself. He could end up kissing her again and he didn't want to do that. She was trouble with a capital T, he thought for the umpteenth time since last night. "I don't know what Neily's up to but be careful," he ordered in clipped tones. "If he mentions me, you let him know we aren't friends. It might even be a good idea for you to make him think we're barely speaking to each other. And it would be best if you led him to believe you don't trust anything I say."

Before Bernadette could respond, Max quickly made his way back to the stairs. Watching the door close behind him, she breathed a frustrated sigh. It would be easy convincing Neily that she and Max were barely speaking because that was the truth. She also felt foolish that she'd tried to flirt with him. Obviously he really didn't want to have anything to do with her. "Someday, some woman may convince him to change his mind about marriage, but it isn't going to be me," she murmured regretfully.

But as she rode with Ben to Neily's house, she found herself thinking that maybe she could still be the one to change

Max's mind. She just needed patience. And a will of iron, she added.

Merriweather Neily was certainly one of the most charming men she'd ever met, she thought as he paused during his very flattering presentation speech to give her a warm smile.

His son was there and Merriweather was talking about instilling civic mindedness into today's youth. Listening to the sincerity in his voice and seeing the warm smile on his face, Bernadette had great difficulty picturing him as the head of a murder-for-hire organization.

Finally the short presentation was over and everyone adjourned to the patio to partake of the elaborate brunch waiting there.

"I do apologize for the short notice," Merriweather said as he, his son, his wife, Ben and Bernadette posed for a few more shots.

"It really wasn't a problem," she assured him.

He smiled down at her, as if tremendously grateful for her understanding, then he politely but firmly shooed the remaining photographers away with a wave of his hand. Turning his attention to his son and wife, he said, "Would you please escort Mr. Kealy to the buffet. I will reserve the honor of escorting Miss Dowd myself."

As the others moved away, Merriweather paused for a moment to show Bernadette a statuette he had recently acquired. When she glanced away from the artwork, she noticed that they were now alone in the room.

"I've always thought the life of a reporter would be exciting," he said conversationally as he shifted his attention from the statuette back to her.

She noticed that he hadn't begun again moving toward the door to join the others. Clearly he'd maneuvered her into a position where he could speak to her privately. Very clever, she silently complimented him. "It has its moments," she agreed, then deciding that caution would be prudent, she added, "but chasing around after Mr. Lang was unusual for me. I doubt I'll get too many opportunities for that kind of excitement. Generally I cover school board and Aldermen's meetings and the openings of parks." Unable to resist, she heard herself saying, "Max Laird is our ace investigative reporter."

Merriweather smiled knowingly. "And an excellent one he is."

Bernadette had to give the man credit. He sounded as if he genuinely admired Max. Doubts began to assail her. Had her feelings for Max clouded her reason and led her to believe things about Merriweather that simply weren't true? Better to be prudent than sorry, she decided. Max had given her an order and for the moment she would obey. "Max is good but sometimes he can get on a person's nerves," she replied, having no trouble sounding convincing on this point.

Merriweather laughed lightly. "I have heard that. But then all strong-willed men are difficult as my wife has pointed out to me on several occasions."

Bernadette managed a warm smile. "I can't believe you would be difficult."

He winked playfully. "I have my moments."

"Everyone does, I suppose," she returned, trying to picture the tall distinguished man in front of her writing himself a note to have someone killed. As farfetched as the image seemed, she managed to do just that. He's too smooth, she realized. Her grandmother had always warned her about men who oozed too much charm. "Charm like that can hide some major character flaws," Grandma Birkely used to say.

"No one is perfect," Merriweather replied philosophically. He suddenly looked apologetic. "And I am being a terrible host. We should be joining the others. My chef was told to create something special for you. I hope you like strawberries. My wife adores them so we grow them year-round in one of our greenhouses."

"He does spoil me," Pauline Neily said from the doorway, coming to join them. Tossing her husband a reproving glance, she slipped her arm through Bernadette's. "And I know how much he likes to show off his treasures. But you are the guest of honor. I wouldn't be accused of starving you. Besides, Peter, our chef, is growing more agitated by the moment. He can be very emotional when he's been creative and he's anxious to present the dish he's prepared for you."

A little later as she sat eating a scrumptious chocolate soufflé garnished with a sweet strawberry sauce and fresh strawberries dotted with whipped cream, Bernadette found herself thinking that adventures could take some very tasty paths.

"I met Max Laird once," Pauline said as she seated herself beside Bernadette.

Bernadette had just taken a bite of strawberry and whipped cream. Turning to her hostess, all she could do was smile in acknowledgment.

"He was rather brusque and pushy," Pauline continued in a thoughtful vein. "But I suppose reporters must be most of the time to get their stories."

Bernadette couldn't be sure if the woman was simply making conversation or probing. If she was poking around to find out if Bernadette was friendly with Max, she was doing it very well, Bernadette admitted. "I think sometimes Max can be a little too pushy and insensitive," Bernadette replied, choosing to continue to follow Max's orders.

Pauline frowned solicitously. "It must be somewhat difficult when you have to work with him." Abruptly she frowned thoughtfully. "Or maybe you never have to work with him. You reporters do mostly work separately, don't you?"

Bernadette felt a chill creep along her spine. Had Merriweather been watching her and Max and was his wife assigned to probe into their relationship? Don't get paranoid, she cautioned herself. The woman could simply be making conversation. Still, her wariness increased. "Mostly we work separately. But sometimes we have to back each other up. In fact, Max backed me up on the Lang story." She forced an edge of aggravation into her voice. "I didn't ask for his help, but he insisted. To tell the truth, we don't get along."

Pauline smiled sympathetically. "He does seem to be a difficult sort."

Pauline's sympathy not only appeared genuine but comradely as well. However, Bernadette's guard remained in place. The thought that maybe Pauline was even an active partner in Merriweather's enterprise crossed her mind. Nothing really seemed impossible anymore.

Riding away from the estate a little later with Ben, she felt tense. Merriweather actually hadn't initiated any conversation regarding Max, she had to admit. She'd been the one to bring up Max's name. But maybe if she hadn't, he would have, she reasoned. She mentally kicked herself for not being more patient.

Pauline Neily was another matter. She'd openly asked about Max. Of course, Bernadette cautioned herself, she couldn't be sure of Mrs. Neily's motives. After all, Max was an attractive man and Mrs. Neily might simply find him interesting in spite of her declaration to the contrary.

"I know Neily's one of our most civic-minded citizens but the man makes me uneasy," Ben said, cutting into her thoughts.

She started to agree but before she could speak she recalled Max's orders. "All men are suspicious of other men who are charming, gracious and rich. You're just too used to the Max Laird's of this world. If a man isn't cynical you don't trust him."

Ben grinned sheepishly. "Yeah, maybe you're right." His grin disappeared and he glanced at her as he stopped at a light. "Is that a subtle way of saying you were impressed by Neily?"

Every fiber of her being rebelled against leading Ben to think she'd been duped by Neily's charm. "Perfection can be boring," she replied.

Ben nodded with approval. "Glad to hear your head can't be turned by a show of opulence. Wouldn't want a reporter who could be bought."

Bernadette wasn't sure how to respond so she didn't. But as they continued into the city, she studied Ben covertly. He seemed relieved by her responses. And that would be reasonable, she argued because he wouldn't want a reporter who was biased. On the other hand, he had asked her about her reaction to Merriweather. Max had indicated that he didn't trust anyone. And he had made her tell Ben a lie about who she'd met the day Martha Jude had contacted her. Surely Ben wasn't one of Merriweather's clients, she argued with herself. Still, a part of her demanded that she remain cautious even with the editor.

I am getting paranoid! she wailed silently.

Five hours later, she was typing in the last revisions on her copy for the day. As soon as she and Ben had returned to the paper, a call had come in about a fire in an apartment complex and he'd sent her to cover the story. The next few hours had been hectic, interviewing fire fighters and residents who'd been driven from their homes. Her own concerns had been pushed to the back of her mind. But now she glanced toward Max's desk to find him frowning at his screen.

He'd been sent to cover a double homicide on the east side of town and she wondered if Merriweather had been involved. "Police have any suspects yet?" she asked.

He scowled at her. She'd never spoken to him before a week ago. He'd told her he wanted them to go back to that arrangement. And hadn't he made it clear this request was for her safety? he fumed. "They're pretty sure it was gang related," he replied, letting his irritation show.

The moment she'd spoken to him, Bernadette knew she'd made a mistake. Still, his sharpness stung. Glancing covertly around the newsroom, she noticed Roger and Gordon had stopped talking and although they weren't looking her way, she knew they were listening. Might as well use this opportunity to further the impression Max and I are again on unfriendly terms, she decided. "I just asked a simple question," she muttered under her breath, anger lacing her words.

Glancing at her, Max couldn't tell if she was really furious with him or just playacting. But the anger had sounded genuine. Which is the way I want it, he assured himself.

But as he watched her leave a few minutes later, a worry began to nag at him. The worry grew as he watched the lights on the elevator flash from floor to floor during her descent to the garage. He raked a hand agitatedly through his hair. Despite his vow to stay away from her, he was going to have to talk to her once more in private.

Bernadette was staring into her refrigerator trying to decide what to eat for dinner when a knock sounded on her door. Glancing out her front window, she saw a florist's delivery truck outside. An elderly delivery man greeted her when she opened the door. "A flower for a lovely lady," he said, handing her a bud vase holding a single red rose surrounded by baby's breath.

Before she could barely say "thank you," he'd turned and left.

"Who would be sending me a flower?" she mused as she closed the door and sniffed the bud on her way back to the kitchen. Noticing the small envelope dangling from the ribbon tied around the vase, she came to an abrupt halt. It read

To Berny. Even if Max hadn't used that nickname he'd picked for her, she would have recognized the handwriting.

Her heart was pounding as she set the vase down and opened the envelope. Had he discovered he missed her? she wondered hopefully.

"No such luck," she muttered, reading the message.

It instructed her to go out her back door, through the yard behind her and onto the next street. The florist truck would be waiting and she was to climb into the back where she wouldn't be seen.

Half an hour later, she was browsing through an assortment of caskets in the storage room of a mortuary when Max joined her. "You do know how to pick interesting spots for clandestine meetings," she remarked dryly.

"I'm trying to make sure you don't end up in one of these," he replied, nodding to an elaborate casket behind her.

His patronizing tone grated on her already taut nerves. "I thought you'd decided the best way to assure that was for us to stay as far away from each other as possible."

"It is," he said, then heard himself admitting, "I'm sorry about sniping at you in the newsroom but I want everyone to know that whatever was going on between us is over."

"I figured that out," she said, surprised he'd apologized.

Max mentally kicked himself. He'd meant to keep the anger between them. His manner became coolly business-like. "I was wondering what happened at Neily's place today?"

A wave of frustration swept through Bernadette. Clearly he was still determined to keep a distance between them. "I got a plaque and a check and their chef made up a delicious chocolate soufflé and strawberry concoction just for me."

Max's nerves grew more tense as the worry that had caused him to arrange this meeting grew stronger. "Did

Merriweather win you over?" he growled. "Have you decided my suspicions are unfounded?"

"I've never trusted men who seem too perfect to be true," she replied.

Max drew a relieved breath.

Unable to stop herself, Bernadette added pointedly, "Since I don't consider you to be anywhere near perfect, you I believe."

"Thanks, I think," he replied, finding himself wanting to convince her he wasn't quite as deplorable as she made him sound. Angry with himself, he fought back this urge. He needed to get her out of his life not invite her back in. In brusque tones, he said, "Now what happened at Neily's. Did he ask about me?"

"He didn't but his wife did. She also wanted to know if we ever worked together," she replied. Interest sparked in her eyes. "Do you think she could be in on his business?"

Max shrugged. "I don't know. Maybe or maybe Merriweather simply asked her to find out more about you and me without telling her why. It'd be safer if you stay away from both of them."

Bernadette frowned thoughtfully. "I don't understand why he made such a big deal out of the Lang affair. That party he threw for me must have cost a pretty penny and he gave me a check for a thousand dollars."

"He's got money to burn. That little gathering this morning enhanced his image as the benevolent civic-minded citizen he wants people to think he is. It also gave him an opportunity to meet you and determine if he should consider you a threat. Any investigative reporter could pose a problem for him."

He looked tired. She found herself recalling how much she'd enjoyed lying beside him watching him sleep. Even when she'd thought she was going to die at any moment, she hadn't been afraid when he was there. "If you're honestly concerned about my safety you could marry me and keep a really close eye on me.'' Bernadette gasped when she realized she'd actually proposed this time.

Max had to admit she was a temptation. Then his gaze shifted to the caskets and a chill ran along his spine. ''I thought I'd already explained to you that I don't want to feel responsible for anyone but myself.''

Fighting down a rush of embarrassment, she forced a nonchalance into her voice and gave a single shoulder shrug. ''As a matter of fact you did. But I thought I'd give you one more chance to change your mind.'' Her gaze shifted around the room. ''This place gives me the creeps. Are you finished so I can go home?''

Max nodded. ''Yeah.'' He motioned toward the door at the rear of the room. ''Joe's waiting for you. He'll drop you off where he picked you up. Just in case Merriweather is having you watched, go in the way you came out...through your backyard and into your back door. As long as you stay away from me, I'm sure he'll lose interest in you quickly.''

I do seem to be easy for men to lose interest in, she mused a little later as she made her way through her neighbors' yard, into her own and then into her house. ''However, I'm sure there's a Mr. Right for me out there somewhere,'' she added firmly as she stripped and climbed into the shower.

Max's image filled her mind. ''But not him!'' she growled, vowing never to make a fool of herself again. He'd made it very clear he didn't want her in his life so from now on she'd stay out of it.

A little later, she found herself wandering restlessly through the house. In spite of her determination not to think of Max, his presence seemed to linger within the walls. ''Maybe it's time I made an even bigger change in my life,'' she muttered. ''Maybe it's time I moved to another town and started out totally fresh.''

Abruptly she halted. No! In the past she'd always taken the easy route. Now every fiber of her being rebelled against that. This was her home. She knew this town and she was doing well at her job. And even if Max would never be interested in her romantically, she still cared about him. She wouldn't leave him with his back totally unguarded.

Of course, she'd have to do her guarding carefully and mostly from a distance. And I should come up with a possible list of clandestine meeting places, she thought as she began turning off lights in preparation for going to bed. "The cemetery at midnight would probably suit him just fine," she muttered.

Chapter Fifteen

Bernadette grinned crookedly at the front page of the newspaper. There had been no earth-shaking events the day before. As a result, in contrast to the thirty seconds she'd received on the television news, Ben had given her award front-page status. A picture of her and him standing with Merriweather, Pauline and their son accompanied the story. It was her sense of irony that was causing her to smile. If Max was right, she was receiving an award of merit from one of the most devious criminal minds of the decade.

"It's nice to be able to print good news once in a while," Ben said, giving her a wink as he passed her desk on his way to his office.

Even though it was Saturday, it seemed as if everyone was on duty, Bernadette thought, noticing that Sabrina had wandered over and perched herself on a corner of Max's desk. As Ben walked out of earshot, the blonde pursed her lips into a pout of critical examination. "Roger could have tried an angle that would have made Bernadette look better." Her gaze shifted to Bernadette. "But then maybe not."

Bernadette was used to Sabrina's offhanded insults. Normally she simply ignored them but today she wished she had a comeback. And next time I will, she promised herself.

"I think I did a great job." Roger's voice sounded from behind Bernadette. Joining them, he handed her a large manila envelope. "Thought you might like a copy of the picture."

Sabrina raised an eyebrow at the photographer as if to say she questioned his objectivity, then turned to Max. "Ever since I learned you'd taken Bernadette to one of the Thursday night poker games, I've been devastated. And now that whatever was going on between you two is ended, I think it's only fair for you to take me next week."

"Sorry," Max replied. "It's back to a men's only night. If you came, we'd have to call you Sam and you're definitely not a Sam."

"But I've been practicing," Sabrina purred. "I was so depressed last week, I complained to Merriweather Neily and he introduced me to a man who gambles for a living."

So that was how Merriweather had connected her and Max, Bernadette realized. She glanced at him and saw him look at her. There was a protectiveness in his eyes that sent a rush of warmth through her. Immediately it was followed by frustration. She didn't want his protection, she wanted his love.

"Hey, no professionals allowed," Roger interjected.

Max gave Sabrina a "there's nothing I can do to help you" look and returned to reading the comics. Silently he breathed a sigh of relief. He'd been a little surprised to hear Sabrina say she'd been the one who'd informed Merriweather of his and Bernadette's recent closeness. However, Sabrina now clearly felt that closeness was finished. Max bet himself, Neily had been told by the blonde that he and Bernadette were again barely speaking. And as long as Bernadette behaved herself, she would be fine.

"Men," Sabrina huffed. "They're totally inflexible. You can never please them. Either you're too experienced or not experienced enough."

Some men could certainly be inflexible, Bernadette agreed silently. Wagering she knew one of the staunchest in that category, she glanced covertly at Max. To her surprise, she noticed there was a more relaxed set to his jaw than there had been a few moments earlier. Then she realized he fully expected Merriweather to have found out from Sabrina that he and Bernadette were no longer a pair. And yesterday's little party had simply been a way for Mr. Neily to confirm the split, Bernadette guessed.

"Hey, kids, time to get to work," Grace called out from her desk. Her gaze shifted to Bernadette. "City hall is open in ten minutes. If you want a good seat, you'd better get there."

"Right," Bernadette called back, finding herself feeling bored already by the thought of covering yet another political press conference. She glanced at Gordon. He'd been talking about retiring to a small town and starting his own newspaper. If he did, she'd talk to Ben about letting her take Gordon's place on the court beat and then work her way into doing overflow on the police beat when Max couldn't cover all the major stories.

She smiled as she punched the elevator button. She might not have Max but at least she had a plan for her future. And a miracle could happen. Max could discover he'd fallen in love with her. In the meantime, however, she was determined to curb her impulsive marriage proposals. Leading a more adventurous life was all well and good but there were some proprieties she wanted to maintain.

And if Max never looked her way again, she'd get over him, she assured herself. It could even be that she was still feeling such a strong attraction to him because he was the first man in her life, she reasoned as she unlocked her car and climbed in. Probably a month from now, she'd wonder what she ever saw in him and be relieved and grateful he never accepted her proposals.

Having had this little talk with herself, she drove off toward city hall.

"I'm bored, bored, bored, bored," Bernadette grumbled much later that night as she sat in her den in her most comfortable cotton nightgown with her feet propped up on the coffee table. She'd made herself a bowl of popcorn. An old science fiction movie was playing on the television. In the past, she'd always loved watching those. She also had a crossword puzzle in her hand and a murder mystery lying beside her. But nothing she'd tried had been able to hold her attention for long.

"I don't know whether to blame Max or my new outlook on life. But whichever one it is, I've never felt so restless," she complained to the actress who was screaming at the top of her lungs because a mutated giant rabbit was stalking her. Bernadette plopped some popcorn in her mouth as the actress escaped from the beast.

But the picture on the screen wasn't fully occupying her mind. Against her wishes, she imagined how nice it would be to have Max beside her and felt more lonely by the minute.

The ringing of the phone was a welcome relief. Flicking the Mute button on her television control, she picked up the receiver.

"I'd like to speak to Bernadette Dowd," an elderly sounding male said from the other end.

"Speaking," she replied, glancing at the clock and seeing that it was nearly ten. A little late for a salesman to call, she thought.

"I saw the story about you in today's paper," her caller continued, a nervous edge entering his voice. "My name's Ted Brown and I know about something you might want to look into. It involves abuse of us old folks."

If her caller had been there with her, she'd have kissed him for giving her something productive to do. "I'm very interested," she assured him, her boredom completely vanquished.

"I can't talk over the phone," the man said, lowering his voice as if afraid he might be overheard.

"I'll meet you," she replied quickly. "Where and when?"

"Tonight. But we can't meet at my home. My son's there. I told him I was going to play bingo and then go out for something to eat with some friends. He won't wait up for me."

He named a corner in one of the nicer residential areas and Bernadette promised to meet him there in an hour. As she hung up, her adrenaline was pumping. Hurrying to dress, she wondered if she should call someone to back her up. Max immediately came to mind but she shoved him out.

Frowning at the phone, she reminded herself it was Saturday night. Probably nobody would be home anyway or if they were, they were relaxing with their families. Besides, she was simply going to meet with an elderly man in a nice neighborhood on a public street corner. "I'm sure I can handle this on my own," she assured herself, pulling on a pair of slacks.

Driving to the meeting she knew Ben would be angry with her. "But I'm sure Max has gone alone to meetings like this a multitude of times," she reasoned, planning to use that as her defense in case Ben did yell at her.

Ahead of her she saw the corner that had been designated for the meeting. A figure stooped with age, using a cane for support, stepped out of the shadow of one of the large trees lining the street. Bernadette pulled up beside him.

Before she could even turn the engine off, he'd opened the passenger door and was peering inside. "Yes, you're Bernadette Dowd," he said in a raspy tone. "Recognize you from your picture." Moving with an agility that surprised her, he slipped into the passenger seat.

He smelled as if he'd doused himself with an entire bottle of after-shave, Bernadette thought, her eyes threatening to tear as the pungent odor permeated the interior of the car. "It's a pleasure to meet you, Mr. Brown," she said extending her hand toward the man now huddled in the seat beside her. She could see that he had a long form but age had bent him cutting several inches from his height. And like her grandmother had in her last years, he obviously suffered from an almost constant chill. Even though the night was pleasant, Bernadette noted he wore an ancient bulky sweater and much used knitted gloves. The feebleness in his touch as he accepted her handshake brought a surge of sympathy and she vowed she'd help him if she could.

Using the cane to prop himself even as he sat, he nodded ahead of them. "We best be going before anyone sees me." He chuckled. "Reminds me of my younger years. My wife's parents objected to me and I used to drive by and she'd hop in before they could see who was picking her up."

Wondering if the girl's parents had objected because of the strength of his after-shave, she forced a smile. "Why don't you tell me what it is you think I should investigate?" she encouraged wanting to get this interview over with before she was overcome by the fumes.

"A friend of mine, Ellie May Wright, wants to talk to you, too," her passenger said. "She's not able to get around much so I told her we'd come see her. She lives on a farm a little ways out of town. I promised her we'd go there and talk over a cup of coffee. Just take the next right."

Glancing at her passenger, Bernadette saw him concentrating on the street ahead. There had been a finality in his voice that told her he'd already decided not to tell her anything until they'd joined his friend. Well, why not? she reasoned. Two sources were better than one.

As they drove, interspersed between his directions on how to get to Ellie May's house, the old man rattled on about how much the city had changed and how it wasn't safe to be out after dark anymore. Bernadette listened politely and commiserated when appropriate. But when they passed the All Night Saloon, she began to get edgy. Maybe her passenger was more senile than he sounded. Maybe he didn't have any information or a friend to back him up. Maybe he simply wanted to have someone to talk to and decided a little ride in the country would be fun as well.

"Just where does your friend live?" she asked when he paused in the middle of a story about walking to school through several feet of snow.

"Not much farther," he replied, a coaxing quality entering his voice. "I know my stories must be boring to a youngster like you but we're almost there."

Bernadette recalled how much her grandmother had enjoyed talking about days past and mentally frowned at herself. "I'm not bored," she lied.

The old man grinned. "Of course you are. But you're much nicer about it than my children. I'd reminisce with old friends but most of them have passed on."

Immediately Bernadette felt another rush of sympathy for her passenger.

"Ellie May's place is on the left just ahead," he said, pointing a crooked finger at a narrow gravel roadway with a single mailbox beside it.

Turning off the main road, Bernadette could see the vague outline of a small house in the distance. On either side of the one-lane driveway, were fields of newly germinating corn. A nice little farm, she thought. But the house could use some paint, she added as she pulled into the wide gravel parking area in front. And the flower beds needed weeding. But that was understandable if the elderly woman lived here alone and couldn't get around too well. Maybe I'll come back tomorrow and put them in order, she thought.

Inwardly she laughed at herself. She'd always hated weeding. But at the moment she was willing to do anything to keep busy and get her mind off Max.

The elderly man had eased himself out of the car by the time she came around to help him.

He waved away her offered aid. "Now don't you worry about me. I'm not totally crippled yet."

Respecting his desire for independence, she stood back while he headed for the house.

After closing his car door, she followed him onto the porch. The blinds had been drawn on all the windows but light showed around the edges indicating that someone was home. Opening the screened door, he rapped a *tappity-tap-tap* with the head of his cane. Glancing over his shoulder, he winked at Bernadette. "We have a little signal so she'll know it's safe to answer. No telling who might come up to your door these days."

"True," Bernadette replied, shifting a little so she was upwind from him and his cologne. In the light of the porch lamp, she had the sudden feeling there was something familiar about her elderly companion. He looks like a hundred other men his age, she reasoned.

"Come on in, Ted," a crackly female voice called from inside. "I've been waiting for you."

"Come on, Miss Dowd," he directed, pushing the door open and motioning for her to precede him inside. "Ellie May has a tendency to doze off. We want to catch her while she's still awake."

Hoping she wasn't on a wild-goose chase, Bernadette entered the house. Immediately inside the door, she froze. She'd entered a living room furnished much as she expected. A couch with a couple of overstuffed, upholstered chairs, outdated in design and their coverings worn with age and use, were the main furnishings. There was a table by the window with a plant. Two straight-back chairs sat on either side of another small table along the far wall. Doilies were on the couch, upholstered chairs and tables and a corded area rug occupied a large portion of the hardwood floor. Darkened prints of landscapes hung on the walls.

But there was no elderly woman waiting for her. Instead she saw Chuck Lang seated in one of the overstuffed chairs looking angry and frightened. Seated on the couch holding a gun aimed at the man was a slender, heavily made-up redhead.

A strong push on her back sent Bernadette stumbling farther into the room.

"Been waiting long?" a familiar male voice asked from behind her.

Bernadette whirled around. Her companion's makeup had been applied expertly. If she'd only seen him and never heard him speak in his normal voice, she wasn't sure she would ever have guessed his true identity. But she'd recognized that carefully cultured voice. "Merriweather Neily," she gasped.

Neily had straightened to his full height. Now he performed an elegant bow. "At your service." Then turning to the woman on the couch, he asked again, "Have you been waiting long?"

"Not very. But this man is a real bore."

Bernadette jerked her attention to the redhead. That voice had been even more familiar. "Sabrina?" She choked out the name.

Sabrina smiled and fluffed the thick, long tresses of her wig. "I've always wondered what I'd look like as a redhead. Stunning don't you think?"

Merriweather laughed. "Modesty has never been one of your faults."

Sabrina wrinkled her nose. "Didn't you overdo the after-shave a bit?"

"I didn't want to take a chance on the lovely Ms. Dowd getting close enough to recognize me." He laughed. "However, you could be right. The way her eyes were tearing, I was worried she might be having trouble seeing the road."

"What the hell is going on?" Lang demanded. He glowered at Bernadette. "And what's that bitch doing here?"

"The same as you," Merriweather replied with a smile. "She's going to die."

Lang paled while Bernadette swore that if she got out of this alive, she was never going out without a backup again even if the person who wanted to meet with her was Mother Teresa.

Merriweather turned his attention to Sabrina. "And how did your part of our little scheme go?"

"Beautifully. If I'd written his lines for him, he couldn't have been better," she replied, giving Lang a grin of approval. "I waited until he'd gone to that diner down the way for supper, then followed him in and asked if he wasn't the guy I'd seen in the newspaper. He flew into a rage. Said he'd kill our Miss Dowd if she ever crossed his path again. Then he called her a few choice names and the owner threw him out for disturbing the rest of the patrons. As soon as he was out the door, I added my own little bit by saying I sure hoped I hadn't triggered him into doing anything rash like maybe harming Miss Dowd. Then I left real fast and followed him. He was such a good little boy. He came directly here."

Looking pleased, Merriweather turned to Bernadette. "If you're wondering where here is, this place belongs to one of Lang's friends. Our Mr. Lang needed a quiet retreat to escape from his recent notoriety. I have to compliment him for making our job so much easier by choosing such a wonderfully isolated spot.''

Bernadette frowned at Neily. The reporter in her refused to die without a few answers. ''Does your wife know how you spend your free time?'' she asked dryly.

Merriweather laughed. ''My lovely wife is perfectly happy to remain ignorant of my extracurricular activities. I married her because she's the perfect society wife and she married me for my money. We have an amicable relationship. If I ask her to find out something for me or even to lie for me about my whereabouts at any particular time, she doesn't ask why, she simply complies with great grace. Of course, she expects a very nice gift for her trouble.''

''I, on the other hand, expect a great deal more,'' Sabrina interjected seductively.

Merriweather shook his head. ''You are insatiable.''

''But why kill Lang and me?'' Bernadette asked, not able to come up with a reasonable answer to this on her own.

''Actually you are the bait and Lang is the red herring,'' he replied.

Bernadette felt a chill run along her spine. ''Would you mind elaborating?'' she requested, maintaining a facade of calmness to cover her growing panic.

Merriweather smiled indulgently. ''Max Laird is my real target. When the bodies are found, it will look as if Lang went hunting for revenge and Laird died because he was in the wrong place at the wrong time. Then in a fit of remorse or hopelessness or whatever....after all, who can understand the criminal mind...'' He laughed at this private joke, then finished, ''Lang killed himself.''

Regret suddenly showed on Merriweather's face. ''I am sorry you have to be involved. But it's the only way to make this look authentic.'' Again his smile returned. ''Of course your death will also serve its own unique purpose. It will cause people to stop and think twice about being Good Samaritans. After all, it will look as if you died because you reported on Lang. Yes, that will definitely give other do-gooders reason to pause." Regret returned as he reached out and touched her cheek. "Still, it is a pity to waste a lovely woman like yourself as mere bait."

"She's not your type," Sabrina said sharply.

"Jealous little thing," Merriweather laughed.

Sabrina gave him an icy look. "It's time for me to go collect Max, isn't it?"

Merriweather nodded in agreement. "Yes, I really need to get home in time to get some sleep. I've got a ten o'clock meeting with the mayor tomorrow morning. We need to discuss the deplorable increase in crime against the elderly."

And now it's time for me to be going, too, Bernadette told herself. She'd noticed a line of woods toward the back of the house. If she could make it to there, they wouldn't find her in the dark.

Spinning around, she shoved Merriweather hard, causing him to stagger backward. Praying he hadn't locked the door, she dashed for it. A crashing blow to the head brought her to her knees. I should have remembered the cane, she thought just before she blacked out.

Max sat slouching in his favorite chair scowling at himself. He hadn't been able to get Bernadette Dowd out of his mind all evening. It was that damned new persona of hers. The old Bernadette Dowd had been predictable, level-headed, conservative. Berny, on the other hand, seemed to enjoy taking risks. "She's not my problem," he told himself curtly, then rubbed his temples where a headache was starting to build.

The ringing of the phone startled him. Glancing at his watch, he noted that it was a little before midnight. His first thought was that the caller was Bernadette and she'd gotten herself into trouble. If that was the case, after he'd rescued her, he was going to have a firm talk with her.

"Max, it's Sabrina. Be a Boy Scout and come rescue me," a female voice pleaded when he answered.

His headache vanished. "What's the problem?"

"I went to this party tonight," she replied, the plea in her voice growing even stronger. "I'll confess, I crashed it. It was on the seedier side of town but I'd heard there might be some people show up who would interest me. I decided a disguise might be appropriate. I'd always wanted to be a redhead and I figured a provocative dress was in order. Anyway, I got myself made-up and went. But I guess I over-did the look. This one guy there hit on me and nothing I could do would make him leave me alone. I thought I was safe because I didn't tell him my real name."

"And now you don't feel so safe?" he asked, when she paused as if embarrassed by the predicament she'd gotten herself into.

"And now I don't feel so safe," she replied contritely. "I think he's trying to follow me home. I'm calling from an all-night diner on the west side of town." She named the place and the location. "I can sneak out the back if you'll just swing by and pick me up around the corner. I'll leave my car here and pick it up tomorrow."

"Sure, no problem," Max replied. "Be there in half an hour."

"You're a sweetheart," Sabrina cooed and hung up.

"Now there's a woman born to trouble," Max muttered.

Half an hour later, as he rounded the corner to the side of the diner and pulled over to the curb, a woman stepped out of the shadows and slid into the front passenger seat of his car.

The woman was Sabrina's size and had her figure prominently displayed in a Lycra mini dress that fit like a second skin. But her face was so heavily made-up and almost hidden by the wild red wig she was wearing, for a moment Max thought maybe he'd picked up the wrong female. "Sabrina?" he asked dubiously.

"In the flesh," she replied.

"The voice and figure I recognize," he said, his gaze traveling over her a second time. "But the rest of you is definitely different."

She smiled coquettishly. "The old me never interested you. How about this new me?"

"It's a little too racy for my blood," he replied.

Her lips formed a pretty pout. "Too bad." Then leaning back in the seat, she said, "How about dropping me off at a friend's house? It's not far from here and I'd feel safer staying with someone tonight."

"Sure," Max agreed, thinking that of all the women he knew, he'd put Sabrina at the top of the list of those who could take care of themselves. "Just give me directions."

Sabrina grinned. "Take the next turn on the right, then straight ahead."

A short time later as they turned onto the gravel lane through the cornfield, Max glanced at his passenger. "I find it hard to picture you spending even one night on a farm. You've always struck me as a city girl."

Sabrina shrugged. "I have my back-to-nature moments."

Yeah, right, Max thought but kept his mouth shut. He could be wrong about Sabrina but he doubted it.

"How about coming in for a drink as a sort of thank-you for rescuing me," she coaxed as they pulled up outside the small old farmhouse.

Max grinned. "I'll forgo the drink but you in this house is a sight I don't want to miss. I'll walk you to the door."

"You are such a gentleman," Sabrina purred.

At the door, she gave the *tappity-tap-tap* knock. "I don't want my friend thinking we're strangers and shooting us," she said as she opened the door without waiting for a response. Stepping aside, she gave a wave of her hand to indicate she wanted Max to precede her.

Stepping inside, his first view was of an elderly man standing near the fireplace with a revolver in his hand.

"Welcome," the man said.

Max would have recognized that voice anywhere. "Neily."

"Come on in and join our little party," Merriweather instructed.

Going farther into the room, Max saw Lang seated in a worn upholstered chair. Then he saw Bernadette lying on the couch. Panic flowed through him. Hatred blazed in his eyes. "What the hell have you done to her?" he growled, rushing to her.

"I had to give her a little tap on the head," Merriweather replied. "I guess I hit her harder than I thought."

"This time I'm going to get you, Neily," Max vowed. "You're never going to hurt anyone again."

"Brave words." Merriweather breathed an exaggerated sigh of regret. "I'll admit, I may miss our little game of cat and mouse. You've kept me on my toes. But I've had to expend a great deal of energy making sure you never had anything tangible to take to the police and lately that has been more and more of a strain. I decided several months ago the time had come to get rid of you but I needed a plan that could never, in anyone's wildest imagination, point to me. Your brief involvement with Miss Dowd and her exposure of Mr. Lang's activities provided me with such a plan."

Max's stomach knotted. He wasn't going to let Bernadette die because of him.

"Look, Mr. Neily, like I've been telling you, whatever your game is, I could be of help to you," Lang butted in.

"He arranges murders," Max informed the man.

"I don't mind killing people," Lang assured Neily. "I killed a man down in Texas and buried the body in the desert. Never bothered me a bit."

"It would seem that in your case I will be doing the public a service by removing you," Neily replied.

"Damn you!" Lang cursed.

Max's gaze narrowed on Neily. "You did arrange my brother's death, didn't you?" he asked.

"He had become an irritant just as you have become an irritant. However, his death was much easier to arrange. A cop's life is always on the line."

"I feel forgotten." Sabrina pouted. She moved toward Max, her gun drawn. "You haven't asked how a nice girl like me could get mixed up with such an unscrupulous character as Merriweather."

Max looked at the .45 Magnum she was holding pointed at him. "To be honest, I've always thought of you as a dangerous woman who likes to play dangerous games. Apparently I was right."

"And I've always thought of you as a man who wasn't afraid of a challenge," she returned. She glanced toward Bernadette and disdain showed in her eyes. "But then you chose to associate with our dowdy Miss Dowd. Really, Max, she's such a bore."

"It's been my experience that every female is a challenge in her own way," Max replied, then heard himself adding, "and all of you are dangerous to a man's peace of mind."

"Well said." Neily smiled. "But enough of this chatter. It's getting late."

Making sure he was positioned to protect Bernadette, Max faced Neily. "Before you do the foul deed. I would like to know what scenario you've devised for my death."

"I realize you're just trying to buy time. But time will do you no good. However, I'm rather pleased with this plan and a little boasting is in order. When Sabrina and I leave, we will set this place on fire. And when the fire is out, the firemen will find the remains of three charred bodies. One of the bodies will be Mr. Lang's and he will still be holding this gun. After talking to the patrons at the diner, the police will have to conclude he captured Miss Dowd and brought her here and you came to rescue her and got yourself killed in the attempt. Or else Lang captured the both of you at the same time and brought you both here then killed you together. Either way works. Everyone at the paper knows something went on between you and Ms. Dowd. It wouldn't be considered unusual for you to have tried to protect her or been caught with her. Finally the police will be forced to conclude that after killing the both of you, Lang, in a final act of desperation, killed himself."

"I'm not going to just sit here and let you shoot me," Lang bellowed, coming out of his chair at Neily.

Neily's attention shifted to the man. Before Max could act, Neily had placed a bullet between Lang's eyes.

Bernadette had been fending unconsciousness for what seemed like forever. She'd allowed herself to open her eyes only the tiniest slit, thus her view was obstructed by her eyelashes. But she had been able to determine Merriweather's and Lang's positions in the room and knew she was on the couch.

She'd heard Max and Sabrina come in. But Max had positioned himself in front of her and she hadn't been able to see what Neily was doing. Hearing the shot, terror that she'd waited too long filled her. Then she realized Max was still standing. Hoping to cause enough distraction to give her and Max a fighting chance, she screamed at the top of her lungs as she lunged at Sabrina.

Startled, Sabrina froze momentarily. That moment was all Bernadette needed to tackle the woman and they both fell to the floor.

Max had been heading for Neily when Bernadette unexpectedly joined the fray. His forward momentum continued while Neily momentarily hesitated, thus giving Max time to reach him. As they, too, crashed to the floor, struggling for control of the gun, several uniformed men burst through the door.

"Everyone freeze!" an authoritative voice ordered.

Bernadette looked past Sabrina's shoulder to see five guns trained on her and the other woman. Five more were on Max and Merriweather.

"It's about time you showed up," Max said, disentangling himself from Merriweather and rising to his feet.

Freeing herself from Sabrina, Bernadette looked up and recognized George Pace.

"We didn't want them to hear or see us approaching so we had to park on the road and make our way along the line of trees on the side of the cornfield," George replied.

Bernadette had shifted into a sitting position. She didn't trust her legs to hold her just yet. Her head was pounding and she was feeling slightly dizzy.

"Just stay sitting," one of the officers directed.

For a moment she thought he was merely showing concern, then she saw the handcuffs he was holding.

"I'm one of the good guys," she said as he started to clasp one onto her wrist.

George's attention shifted to her. "She's one of us," he informed the officer who was regarding her dubiously, the handcuffs still out ready to use. Then concern spread over his face. "Are you all right, Berny?"

"Just a little headache," she replied, attempting to rise.

She swayed slightly. A strong arm immediately was wrapped around her waist. Turning to her rescuer, she found herself looking up into Max's grim features.

"You are not all right," he said gruffly. "Your eyes look glazed. It's my guess you have a concussion." He turned to George. "Merriweather knocked her out. We need to get her to a hospital."

Bernadette's dizziness was subsiding. She started to protest being taken to the hospital when she saw the protectiveness in Max's gaze. Her words died in her throat as a warmth spread through her.

"Give me your wire. Then you drive her. I'll send one of the cars ahead to clear you a path while I stay here and make sure our prisoners are read their rights."

Max eased Bernadette into a nearby chair, then unbuttoned his shirt and took off the microphone and the small recorder hidden beneath.

"You knew this was a setup?" Sabrina glowered at him. "How?"

"I knew Merriweather had to have a spy at the newspaper. You've always liked money and the people who have it. And, while you were always eager to report any scandal among the elite, you treated Merriweather as if he was as pure as snow. I figured I could be mistaken about you being bought by him. You might simply have been enamored by his charm and wealth. But I've always been the cautious type," Max replied. "When you called tonight, I called George for backup, just to be on the safe side."

Max regarded her thoughtfully. "I guessed you were Merriweather's spy but I'd never have guessed you would involve yourself in an actual murder."

"I've always believed that to keep the bond strong in a relationship, people should take an interest in each other's careers and help when possible," she tossed back flippantly.

"Women," Max muttered as he slipped an arm around Bernadette's waist to help her to her feet.

She saw the impatience on his face as if he considered all women to be nuisances and it grated on her nerves. "I can walk just fine on my own," she said slipping out of his hold. "It was just the scuffling after lying still for so long that caused me to be so shaky. But now I'm perfectly all right. I'll just drive myself home."

Max's hand closed around her arm. "You will do no such thing. Give your keys to George. He'll see that your car gets back to your place. In the meantime, I'm taking you to a hospital." The guilt he had been feeling ever since he'd walked into the farmhouse and found her there showed on his face. "You nearly got killed because of me."

His guilt bothered her more than his impatience with her gender. She started to lodge another protest but before she could speak she found herself suddenly tossed over his shoulder like a sack of flour.

"Why can't women simply do as they're asked without an argument," he grumbled as he strode out the door with her.

Fury enveloped her. The problem was she didn't know who she was most angry with . . . him or her. He was only concerned about her because he felt guilty and yet every fiber of her being was aware of him.

"Get in," he ordered, setting her on the ground beside his car and opening the door.

Relieved to be free and knowing that protesting would do no good, she obeyed.

Max felt shaky as he rounded the car. She'd come to within an inch of death and it was all his fault. "How'd they lure you here in the first place?" he demanded as he climbed in behind the wheel and maneuvered the car back onto the road.

"I got a call from Merriweather disguised as an elderly man wanting to give me a lead to a story," she replied, bracing herself for the lecture she knew was coming. Almost in a mumble, she added, "He asked me to meet him. The neighborhood was a nice one."

"And so you didn't call for a backup," Max finished curtly.

"And so I didn't call for a backup," she confirmed grudgingly.

Max wanted to shake her and the urge to bluntly point out how close to death she'd come was strong. But glancing at her, he saw the strain still etched into her features. Reminding himself she'd get a lecture from Ben, he simply said, "I hope you've learned your lesson."

"I've learned my lesson," she replied honestly.

Chapter Sixteen

Bernadette frowned at Max impatiently. "I'm fine. The doctor says I have a head like a rock. You can stop baby-sitting me. I can take a taxi home." At his and the doctor's insistence, she'd spent what remained of the night in the hospital for observation. Now morning had fully arrived. The sun was shining and she'd been given the okay to go home.

When Max had first brought her to the hospital, he'd stayed until she'd been checked in. Then he'd gone to the newspaper offices and written the story of Merriweather's arrest. But once he'd handed in his copy, rather than going to his place, he'd returned to the hospital and hovered over her. He had not, however, been solicitous. Instead he'd paced the room like a caged beast. When she'd complained that he was making her dizzy, he'd sat down in the lounge chair but, even seated, there had been nothing relaxed about him. And, when he'd finally fallen asleep, his expression had remained grim. He made her feel like the top nuisance of all time and his presence was grating on her nerves.

"I'm going to take you home," he said, his voice holding no compromise. Ever since they'd left the farmhouse, the thought of her lying dead had been taunting him. Even asleep it had never left him and he'd woken in a cold sweat. He needed to put distance between himself and her but he couldn't do that until he'd seen her safely home. Then, he promised himself, for her own good he would walk away and never look back.

Realizing that arguing would be futile, Bernadette gave him a final impatient glance, then suggested that while she dressed, he call George Pace and find out what was happening with Merriweather and Sabrina.

Max nodded in agreement and started toward the phone by the bed. Almost immediately, he stopped himself. Being in the same room with her while she dressed, even if she was behind a curtain, was a strain on his control. "You'll want some privacy. I'll use the pay phone in the hall," he said and strode out of the room.

Bernadette frowned at his departing back. "The sooner we part company, the better," she muttered, then hurriedly pulled on her clothes.

"What did you find out from George?" she asked as she slid into the passenger seat of Max's car a few minutes later.

"George assures me that no matter how many influential friends Neily has, they are both going to stand trial for first-degree murder." Anger mingled with frustration on his face. "But they didn't find Neily's files. The consensus is that he keeps them in his head. They picked up his chauffeur and one of his gardeners. The police suspect both men of being shooters. But even if they talk and name names of victims, and right now it looks as if they won't, there is no way to know for certain who hired Merriweather for any particular hit. The shooters wouldn't know the buyer."

"Well, at least they've got him for Lang's killing," Bernadette said encouragingly. "And he confessed to arranging for your brother's death, too."

"And our attempted murders," Max reminded her. Again the thought of how close she'd come to getting murdered sent a chill through him. As he pulled out onto the street, he couldn't stop himself from asking curtly, "Have you had enough excitement? Are you ready to let Berny take a rest?"

During the night she'd asked herself that same question. But she knew Max wasn't going to be happy with the answer she'd arrived at. "I have to admit last night was more than I'd bargained for," she replied evasively.

Max glanced toward her. She had that set to her jaw that always made him uneasy. "Is that a 'yes, I'm going to settle back into being Bernadette Dowd' or 'no, I'm going to stay Berny and turn everyone's hair prematurely white with my antics'?"

Bernadette glowered at him. "I'm going to strike a happy medium," she informed him coolly. "I won't go out on any investigations without a backup and I'm going to take some courses in self-defense just to be on the safe side." A pointedness entered her voice. "And there is no reason for *your* hair to turn prematurely white because of me." Pronouncing each word distinctly and with force, she finished, *"I am not your responsibility."*

"No, you're not," he replied, more as an admission to himself than to confirm her words.

Bernadette experienced a strong wave of regret. He really was going to walk away from her and never look back. Irritated with herself, she realized that down deep she'd continued to cling to the hope that he would learn to care for her. Now she forced herself to face the cold, hard truth once and for all: He was never going to fall in love with her. He was determined to be a loner.

"Well, I'm glad we finally have that settled," she said wishing she felt as relieved as she'd forced herself to sound.

A little later, she stood alone in her living room as Max drove away. He'd seen her as far as the door, informed her that Ben wanted her to take the next couple of days off and rest, then left.

"This is the first day of the new me," she announced to the room as she watched Max's car disappearing down the street. "I should be excited." Her jaw tensed defiantly. "And I am."

She'd get Max out of her system. It might take time. Or it might not, she mused. That distant, patronizing manner of his could get on a person's nerves fast.

Still, he had a lot of good qualities. He was certainly someone she'd want on her side in a dangerous situation. A heat rushed through her as memories of other times spent with him filled her mind. He could also be gentle and fun, she admitted.

A low groan escaped. "That man makes me crazy!" she wailed in frustration.

"I will find someone better than him who is much easier to get along with," she assured herself. "Well, at least easier to get along with," she amended.

"But not right now," she muttered, glancing down at herself. She was still in the clothes she'd worn the night before. "Right now I need a bath."

Max stood in his shower letting the water cascade over him. He felt as tense as a bowstring. He should feel relaxed. Neily was behind bars and the case against the man was rock-solid.

"I can take a vacation that doesn't involve following up on a lead," he pointed out to himself. "I can go fishing and concentrate on the fish instead of working out plots to trap Merriweather. I'm free, unencumbered.''

Bernadette's image suddenly loomed in his mind. Now there was a woman who was real trouble, he thought. He'd be a wise man to cross the street whenever she came walking his way. "But I don't need to worry about that. I'm the last person in the world she'll ever come looking for," he reminded himself.

Bernadette pulled the final weed from her front garden. She'd napped after her bath. Then, in an effort to get her life back on a smoother track, during the afternoon she'd done her laundry, mowed her lawn and worked in her flower garden. It was early evening now. She was tired but felt a sense of normalcy was returning to her life.

The sound of a car pulling into her driveway surprised her. Glancing over her shoulder, she breathed a frustrated sigh. How was she ever going to stop picturing Max in her life when he kept showing up on her doorstep! The urge to scream at him to go home was strong. Instead, rubbing the dirt from her hands, she rose and faced him coolly. Afraid her frustration would show if she spoke, she remained silent as he approached.

Max had expected a cool reception. I've faced tough challenges before, he told himself. "Nice flower garden," he said.

Small talk! He was making small talk, Bernadette fumed looking up into his grim-featured face. Obviously he was finding it easy to put what happened between them out of his mind and get back to business as usual. Except business as usual didn't involve him showing up at her place. "Why are you here?" she asked bluntly.

"I'm hoping I'm not too late," he replied.

She saw the uncertainty in his eyes. "Too late?" she asked, afraid to let herself speculate on his meaning.

Max searched her face. The fear he'd killed any feelings she'd had for him was strong. "You once told me you wouldn't wait forever for me to admit I couldn't live without you."

Joy surged through her. It was quickly followed by a wave of caution. "And are you ready to admit that?" she asked, needing to hear him say it before she'd allow herself to believe it.

Crossing the distance between them in one long stride, he cupped her face in his hands. "I can't stop thinking about you. Maybe it's not fair to you for me to ask you to be a part of my life. There will always be dangerous investigations I'll feel I have to pursue. But at least you'll know the risks before you make your decision."

Suddenly worried she might be misinterpreting the extent of his offer, she asked, "Just how much a part of your life are we talking about?"

"I was thinking in terms of a legal bond," he replied.

She smiled up at him. "A legal bond sounds nice."

A shadow seemed to pass over his features. "But like I said, I can't promise you the kind of security you were probably looking for in a husband. I won't always take the safe road."

She frowned at him. "If there is one thing I've learned during the past couple of weeks, it's that life is a chance situation. Besides, you aren't the only one who's going to be pursuing investigations."

He grinned down at her. "That was one of my strongest arguments for coming here. I figured if I didn't marry you so I could keep a close eye on you, I'd never get another decent night's sleep for worrying about what you were up to."

Remembering how protective he could be, the sudden thought he might be there for the wrong reason filled her.

Her eyes searching his face, she said, "I was hoping your strongest argument was that you'd fallen in love with me."

A gentleness spread over his face. "I have. I love you, Bernadette Dowd, totally and completely."

Happiness flowed through her. "Well, it certainly has taken you long enough to admit it," she said, wrapping her arms around him. "Now would you please kiss me. I've missed you so much."

"I've missed you, too," he replied, as his lips found hers.

Bernadette propped herself up on her arm and smiled down into Max's face. They had spent an invigorating evening but she didn't feel tired. Instead she felt happy and content.

Running his hand along the line of her hip, he smiled up at her. "You look like a woman with something on her mind," he said huskily, recalling how good making love to her had felt and knowing with certainty that he belonged with her.

"I was just thinking that I get all this—" she paused to kiss him, then finished with a twinkle in her eyes "—and free dental care, too."

Max laughed and pulled her down on him. "I hope it wasn't the health benefits that persuaded you."

"No," she assured him, then added playfully, "but it was a point in your favor."

Again he laughed. "How could I ever have thought of you as being dull?" he mused, caressingly exploring the contours of her body and thinking nothing could feel as soft and inviting as she did, nor be as much fun.

Desire ignited anew within Bernadette. "I do enjoy spending my weekends in bed with you," she confessed, nipping at his earlobe.

"As I recall, you've agreed I get to stay the rest of our lives as well," he reminded her.

She lifted her head and smiled at him. "I remember."

His touch became more intimate and she giggled with delight. Her lips were heading for his mouth when the ringing of the phone interrupted. With a groan of impatience, she picked up the receiver.

Max saw the blush begin to build on her cheeks.

Cupping her hand over the receiver, she said, "It's George looking for you."

He grinned at her, finding himself pleased that the modest Ms. Dowd was still a part of her, too. Continuing to hold her against him with one arm, he took the call.

She felt his body tense and saw the grimness return to his features. "What's wrong?" she asked when he handed her the receiver so she could hang it up.

"Neily committed suicide," he replied.

She frowned down at him. "He didn't seem like the type."

Max nodded. "My feelings exactly."

He was massaging her back with a touch that was igniting fires but she could see his mind was elsewhere. "Shouldn't you be going down to police headquarters?" she asked, fighting to keep the regret out of her voice. "After all, this is your story."

Apology showed on Max's face. "Yeah, I should. And what makes George's call even more interesting is that I have a feeling he isn't so sure Merriweather's death is a suicide, either. He told me he's put an extra guard on Sabrina."

Bernadette started to move away from him, but his hold tightened.

"Nothing has ever kept me from racing instantly to the site of a story," he said, then added huskily, "until now. You and I have some unfinished business and until we're both satisfied, I won't be able to concentrate on anything. Keeping you happy is going to be rule number one on my list from now on."

Bernadette grinned with pleasure as his fingers wove into her hair and he drew her mouth to his. "I like your new rule," she murmured against his lips. Then everything but the heat of his body and the delight of his touch was forgotten as she let herself get lost in a world of sensations.

* * * * *

A Note From The Author

I'm so pleased that Special Edition has created THAT
SPECIAL WOMAN! to honor heroines. My grandmother
and my mother both instilled in me a belief that, while some
men may be physically stronger than women, women possess an intense inner strength. And when called forth, this
strength enables them to nurture those who are dear to them
through difficult times. It is also this strength that enables
women to meet adversity and not allow it to conquer them.

Max Laird, the hero of this story, recognizes this strength.
He has never been fooled into thinking of women as the
weaker sex. He knows they can be tough as nails and when
their minds are set on something, they can be more tenacious than a hound on the scent of a fox.

And Bernadette Dowd, my heroine, surprises herself by
being just that. I think many women surprise themselves by
how strong they can be when the need arises. And in Bernadette's case, finding this inner strength opens up a new life

for her. It allows her to fully discover herself and find the path she most wants to follow.

I hope Bernadette and the other heroines of the THAT SPECIAL WOMAN! promotion inspire others to reach within themselves and find their own strength. For those of you who have already tapped this source of power, I hope our heroines reaffirm your belief in yourself.

Silhouette

SPECIAL EDITION

COMING NEXT MONTH

#877 MYSTERY WIFE—Annette Broadrick

That Special Woman!

Sherye DuBois awoke in a hospital with amnesia—and discovered she was married with children. Could the love of her sexy husband, Raoul DuBois, help to unravel the mystery of her life?

#878 SHADOWS AND LIGHT—Lindsay McKenna

Men of Courage

As a marine, Capt. Craig Taggert had faced many trials. Now his greatest challenge was ahead of him—convincing Lt. Susan Evans that this time, hell or high water wouldn't keep them apart!

#879 LOVING AND GIVING—Gina Ferris

Family Found

Finding his real family was just the first surprise in store for Ryan Kent. True love with the beautiful Taylor Simmons would be the second—and best—discovery of all!

#880 MY BABY, YOUR CHILD—Nikki Benjamin

Everything was at stake when Tess McGuire saved the life of Will Landon's nephew—the child she gave up for adoption. Will's tender, loving care proved he wasn't just grateful, but a man in love....

#881 WALK IN BEAUTY—Ruth Wind

Jessie Callahan never expected Luke Bernali—her lost love and father of her child—to return. But Luke was a changed man, and eager to rekindle a love that never died!

#882 THE PRINCESS OF COLDWATER FLATS —Natalie Bishop

Single-minded Samantha Whelan's only mission in life was to save her bankrupt ranch. Prairie-tough Cooper Ryan also had designs on the ranch—and on ex-rodeo princess Samantha!

Take 4 bestselling love stories FREE

Plus get a FREE surprise gift!

MYSTERY WIFE
Annette Broadrick

She awoke in a French hospital—and found handsome Raoul DuBois, claiming she was his wife, Sherye, mother of their two children. But she didn't recognize him or remember her identity. Whoever she was, Sherye grew more attached to the children every day—and the growing passion between her and Raoul was like nothing they'd ever known before....

She's friend, wife, mother—she's you! And beside each Special Woman stands a wonderfully *special* man. It's a celebration of our heroines—and the men who become part of their lives.

Don't miss **THAT SPECIAL WOMAN!** each month— from some of your special authors! Only from Silhouette Special Edition!

If you are looking for more titles by

ELIZABETH AUGUST

Don't miss this chance to order additional stories by
one of Silhouette's great authors:

Silhouette Romance™

#08809	A SMALL FAVOR	$2.50	☐
#08833	THE COWBOY AND THE CHAUFFEUR	$2.59	☐
#08857	LIKE FATHER, LIKE SON	$2.69	☐
#08881	THE WIFE HE WANTED	$2.69	☐
	The following titles are part of the Smytheshire, Massachusetts miniseries		
#08921	THE VIRGIN WIFE	$2.69	☐
#08922	HAUNTED HUSBAND	$2.69	☐
#08945	LUCKY PENNY	$2.75	☐
#08953	A WEDDING FOR EMILY	$2.75	☐

Men Made In America

#45158	AUTHOR'S CHOICE	$3.59	☐

(limited quantities available on certain titles)

TOTAL AMOUNT	$
POSTAGE & HANDLING	$
($1.00 for one book, 50¢ for each additional)	
APPLICABLE TAXES*	$ _____
TOTAL PAYABLE	$ _____
(check or money order—please do not send cash)	

To order, complete this form and send it, along with a check or money order
for the total above, payable to Silhouette Books, to: *In the U.S.*: 3010 Walden
Avenue, P.O. Box 9077, Buffalo, NY 14269-9077; *In Canada*: P.O. Box 636,
Fort Erie, Ontario, L2A 5X3.

Name: _____

Address: _____ City: _____

State/Prov.: _____ Zip/Postal Code: _____

*New York residents remit applicable sales taxes.
  Canadian residents remit applicable GST and provincial taxes.   EABACK2

Silhouette ®
™

As seen on TV!
Free Gift Offer

With a Free Gift proof-of-purchase from any Silhouette® book,
you can receive a beautiful cubic zirconia pendant.

This gorgeous marquise-shaped stone is a genuine cubic
zirconia—accented by an 18" gold tone necklace.

(Approximate retail value $19.95)

Send for yours today…
compliments of ▼ *Silhouette*®

To receive your free gift, a cubic zirconia pendant, send us one original proof-of-
purchase, photocopies not accepted, from the back of any Silhouette Romance™,
Silhouette Desire®, Silhouette Special Edition®, Silhouette Intimate Moments® or
Silhouette Shadows™ title for January, February or March 1994 at your favorite retail
outlet, together with the Free Gift Certificate, plus a check or money order for $2.50
(do not send cash) to cover postage and handling, payable to Silhouette Free Gift Offer.
We will send you the specified gift. Allow 6 to 8 weeks for delivery. Offer good until
March 31st, 1994 or while quantities last. Offer valid in the U.S. and Canada only.

Free Gift Certificate

Name: _____

Address: _____

City: _____ State/Province: _____ Zip/Postal Code: _____

Mail this certificate, one proof-of-purchase and a check or money order for postage
and handling to: SILHOUETTE FREE GIFT OFFER 1994. In the U.S.: 3010 Walden
Avenue, P.O. Box 9057, Buffalo NY 14269-9057. In Canada: P.O. Box 622, Fort Erie,
Ontario L2Z 5X3

FREE GIFT OFFER
ONE PROOF-OF-PURCHASE

079-KBZ

To collect your fabulous FREE GIFT, a cubic zirconia pendant, you must include this
original proof-of-purchase for each gift with the properly completed Free Gift Certificate.

079-KBZ